THERE WOULD BE A CONFRONTATION, TALIA COULD FEEL IT . . .

There were three large, hooded figures, and they were rapidly walking toward the party of genteel telepaths and one security officer.

She didn't want to pry into their minds, but she had to know what the three strangers were thinking as they strode briskly toward them. She could see them clearly now, even in the dim light, and she tried to hear their voices.

Talia gasped. Their minds were cold and alien! They were not human!

"I know," said Malten, hearing the alarm sounding in Talia's head.

The security chief quickened his step to get out in front of the others. He waved jauntily as the first hooded figure drew abreast of him. "Top of the mornin'!" he called.

The alien never stopped moving as he slammed his shoulder into Garibaldi and crushed him into the bulkhead. A huge knife flashed under the dark robes, and Emily screamed.

The other hooded thugs rushed toward the telepaths, knives gleaming in their gloved hands!

BABYLON 5: VOICES

John Vornholt

**Based on the series by
J. Michael Straczynski**

A Dell Book

For Richard Curtis

Based on the Warner Bros. television series *Babylon 5*, created by J. Michael Straczynski. Copyright © 1994 by Warner Bros. Television.

Published by
Dell Publishing
a division of
Bantam Doubleday Dell Publishing Group, Inc.
1540 Broadway
New York, New York 10036

The trademark Dell® is registered in the U.S. Patent and Trademark Office.

ISBN: 0-440-22057-2

Printed in the United States of America

Published simultaneously in Canada

March 1995

10 9 8 7 6 5 4 3 2 1
OPM

Special thanks to Katherine Lawrence and Jean Reich

Historian's note: The events of this novel take place shortly after the events depicted in the second-year episode, "Points of Departure," and prior to the events in "A Race Through Dark Places."

CHAPTER 1

"WELCOME to Mars," said the sultry, automated voice. "The time is 24:13 Martian Central, and the temperature is currently 201 degress Celsius. Tomorrow's high temperature is expected to be 274, with light winds and dust. Please watch your step as you disembark, as Martian gravity is thirty-eight percent that of Earth. Have a pleasant stay."

Yes, thought Harriman Gray, his step did indeed feel springier as he negotiated the moving walkway. A shy, reserved person, Gray did not usually have a bounce in his step, nor did he whistle while he worked. His job as a telepath for Earthforce required a demeanor slightly less serious than that of an undertaker.

But he couldn't help feeling rather chipper tonight, as he was about to embark on a new assignment—liaison to Mr. Bester. Bester was the top Psi Cop, the one who got the tough cases chasing down rogue telepaths. But he was much more than a Psi Cop, as Gray well knew. Bester was one of the most powerful figures in Psi Corps, the closely guarded organization charged with training and regulating both military and civilian telepaths. Although Bester's name did not appear on any list of prominent citizens, a more powerful man in the Earth Alliance would be hard to find.

Gray was distracted by some children bounding several strides ahead of their parents in the light gravity. He was glad that he didn't have any of *those* to worry about, although, lately, he had been feeling unaccountably paternal. It was Susan, he thought, Susan Ivanova from Babylon 5. She had brought out these strange feelings in him, and what had he brought out in her? Loathing and disgust. He was afraid to give himself encouragement when it came to Susan, but toward the end of his eventful visit to Babylon 5, there had been a twinge of sympathy, a smidgen of understanding in her response to him. Or so he imagined.

After all, nobody *chose* to be telepathic. Better than anyone, Susan Ivanova should know that. She could have unlimited sympathy for her mother, a rogue telepath, so why
couldn't she have some for him? Was he any different, just
because he had chosen to accept his gift and allow the Corps
to train him and place restrictions on his behavior? Was he
any different than a soldier, trained to kill one moment and
keep the peace the next? They lived in a society that had
rules, and the rules were for the good of everyone.

Okay, Mr. Gray had to admit, the rules worked better for
some people than for others. But nobody wanted anarchy,
such as the revolt on Mars a few weeks earlier. The fighting
was over, he reminded himself, and most of the real damage
had occurred on another part of Mars, not this region. Stopping the dissension on Mars would be easier than winning
Susan's heart. If only he could return to B5 and have another
chance to talk to her, to convince her that he wasn't a monster.

A moment later, another female intruded into his mind. It
was the security guard at the end of the walkway, and Gray
separated her voice from the innumerable voices which bab-
bled inside his head whenever he was in a crowded place.
They weren't real voices—they were thoughts—but his mind
translated the thoughts into an interior monologue. If he concentrated, he could pick out the voice he wanted, amplify it,
and even look behind it at the emotions and motives which
informed it.

He produced his identicard a moment before she asked for
it. Then he felt a jab of fear from her in response to the card
and his Psi Corps insignia, although her smiling face said,
"Have a pleasant stay on Mars, Mr. Gray."

Many telepaths loved that instantaneous fear they inspired
in total strangers. They got off on it and were disappointed if
a person's psyche didn't cower before them. Gray only found
it depressing.

With his guard down, he was struck by a mind-scan so
severe that it staggered him. If it hadn't been for the Martian

gravity, which bounced him harmlessly off a wall, he would've fallen to the floor.

"Are you all right?" asked the guard as she grabbed Gray's elbow and steadied him.

"Yes, yes," he rasped, trying to clear his head. Who the hell had done *that* to him?

A small, middle-aged man in a black uniform stepped from behind a pillar. He smiled, trying to look friendly, but he only succeeded in looking heartless.

"Your friend will look after you," said the guard cheerfully, literally pushing Gray into the man's gloved hands.

"So pleased to meet you," said Mr. Bester without speaking a word.

Gray blinked in amazement and answered telepathically, "I didn't expect you to meet me personally, Mr. Bester."

"You'll find," said the Psi Cop in spoken words, "that I believe in the axiom 'If you want something done right, do it yourself.' "

Gray almost protested over the way he had been scanned without permission, or warning for that matter. But he knew it wouldn't do any good. Bester was above the law, if anyone was, although he preferred to work from behind pillars and politicians, not in front of them. In a privileged class, Bester was the most privileged.

Harriman Gray was a slight man, and he took some comfort in the fact that Mr. Bester was no taller than he. In fact, without the considerable amount of hair that Bester possessed, he might have been even shorter.

The Psi Cop frowned. "Yes, but I'm a P12, and you're only a P10."

"I didn't mean anything by that," said Gray apologetically.

Bester smiled and started down the corridor. "Of course not. Do you know, there have been studies showing that shorter men are actually more predisposed toward telepathy. Do you suppose that could be evolution making up for a height disadvantage?"

"I read the Berenger Study, too," answered Gray, "but I

didn't think that he proved his hypothesis. For example, the same study showed that taller women were predisposed toward telepathy. It looks to me like a statistical aberration."

"That's why I wanted to pick you up myself," said Bester with satisfaction. "To have some time to talk with you. You know, this assignment won't last very long, just until we iron out the details of the conference and get the weekend started. However, I am looking for a new assistant."

Gray was caught off-guard by Bester dangling a ripe promotion in front of his nose, but he blocked his reactions as best he could. He could feel the Psi Cop probing his mind for a reaction, but he thought he had a very effective way to shut the probing down.

"Yes, I heard about poor Ms. Kelsey," said Gray, shaking his head. "Terrible tragedy."

Bester shrugged and stopped his scan. "She knew the risks. We got our man, that was the important part. Of course, when *you* went to Babylon 5, you also came back minus one."

Touché, thought Gray. "Yes, that was also a tragedy," he said with all sincerity.

"Nonsense," snapped Bester. "Ben Zayn was a weakling, a war burnout. Just like Sinclair."

The man in the black uniform swept down another corridor, and Gray hurried after him. Except for the ease of moving in the light gravity, there was no indication that they were on Mars. The docking area looked like any other space facility designed for oxygen-breathers; there were the usual crowded corridors, gift shops, florists, newsstands, restaurants, and credit machines. One had to go to an observatory dome to see anything of the red planet.

Bester went on with his diatribe about Babylon 5. "Neither Sinclair nor Ben Zayn was right for that post on B5. Now we've got another war hero there—John Sheridan. That's the trouble with the Senate and the President, always appointing war heroes to positions of command, just because they're popular."

"You don't think much of Captain Sheridan?" asked Gray with surprise. "Everyone at Earthforce think it's finally the right move."

"At least Sheridan is by the book," conceded the Psi Cop. "An honest plodder. But he may find that Babylon 5 is not covered in the book. I'll reserve judgment until I see how he handles the pressure."

"You would rather have someone from the Corps running B5?"

"No," answered Bester. "We work better behind the scenes. But it would be nice to have a *friend* in that post."

Gray cleared his throat and thought that he had better turn the conversation back to the promotion. "If you get a new assistant, doesn't he or she have to be a Psi Cop?"

"That has always been the conventional thinking—Psi Cops sticking with other Psi Cops. But it's not official policy. In some respects, it would be better to separate my assistant from my backup person. I can always find new cops to go after the rogues, but an able assistant is a bit harder to replace."

After negotiating another corner, Bester continued, "My assistant has to be a member of the Corps and be willing to undergo a deep scan. That goes without saying. Otherwise, it could be anybody."

The older telepath turned abruptly, stepped in front of Gray, and looked him squarely in the eyes. "I've done a lot of research on you, Mr. Gray. I especially like the way you manage to come out on the winning side of every skirmish. That quality, plus your military background, is very appealing to me."

Gray waited for the blast of a deep scan, but it never happened. Bester just looked at him, a satisfied smile on his surprisingly youthful face. It was as if he was saying he could jump his mind anytime he wanted to, but he wasn't going to, for now. So the liaison official took the offer at face value—he was on a trial period to be Mr. Bester's full-time assistant.

However, Gray couldn't forget the fact that he had a job to do, and that was to promote the military's needs in the upcoming conference of high-level telepaths. Press releases claimed the focus was on commercial applications for telepaths—and there would be representatives from the commercial firms—but everyone knew who really controlled the Corps these days. Military and corporate telepaths were fighting for crumbs of power compared to what Bester already had. They controlled their own domains, but Bester and the Psi Cops controlled them.

"The monorail is this way," said Bester. "We have a private car."

"My luggage," said the young telepath.

Bester smiled. "It's being delivered to your suite. I think you will find that the Royal Tharsis Lodge is being quite accommodating."

Once inside the security of the sealed monorail car, Harriman Gray finally relaxed and took in the sights, such as they were on a dark Martian night. The angry red planet didn't look so angry when it was crisscrossed with monorail tubes, prefabricated dwellings, and shielded domes. It looked like a giant gerbil habitat on a dusty parking lot.

A canyon yawned beneath the monorail tube, lit up by a science station perched on the rim. The canyon was, Gray estimated, about six kilometers deep, or about three times the depth of the Grand Canyon. The canyon faded into the distance before Gray could get a very good look. With a minimum of gravity and friction, the monorail was breezing above the surface of Mars at a speed of four hundred kilometers per hour.

Gray shifted his gaze toward the distance and their destination, the famed Tharsis Rise—a jutting plateau of volcanic ridges that was five kilometers high. It was lit up like the Pyramids, but the lights failed to convey even one-tenth of its size. By daylight, it was a monstrous thing that seemed to go on forever, but Gray knew it was only about three thousand kilometers across.

Tharsis Rise was a bona fide tourist attraction, no one could deny that. And the Royal Tharsis was a posh resort, so posh that both the manager and the chef were Centauri. Fine, thought Gray, but once you got past a few Centauri luxuries, there wasn't anything out here to see but a big flat rock. He would have preferred an Earth setting for the conference—with greenery and water—not hot, dusty rocks.

Bester was quiet and thoughtful as he gazed out the convex window. "You don't see anything of interest out there, do you," he remarked.

"I'm afraid I don't," answered Gray. "I've always found the mystique of Mars to be sadly lacking. Behind all these sleek tubes, there's a lot of poverty, dissension, and . . . nothing. People came here looking for something, and only a few found anything of value. Now they want to blame the planet they came from for all their problems."

"Yes," said Bester, staring at the vast, rose-hued horizon. "But if you find something of value here on Mars, it may be priceless."

Even though the two men were totally alone in the private car, Gray leaned forward conspiratorially and whispered, "There are rumors about what's going on at our facility in Syria Planum. If I may ask, Mr. Bester, what's going on out there?"

The little man bristled. "That information is on a need-to-know basis, and you don't need to know."

"Sorry, sir," said Gray, straightening in his seat.

Actually, the military had a good idea what was going on at the Psi Corps training center, and Gray had been secretly briefed about it. But this was not the time or place to pursue the matter.

Bester relaxed a bit, but he still looked preoccupied. "Don't you see," he explained, "we can't tell anyone about Syria Planum, because *we're* the only ones who can keep a secret."

"Yes," admitted the young telepath, nodding his head

sagely.* It was their burden, in a way, that all the mundanes, the nontelepaths, were doomed to become a second class under the telepaths. He didn't really like it, but he understood it as a sort of natural evolution of society. Who could stand in their way?

"It's late," said Bester, "but I can arrange a tour of the hotel for you right away, if you like."

"I've been here before," answered Gray, "although I was only here for the day. It's a beautiful facility."

"Secure, too," said the man in the black uniform. "The monorail is the only way in or out. Except for overland, which would be insane. During the weekend of the conference, we can make sure that only the Corps and our handful of invited guests even get off the rail."

Gray shook his head apologetically. "I've been traveling around so much, I haven't kept up. Are we still worried about the separatists?"

"Bloody idiots," muttered Bester. "They haven't got a chance. We're not going to give up Mars to a bunch of illiterate miners, I can tell you that."

Gray cleared his throat. "Of course, the military would have preferred to go to Earth for the conference. West Point or Sparta, some place like that."

Bester smiled. "Have you ever played Martian basketball?"

Now Gray sat forward eagerly. "No, but I've heard about it."

"It's just like Earth basketball," said Bester, "only with the low gravity, *everybody* gets to dunk it. They have some lovely courts here, and perhaps you and I can take some time for a match in the morning. We don't have to sign the contracts with the hotel until tomorrow afternoon."

"I'd like that," answered Gray, beaming.

---

* For six generations since telepathy had been scientifically proven, Psi Corps had been testing and monitoring telepaths. It had grown from a minor subdepartment into the most feared organization in the Alliance, and most telepaths considered themselves genetically superior.

The young man was feeling more relaxed already. Certainly all those terrible stories about Mr. Bester were simply not true. He could see the hotel very clearly now, an art-deco monstrosity that looked nothing like a lodge, as he thought of a lodge. Only the jutting ridge of Tharsis gave the complex any perspective whatsoever.

An explosion suddenly lit up the jagged rock face, and a flaming section of the hotel spewed outward, along with tables, chairs, and other objects that were sucked into the thin atmosphere.

The flames went out immediately, but debris continued to fly out. The shock wave jarred the monorail and would have knocked them out of their seats, if not for their restraints. Lights flickered in the car, and the monorail screeched to a bumpy halt.

The oxygen wasn't gone yet, but Gray was already panting for breath.

"Stay calm," ordered Bester. "Whatever you do, don't take your restraints off. What's the matter with this thing?"

He pounded on the panel over his head, and a dozen oxygen masks fell out, hanging from the ceiling like the tentacles of some bloated jellyfish. Swift changes in air pressure made papers and cups fly around the room.

"Put a mask on," ordered Bester, although Gray already had four of them in his hands.

They secured their oxygen masks and waited in the flickering lights. Gray felt a tug at his clothing, and the hair on his arms and neck seemed to rise with the drying of the air. They were going to be in oxygenless, 200-degree heat in a few minutes, he thought in a panic! He glanced at the gaping hole in the Royal Tharsis Lodge, and he saw things still flying out of it—things that might be human bodies! Or Centauri bodies. The voices started to bombard his head, and Gray closed his eyes and concentrated on breathing.

Bester ripped his mask off and sniffed the air. "Stay in your seat," he barked. "That is an order. I am going to loosen my restraints and try to get this thing into reverse."

Gray lifted the lip of his mask. "No, Mr. Bester! If the air gets sucked out, you might, too!"

"Do you think I want to sit here and bake to death?" asked Bester, unsnapping his restraints. He sprang to his feet and ripped out an entire bank of panels over his head. "Although," he remarked, "dying of dehydration is supposed to be one of the more pleasant forms of death."

"I wouldn't know!" shrieked Gray. He gulped and drew the oxygen mask back over his face.

Bester was like a man possessed, ripping out panels in the ceiling, on the floor, in the storage bins, and the bathroom. He occasionally had to grab a mask for a hit of oxygen, but he never faltered from his task. Finally, in the panel above the water dispenser, he found what looked like a pair of old-fashioned levers.

"Manual override," he panted. "Undocumented feature. It's amazing what you learn when you read people's minds all day."

Bester took one more breath of oxygen from a nearby mask and reached over the water cooler to grab the levers. His normally coiffed hair was plastered across his forehead in dripping ringlets, and the sweat drooled off his chin. The Psi Cop braced himself to give the levers a forceful jerk.

He needn't have tried so hard, because the levers moved easily in his grasp. There was a comforting clunk, and the car shuddered on its overhead track. One second later, the car flew into reverse so quickly that Bester was dumped on his backside. Gray considered himself fortunate that he was still strapped in.

Bester sat up groggily and staggered like a drunk into a seat, any seat. He strapped himself down, reached for a gas mask, and gratefully sucked oxygen.

Gray suddenly realized that he was a quivering rag of sweat, too. He tried to remain composed, but it was difficult with the dark hotel and its gaping wound in his direct line of vision. That was when the voices, the screams, and the agony grew louder! Gray put his hands over his ears and shrunk down into his seat.

"Don't give in to them!" growled Bester. "Block it. You can't help them now."

The assured words helped to calm Gray and give him some control, which he used to push the voices into the background while he tried to concentrate on his home in Berlin. His home was a grim little apartment, on the second floor, with stark furnishings and one window with a flower box that looked down upon a koi pond. He loved it. Gray had just gotten the apartment a few months ago, and he was very proud of it, even though he had only spent a handful of nights there between assignments.

He wanted to bring somebody to his apartment for dinner. Somebody like Susan. He tried to concentrate on Susan Ivanova until the terrified voices faded from his mind.

Bester coughed and cleared his throat. "Well, the Royal Tharsis Lodge is off the list. Where do you think we can hold this conference on short notice? No, do not suggest Earth or the training center at Syria Planum."

"If not Earth," said Harriman Gray, "I was going to suggest Babylon 5."

Bester took out a handkerchief and wiped his face. "Hmmm. You want to go to B5, eh?"

"Yes," said Gray, straightening up in his seat. "We'd both like to see how Sheridan is getting along there. The station is self-contained and relatively secure. I know Mr. Garibaldi has an attitude problem, but he gets the job done and has a good staff. We have a resident telepath there, Talia Winters, who can act as our coordinator."

"Let me get this straight," said Bester. "You'd like to invade B5, on a few days' notice, with the four hundred highest-ranking telepaths in Psi Corps?"

"Yes, sir."

Bester tapped his finger to his lips and smiled. "Even though we can't play Martian basketball there, that does sound like fun. You approach Ms. Winters, and I'll work through my channels. We want her to ask Captain Sheridan for permission, but we want to make sure he won't say no."

Gray swallowed and started to say, "Commander Ivanova . . ."

"Will be difficult as always." Bester clicked his tongue with disapproval. "A spotless record, except for her strange aversion to Psi Corps. You would think her mother was the only telepath who had ever been put to sleep."

Gray shook his head and decided not to mention Susan again. Bester didn't have to know about his personal life, although he might have already found out about his crush on Susan during that unexpected mind-scan. Well, thought Gray, he was on a new assignment and headed back to B5, and that was all that was important.

The young man chanced another look out the window. Half of the hotel on the great ridge was illuminated again, which was encouraging. The emergency systems and airlocks must have kicked in. Best of all, thought Gray, the voices had died to a whimper.

"Do you think the Mars separatists did that?" he asked softly.

"Who else?"

"I wonder how many people died in that explosion?" Gray mused.

Bester closed his eyes. "I counted twenty-six."

CHAPTER 2

"27 PERISH IN MARS HOTEL BOMBING!" exclaimed the banner headline in the *Universe Today* newspaper.

Talia Winters paused in her stroll down the mall to stare at the newspaper displayed on the newsstand of a small gift shop. The statuesque blonde only had to glance at the first few paragraphs to know that her all-expenses-paid trip to Mars was in serious jeopardy.

The report began:

> "The Royal Tharsis Lodge in Central Mars was the target of a terrorist bombing early this morning, in which 27 people, mostly hotel employees, died. Authorities have yet to make an arrest, but a previously unknown terrorist organization has claimed responsibility.
>
> "The organization, calling themselves Free Phobos, issued a communiqué saying that the purpose of the bombing was to prevent a scheduled conference of Psi Corps officials at the hotel. A Psi Corps spokesperson said the hotel was only one of several facilities under consideration.
>
> "Authorities believe the attack was made overland, because suspicious tracks were found on Tharsis Rise."

Talia Winters looked away, wondering if the problems on Mars would ever end. She had an appointment, so she couldn't dwell on her own little problems. With a sigh, she continued her stroll down the main corridor.

As usual, heads turned to watch Talia, but she paid them no attention. She was a beautiful woman, with sleek blond hair, an intelligent face, and a long-legged body wrapped in a tailored gray suit. Her P5 psi-level was only average, but her classy presence at a meeting or negotiation was as much in demand as her telepathic abilities. Even when both sides were friendly and had no intention of lying to one another, Talia brought an aura of professionalism and importance to the meeting. And she knew it.

However, her confidence was at a low ebb this particular day. Not only was she upset about the conference on Mars having to be postponed, in all likelihood, but she was mystified by the client she was going to see.

Talia was accustomed to not understanding the intricacies of every business deal—that was normal. In those cases, she would merely concentrate on trying to decide if the opposing party was sincere and truthful. Did they want to make a deal for mutual gain, or were they running a scam for their own personal gain? On most occasions, she didn't need to know the difference between a Brussard hydrogen scoop and an ice cream scoop.

This client was different. Not only didn't she understand Ambassador Kosh or his negotiating partners, but she often didn't understand the purpose of their meetings. For a telepath, being in the dark was the most irritating sensation in the universe. She had hoped to ask for opinions about Kosh from her colleagues at the conference, but now that was off. No conference, she thought glumly, and nothing to look forward to but a mind-bending encounter with Ambassador Kosh.

The attractive telepath finally reached the small cafe on Red-3. It was a local place, frequented by residents of the Red Sector looking for refreshments that were simple and quick. Why Kosh liked it so much, she didn't know; his ambassadorial quarters in the Alien Sector were on the other side of the station.

But she had a theory as to why he called the time they often met the Hour of Scampering. Briefly, between shifts, the cafe on Red-3 did turn into a pick-up bar, especially for the people who lived there and were headed home. Even Earthforce personnel felt comfortable on Red-3 during the Hour of Scampering.

Talia sauntered in and stopped. Kosh always stood out like a statue in the park, covered with a tarp to keep the birds off.

He was right there at his usual chest-high counter. Rather his ornate, bulky encounter suit was there—no one on the station had any idea what he looked like under it. Talia envisioned Kosh to be *big,* because a weakling could never carry that enormous suit around. She had no proof that he was big, but that was her theory.

The suit had a collar, carved from a gorgeous marblelike stone, and the collar was bigger than most of the tables in the restaurant. A mountain of rich fabrics cascaded off this neckwear, including a breastplate festooned with lights. The breastplate looked like an affectation, until one witnessed a precision instrument issue from it to perform some intricate operation. The breastplate also housed Kosh's communicator, which translated his musical squiggles of a voice into standard Interlac.

She took a deep breath and strode up to his table. "Pleasant Hour of Scampering, Ambassador Kosh."

"To you, Ms. Winters." The enormous head-gear nodded. It looked like an artistic rendering of a viper's head, without eyes or orifices. All the orifices were on his collar, and they were constantly revolving, sucking, expelling.

"Has your guest been detained?" asked Talia, looking around for the other half of this meeting.

The notes twinkled, and the lights flashed. "She is here," answered the communications device. The immense head-gear nodded toward the other corner of the counter.

"She is?" asked Talia, shaking her blond hair. Then she winced and put her hand to her head. "Don't tell me, your friend is invisible?"

Kosh nodded.

Talia tried to smile, but her fingernails drummed the countertop. "Isn't that special, an invisible friend. Look, Ambassador, I'm a licensed commercial psychic, not an escort service. If you want to ask me for a date, I may not even charge you. You don't have to pay my top rate just to get me out for a drink. Especially during the Hour of Scampering."

Kosh nodded insistently toward the empty space at the counter. "Her name is Isabel," said the synthesized voice.

"Invisible Isabel," Talia muttered. "Okay, Ambassador Kosh, that's it. I don't need any more commissions from you. You've jerked my chain for the last time."

The encounter suit seemed to rise up a few centimeters and pause in the air, commanding her attention. "Scan her," ordered the voice.

Talia swallowed. It would only take a second, she thought, and then she could leave and collect her paycheck. Scanning an imaginary person wasn't as bad as talking to one, she supposed. Could there really be someone there?

She had heard of cloaking suits, but she had also heard that they weren't very effective at close quarters. Thus far, Talia hadn't heard any other voices in this quiet corner of the room, and she was certain that Invisible Isabel was nonexistent. But she took a deep breath and tried to concentrate on the blank space at the end of the counter. Kosh would know if she faked it, even for a pointless purpose. Many of the other scans she had performed at his request had been pointless, although perhaps not as pointless as this.

Scanning something nonexistent proved to be more difficult than anticipated, and Talia had to concentrate to shut out the other voices in the room. If Isabel were invisible, she reasoned, then her psychic voice would be the only thing there was to pick up of her. Eliminating every voice in the room would prove that she was correct, and that Ambassador Kosh was crazy. At least that was Talia's rationale as she began her scan.

One by one, Talia isolated each voice in the room, determined who possessed the voice, and eliminated it. It took a lot of concentration, and she found herself shifting her eyes from one person to another. That Narn gone, that Antarean, that Centauri, those tourists, the two security officers, the waiter, the bartender—one by one she knocked them all out of her mind—until there was just her, the massive suit that was Kosh, and one other.

There *was* one other voice in the room.

As soon as Talia isolated the voice, it was gone. She

looked back at Kosh, startled. "What happened to her? Where did she go?"

The Vorlon shook his head-gear. "Gone."

That was not what Talia wanted to hear, and she was shaken. Had there been someone, or hadn't there? She had done a fifteen-minute scan that had given her a tremendous headache, but it was inconclusive.

She pointed a manicured finger at Kosh. "I'm thinking about raising my rates on you."

"Your rates are not the problem," remarked the Vorlon.

No, she thought, that was the truth. Playfully she said, "I would like to meet Invisible Isabel again."

"When the time is right," answered Kosh. "You will be very busy."

Talia sighed and put her elbows on the bar. "No, I don't think so. I cleared my schedule for a conference on Mars, but now it's not going to happen. *C'est la vie.*"

"Tous les jours," answered Kosh.

The young woman gave the Vorlon ambassador a friendly smile. "Today was better than most of the scans I do for you, although I couldn't say why. What happened?"

The twinkling notes sounded, and the Vorlon bowed his bulky suit. "Our business is concluded."

Without another word, the mountain of armor and fabric glided out of the room.

A tall, balding man in an Earthforce uniform strolled jauntily down the corridor toward the briefing room. He began to whistle. The worst thing he could imagine happening had happened, and he had lived through it! His best friend, the man who had gone out on a limb to make him the security chief of Babylon 5, was gone. But Michael Garibaldi still had a job.

The security chief couldn't believe it, but it was finally sinking in. Jeff Sinclair was gone, but he was still here. If anyone had told him a month ago that Jeff would be leaving and he would be staying, he would've laughed in his face. Jeff was the war hero, the handpicked savior of the Babylon project, and Garibaldi was a broken-down drunk, bouncing from job to job, coasting into the sewer. It was all thanks to Jeff that he'd gotten the job in the first place, and he was certain that if Jeff ever left, he would be handcuffed to his trunk. Would a new commander, a complete stranger, want to keep him on as chief of security? Not bloody likely.

Yet here he was! Sinclair had wanted him to stay on B5, and, miracle of miracles, so had Captain Sheridan. The captain had reviewed his reports and found his conduct and actions to be acceptable. Not great, mind you, but acceptable. According to Captain Sheridan, there was always room for improvement.

The captain had made it clear that Garibaldi served at his pleasure, to be replaced at a moment's notice. But Garibaldi had been replaced so many times in his career, he figured he was on probation for the rest of his life, anyway. Having it official didn't matter.

Hell, thought Garibaldi, *I'm still here!* Wasn't there a song with that title? He tried to remember the words.

"Mr. Garibaldi," said a no-nonsense female voice.

He turned to see an attractive brunette woman in an Earthforce uniform striding to catch up with him. He stopped and waited.

"Hi, Susan."

"Please," she whispered, "we're on our way to a briefing. Let's try to show some decorum. Call me Commander." She raised an eyebrow. Ivanova's eyebrows were famous for what they could do to people.

Garibaldi smiled and leaned down. "Tell me, Commander, how come when I had a friend running the station, I was relaxed about it. Now that you've got a friend running the station, you're all uptight."

"He's not my friend," she whispered, "just my former CO. And I'm worried about *you,* not me."

"Well, don't be," said Garibaldi with confidence. "What could Captain Sheridan possibly tell us that would spoil this beautiful day? I mean, the worst thing that can happen has already happened, right? Jeff is gone, but I'm still here, and you're still here. The station is still here. No ka-boom."

"Yet," added Ivanova grimly.

Garibaldi grinned. "And Captain Sheridan has had a salutary effect on the other races. I love the way he's not trying to make friends with them, or coddle them. They hate his guts, but they think you and I are great!"

Ivanova cleared her throat, put her hands behind her back, and strode toward the briefing room. She waited for the door to open, then charged in, followed by a grinning Garibaldi.

The captain was already there, leaning over a computer screen. He looked as handsome and distinguished as always, thought the security chief. Garibaldi was about the same age as Sheridan, around forty, but he didn't think he would ever be able to look as distingished as that, even if he had all his hair. The junior officers saluted, and Sheridan snapped off a salute of his own.

"Commander, Chief, have a seat."

"Are we expecting anyone else?" asked Ivanova, slipping into a chair at the conference table.

Sheridan smiled. "I believe we will have one more before too long, but essentially it's the two of you I want to see. I brought you down here because we have several consoles at our disposal; and I think we may be looking up schedules and personnel files long into the night."

Garibaldi started to say something sarcastic, like "Great!" Then he remembered that this wasn't Jeff Sinclair. He folded his hands and waited patiently.

"I've just been talking with Senator Hidoshi," the captain began. "And a most interesting opportunity has come our way. You must have heard about the hotel bombing on Mars?"

"That made no sense," muttered Garibaldi. "Who are these Free Phobos people? I never heard of them. Almost everyone they killed in that blast was just a working stiff, most of them *from* Mars!"

Ivanova shot him a glare at his outburst, and Sheridan

stiffened his back and cleared his throat. "Mr. Garibaldi, you have served on Mars, I take it?"

The chief lowered his head and scratched behind his ear. "Yeah, for about a year."

"Then you know," said Sheridan, "the problems of Mars are very complex. Ivanova and I served together on Io, far removed from most of the difficulties, and that was bad enough. The thing is, the infrastructure of Mars is so fragile that we can't really wage war there. We can't wipe out the terrorists, so they have all the advantages. They can destroy targets—and the Royal Tharsis was a very astute target—but if we destroy anything, we'll kill thousands and create a mess that will never be cleaned up."

"In other words," said Garibaldi, "we could win it, but there wouldn't be anything left to take home."

"Precisely," agreed Sheridan. "So let's not get too riled up about Mars, because the Senate will just have to suck it up and find a political solution. In one small way, though, we can help."

"What is that, sir?" Ivanova asked brightly.

The captain wiped a speck of lint off the table. "Did you know that Psi Corps was planning to hold a conference at the Royal Tharsis? And now they can't."

"Yes?" answered Ivanova, suddenly very grim.

Gabibaldi wasn't about to say what he thought of that. It was hard to hate someone who made Psi Corps squirm.

"Anyway," said Sheridan cheerfully, "we have a chance to thumb our noses at the terrorists. We can make sure that Psi Corps has their conference—right here on B5!"

Ivanova squirmed in her seat. "How many telepaths are we talking about, sir?"

"Only about four hundred."

Garibaldi's elbow dropped off the table, and he very nearly hit his jaw on it. "But, sir, in a few days—four hundred guests. I'm not sure the station can accommodate . . ."

"Housekeeping informs me there's no problem," said Sheridan. "We've been remodeling Blue-16, and we simply step it up in the next forty-eight hours and get those rooms ready."

Ivanova looked truly stricken now. "Are we talking about Psi Cops, like Bester? Or commercial telepaths, like Ms. Winters?"

Sheridan crossed his arms and stared at his subordinates in amazement. "Who do you think we're talking about? The four hundred highest-ranking telepaths in Psi Corps, that's who! No, they're not Snow White and the Seven Dwarves, but they're a damned important bunch of people."

"But why do they want to come here?" asked Garibaldi suspiciously.

The captain shook his head puzzledly. "I thought you would welcome this as a golden opportunity, which it is. It's a chance for us to show everyone that B5 is past her growing pains, that we're a suitable place for a high-level conference. You know, everybody thinks we're a jinx! Psi Corps is doing *us* a favor by coming here."

Garibaldi glanced at Ivanova, but the commander's lips were clamped tight. He knew that she had decided to withhold comment about Psi Corps for the moment.

He gingerly held up his finger. "Sir, it's just that, in the short time we've been open, Psi Corps has shown unusual interest in us."

"Nonsense," snapped Sheridan. "Psi Corps shows unusual interest in *everybody*. But what are we going to do about it? Make them mad, so they show even more interest? The next time the Senate considers our appropriations, it would be very nice to have Psi Corps in our corner. Besides, all telepaths are not cut from the same cloth as Bester. Our own Ms. Winters is highly respected, and so are hundreds of other private telepaths. And, Chief, unless you lied in your report, Harriman Gray saved your life."

"Yes, he did," admitted Garibaldi. He appealed to Ivanova. "Are you going to say anything here, or do you want Bester and four hundred of his friends to show up tomorrow?"

The second-in-command sat up in her chair. "Captain," she began, "if I may speak freely."

Sheridan sighed. "Mr. Garibaldi has no problem speaking freely, so why should you?"

"I have a revulsion to Psi Corps," she declared. "It's personal. I have never let this interfere with my duty, except for the fact that I will not submit to a scan, for any reason. I'm sure this will hamper my career advancement at some point, but I will not let it interfere with my duty."

Ivanova took a deep breath and concluded, "I will get all of their ships in safely and assist in the Psi Corps conference however I can. I will do my best to put the station in a good light. However, if one of those buggers tries to scan me, I will rip his lungs out."

Garibaldi nodded in agreement. "Yeah, and it'll take five guys to pull her off. And another five guys to arrest her, then all those doctors in medlab. Do we really want to risk it, sir?"

Sheridan rubbed his eyes. "I have sympathy for your feelings, but they can't stand in the way of this opportunity. Therefore, Commander, you will be restricted to quarters during the duration of the conference, except for your normal hours of duty. In fact, Commander, you are under orders not to talk to the attendees. If they don't like that, you can talk to them just long enough to tell them to come see me."

"Uh, sir," asked Garibaldi hopefully, "could we arrange it so that *I* don't have to talk to them either?"

"I'm afraid not, Chief. They're going to be paranoid about security, especially after this Mars thing. To put it bluntly, it's going to be a nightmare for you. I could requisition some outside security to help you, but I don't want to risk it. We don't know who they might send."

"No, that's okay," said Garibaldi, his shoulders drooping. "Hundreds of paranoid Psi Cops, just what I always wanted. I don't suppose there's any way you could be talked out of hosting this shindig?"

"Well," said the captain, "if you had offered reasoned arguments against it, I might have listened. If your only objection is that you hate Psi Corps, that's not unusual enough.''

Sheridan tapped the link on the table console. "Captain Sheridan to Ms. Talia Winters.''

"Captain!'' said her startled voice a moment later. "I was just about to call you! Did you hear about the conference? Isn't it wonderful!''

The captain surveyed the long faces of Ivanova and Garibaldi. "Oh, yes, we're jumping up and down here. You are supposed to make an official request, I believe, on behalf of Psi Corps.''

"Oh, I'm so relieved to hear you say you will accept! I had the silly notion there might be some problem.''

"Of course not,'' said Sheridan magnanimously. "We're down in the briefing room now, and perhaps you'd like to join us and get the ball rolling. Oh, Mr. Garibaldi wonders how many of the attendees will be actual Psi Cops, like Mr. Bester.''

"About a hundred or so.''

Garibaldi buried his head in his hands.

"The theme is commercial applications,'' Talia added. "I'll be right down to tell you all about it!''

"I look forward to it,'' answered Sheridan. "Out.''

The captain looked grim as his gaze traveled from Ivanova to Garibaldi. "An advance team from Psi Corps is already on its way to help coordinate, and the rest will follow in the next day or two. Listen, people, for the next six days, you *love* Psi Corps. And your mission in life is to make sure they have the best conference they ever had. Do you understand?''

Garibaldi and Ivanova just looked at each other and sighed. "Yes, sir,'' they muttered.

CHAPTER 3

"WELL," said Garibaldi, leaning over a stack of diagrams, "we've got the Blue recreation room. You can have that. Unless our work crews fall asleep, a couple of Blue meeting rooms will be ready. The cafe in Blue Sector is under private contract, but the proprietor says he'll have it open in time for the reception."

"We'll want to run a security check on the proprietor," said Talia Winters. "And we'll need more than a couple of meeting rooms. The idea of this conference is to break off into smaller discussion groups. Intimate gatherings."

Garibaldi cocked an eyebrow. "I'll bet."

Talia pursed her lips, but she let it pass. "What about the meeting rooms on Red and Yellow?"

The security chief scowled. "I'm trying to keep all of your people in the Blue Sector, and pretty much seal it off. For their own safety."

Talia smiled even while she shook her head. "No way, Mr. Garibaldi. These people don't like to be told that certain places are off limits. No place is off limits for them."

"Wait a minute," he protested, "I can't give them complete run of the station! You don't want them Down Below, do you? With that element. Or in the Alien Sector. What if they meet up with the carrion-eaters? I can't protect them on every square centimeter of every cargo bay of B5."

"I think you will find, Mr. Garibaldi, that most telepaths are capable of taking care of themselves. Besides, most of them have never been to Babylon 5. They'll be disappointed if they don't receive the full experience."

"Is that so," grumbled Garibaldi. "You know, Ms. Winters, we've had our share of murders and disappearances here, and a couple of the other Babylon stations were blown to bits. The *full* B5 experience is not what I really want them to have. I want them to have a safe, boring experience. I want them to go back to their slimepits and say, 'Gosh, that B5 was the most boring place I've ever been. There is certainly no reason to go back *there* again.' ''

Talia's icy-blue eyes burned into him. "This is only our first day of planning, Mr. Garibaldi, and I will not allow you to start insulting the Corps. If we have a problem we can't resolve, I suggest we get Captain Sheridan to arbitrate it."

"I'm doing exactly what the captain wants," the chief countered. "He wants us to look like grown-ups, no more Wild Frontier stuff. He wants B5 to look like a proper place to hold a high-level tête-à-tête, and I don't blame him. The more money we can bring in by ourselves means the less we have to rely on our allies and the Senate."

Now Garibaldi looked into Talia's eyes, something he did not mind doing whatsoever. "Look, Talia, B5 is not a swank resort, and that was their first choice. Security is going to be stretched like we've never been stretched before, just dealing with the arrivals. We haven't had time to get the word out, so all of our regular traffic will be piling up at the docks. I'm not saying we can't do it, but have a heart!"

"All right," conceded Talia, "we will label certain areas, such as Down Below, cargo bays, and the Alien Sector as 'Travel at Your Own Risk.' In the handouts, we'll advise the attendees not to go there. Satisfied?"

"Not exactly," muttered Garibaldi. As Talia was not going to back away from him, and her closeness was making him nervous, he found a chair and began to go over the diagrams again.

"Okay," he told her, "Green Sector has a business park that hasn't been opened yet. It has a lot of standard offices and meeting rooms, even a few larger rooms for light manufacturing. Hey, that's nice—a few of these offices have dual-atmosphere. Anyway, I guess your folks could take over the whole business park. So you'll sleep in Blue-16 and party, or whatever you do, on Green-12."

Talia sat on the desk and crossed her legs, and the tight gray skirt rode up to midcalf. "Panels mostly. I'm moderating a panel on currency exchange, and I'm going to attend two seminars on mining law. You know, everybody thinks when telepaths get together, they study telepathy. Hell, we already know about that. We have to bone up on the other stuff, that everybody else knows.''

"Okay," said Garibaldi, "so maybe this won't be so bad. And if it gets too boring, we can always send for some Martian terrorists to liven things up."

The telepath sat forward, looking grim. "You won't let that happen, will you?"

Garibaldi lowered his lofty forehead at her. "Let us say that nobody will get into Blue-16 or Green-12 except your people and my people. But you had better give the attendees an advisory about the rest of the station."

He frowned. "And I'll give the rest of the station an advisory about them."

"We do want to be able to use one more room," said Talia. "The casino."

"Whoa, wait a minute. Telepaths aren't allowed to gamble. Why would they want to go there?"

Talia insisted, "Just to have someplace fun and cheerful to go. Would you like to be cooped up in a bunch of boring offices and crew quarters? You said it before, this isn't a luxury hotel, but we should go the extra centimeter to make it pleasant. The casino would simply give them someplace to go, to mingle with the populace. As for the gambling, shut down the games."

"Shut down the games?"

"Out of consideration." Talia tossed her sleek blond hair and leveled him with her firmest gaze. "Look, Garibaldi, I've given in on everything. You are getting it as easy as I can make it. Don't you think you can give me one thing—a place to party, as you call it. I will go to the captain with this, if you insist on fighting me."

"No, no, leave the captain alone," said Garibaldi. "He's up to his eyeballs in VIPs, and they're not VIPs I want to see."

"Yes, I know," replied Talia, pulling up the flap on her

leather glove to check her timepiece. "I really should be going to meet them."

Garibaldi pushed the link on the back of his hand. "Link, take a memo. For the benefit of our conference guests, the station is assigning extra security to Blue-16, Green-12, the docking area, connecting corridors, and connecting tubes. Oh, and the casino. The attendees will be told that all other areas are to be entered at their own risk. They are not protected in the other areas."

He lowered his hand and smiled at Talia. "I believe in getting things in writing."

"So do I," agreed Talia. "Make sure you mention that gambling in the casino will be prohibited all weekend."

"Yeah, yeah," muttered Garibaldi. He spoke into the back of his hand. "Gambling will cease in the casino in exactly twelve hours, not to be resumed except by my authority. End memo. Priority distribution."

Talia grabbed the diagram of the business park in Green Sector and studied it. "Are these spaces expensive? Maybe I'll lease one, when this is all over."

"Lady," said Garibaldi, "you get me through this, and I'll make sure you get the nicest one—for free."

Talia gave him her professional smile, the one that dazzled the opposition and made them realize they had been beaten. Garibaldi was suitably dazzled.

"Thank you, Michael," she replied. "It's been a pleasure doing business with you." Talia sauntered to the door and tossed over her shoulder, "I'll get you a schedule of the panels."

"Thanks!" he said, as if he really wanted one.

When the door finally shut, Garibaldi rolled his eyes toward the heavens. As miserable as this black cloud was, even it had a strand of silver lining. No matter what else happened in the next six days, he was going to be spending a lot of time with Talia Winters.

"Be still, my heart," he told himself with a chuckle.

* * *

Talia Winters was a bit surprised to find no one waiting at the docking bay except for Captain Sheridan and half a dozen extra security officers. She didn't expect a brass band exactly, but a small show of ambassadors or dignitaries would have been in order.

"Captain," she said. "Are more people coming?"

"Hello, Ms. Winters," he said, not dispensing with the niceties simply because she had. "We've got everyone working double shifts down in Blue Sector just to get it ready. Mr. Bester will have to be content with you and me."

"What about Ambassador Mollari?" she asked. "Or Ambassador G'Kar?"

"What about them?"

Talia started to say that Commander Sinclair would have gotten the ambassadors to come, but she squelched that thought before it left her lips. Odd, she mused, how you didn't notice certain qualities in people until they were gone. On the face of it, Captain Sheridan was a cultured, charming man; but underneath he was intractable, like a sword in a supple leather scabbard. Commander Sinclair had been intractable on the surface, but underneath he was open-minded, ready to sympathize and take risks. Perhaps too ready.

The captain gave her a pleasant smile. "Are you scanning me?"

"No," she said defensively. "But I was comparing you to Commander Sinclair. I'm sorry."

Sheridan nodded. "That's understandable. When I came here, I was surprised to learn how popular my predecessor was. On Earth, they said he was crazy, a loose cannon, but here people thought he was a saint. Now compare that with the way General George Armstrong Custer was perceived during the conquest of North America. His commanders in Washington thought he was brilliant, but in the field, everybody knew he was crazy."

"Perceptions are not what they seem," remarked Talia. "That's why we need telepaths."

"You've never regretted joining Psi Corps?"

"No," she answered, taken aback by the very idea. "Do

you regret the training you had? Does a musical prodigy regret his musical training? We are seeing the emergence of a new talent in thousands of people, and it must be nurtured and regulated. Psi Corps is everything anyone could hope it would be.''

"But Psi Corps has become an issue," the captain declared. ''People fear it, people discuss it. People try to stop it. My predecessor at this station became an issue, and that's what ultimately hurt him. That's where I'm different—I want my presence here to be neutral, just enough to make the station run efficiently. So don't expect me to go overboard, on anything.''

"Understood," said Talia. ''I sincerely appreciate your cooperation on this conference. However, Captain, I don't think that Psi Corps can take a backseat any longer. We have a certain destiny to fill, and we need to be up-front about it.''

Sheridan nodded thoughtfully. ''I would suggest you remember one thing, Ms. Winters—when you're up-front, they'll shoot at you first.''

Talia nodded curtly and stared down the walkway at the closed air-lock. On the eve of this important conference, she didn't need to hear ominous warnings from her station commander. On the other hand, it was evident that they wouldn't be here if terrorists hadn't bombed that Martian hotel. Was Sheridan trying to tell her the same thing Garibaldi had been trying to tell her? Keep it safe. Keep it low-key.

Talia had been thinking just the opposite. She wanted to show the world that Psi Corps was more than a few failed cases of telepaths gone rogue, or sleepers getting depressed. Psi Corps meant commerce, diplomacy, military preparedness, and, yes, a more efficient government. Telepaths had their place everywhere, in every endeavor. That was the message she wanted the conference to spread.

But maybe Sheridan was right. Talia often ignored the backlash against Psi Corps as being mere jealousy from the mundanes. Perhaps it was more ingrained than that—perhaps people really did want to stop them. Although she didn't agree with Captain Sheridan, she would heed his warning.

The affair would be low-key, manageable, without controversy. Maybe it would even be slightly boring.

Sheridan's link chimed, and he lifted his hand to answer it. "Yes?"

"Captain," said Ivanova, "transport *Freya* has just docked. Your party should be disembarking any moment."

"Thank you, Commander. Any word from the ambassadors about our invitation?"

"No, sir."

"Sheridan out." He lowered his hand, looked at Talia, and shrugged. "I did invite the ambassadors to attend the reception tomorrow night. But I never know what they'll do. If you would like to talk to them . . ."

Talia shook her head and smiled. "No, Captain, let's keep it low-key, shall we?"

He nodded. "I agree."

The air-lock opened, and a man in a black uniform strode off the dock and down the walkway. He was followed by a slight man, who looked expectantly around the docking area, as if he was looking for someone. A handful of other passengers followed, and a few of them were also wearing Psi Corps insignia. None but Mr. Bester wore the black uniform of the Psi Police.

"Captain Sheridan," said Bester as he produced his identicard. "Congratulations on your new command."

"Thank you, Mr. Bester."

The security guard nervously finished with Mr. Bester and sent him on his way. "Ms. Winters," said the Psi Cop with a nod.

She smiled. "Mr. Bester."

Talia was waiting for Bester to scan somebody, anybody, because he hardly needed any preparation. He did it with as much effort as it took to brush the lint off one's sleeve. Plus, he had the authority to cut corners, which usually meant that he took what information he needed, from wherever it was in people's minds. But the famed Psi Cop was on his best behavior; he waited patiently for the other members of his party to be checked through.

"Mr. Gray, how are you?" Captain Sheridan called to the young man in a chummy tone.

The military liaison stopped looking around long enough to smile. "I'm fine, Captain, thank you. Let me also congratulate you on your new post. Everyone at headquarters is pulling for you."

Bester looked at the telepath with amusement on his ageless face. "Come now, Gray, not everyone. You were thinking about a certain general, for instance."

Gray bristled. "I don't believe I was. Excuse me, Captain, but where is Commander Ivanova?"

"Busy," snapped Sheridan. "You won't be seeing much of her, I'm afraid."

Talia looked away from the flustered Mr. Gray to see who else from Psi Corps had arrived on the *Freya*. There was a small, dark-skinned woman, who fumbled with her identicard. Instead of her making the guard nervous, the guard was apparently making her nervous. Behind her, waiting patiently, stood a tall man with a professorial air to him, no doubt helped by his graying goatee. He looked older than the last photograph she had seen of him, but there was no mistaking the profound intelligence in his sad, dark eyes.

"Mr. Malten?" she asked.

He smiled apologetically but boyishly. "Pardon me, but I'm terrible with names. Isn't that an awful thing for a telepath to admit?"

"Not at all," she said, extending a gloved hand, "because we've never met. I'm Talia Winters, resident telepath on B5."

The guard motioned Malten through as quickly as he could, so that he could complete their handshake. The distinguished telepath was beaming. "I was hoping I would run into you right away, Ms. Winters! May I present my associate, Emily Crane. She'll be assisting you this week."

The small, dark-skinned woman held out her gloved hand, and Talia took it. "Very p-pleased to meet you," stammered Emily.

Talia smiled. "Likewise." If it hadn't been for the Psi

Corps insignia on Emily Crane's collar, Talia would never have guessed she was a telepath. She barely seemed the type who could tie her own shoelaces.

"Yes," said Malten, "I'm turning Emily over to you. You'll find her quite a whiz with newsletters, press releases, and such. I always find that a conference goes better when there are plenty of newsletters to keep everyone abreast of changes. Don't you?"

"Oh, yes," agreed Talia.

Malten smiled proudly at the tiny woman. "Emily's real job is chief copywriter for our firm."

Our firm, Talia repeated to herself. It was amazing how blithely Malten could refer to Earth's biggest and most prestigious conglomerate of commercial telepaths. The Mix, as it was known across the galaxy, had offices in virtually every corner of the Alliance, and on some nonaligned worlds.

Talia turned to Emily. "I've been reading about telepathic copywriting. How does that work?"

"Well," said Emily, "say the client has an advertising campaign in mind, but they c-can't express it in words. Or it's only half-formed in their minds. We d-do a scan. We learn what they really want, even when they don't know what they really want." She grinned, happy to have gotten that speech out.

"Yes," said Malten, "we started out thinking we could do the finished ads in-house, but it turned out to be more cost-effective to contract our services directly to the ad agencies. By the end of the year, we'll have seven branch offices doing nothing but this."

"You'll have to c-come to my panel," Emily added. "We'll d-do a demonstration."

Malten gave both women a gentle push down the corridor. "Looks like they're leaving us behind."

Talia turned around to see Captain Sheridan, Mr. Bester, and Mr. Gray walking briskly down the corridor about fifty meters ahead of them. All of a sudden, none of those three men seemed very important to Talia, not when the man beside her was pioneering the invasion of telepathy into every-day life and business.

"They're just going to look at security grids and the like," said Talia. "But I know a great place where we can get a Jovian Sunspot."

Arthur Malten laughed. "I presume we can pick up our luggage from customs later tonight. Lead on!"

Needing the computer consoles, Garibaldi turned the briefing room into his temporary headquarters. For the umpteenth time, he rubbed his eyes and squinted at his screen. "Come on, Baker, are you going to tell me that you need four guys around the clock on one lousy access port?"

"That's the primary access port for Green-12," answered Baker. "If we're going to seal it off, but let the VIPs through, we've got to have lots of eyes."

"I'll give you two guys," growled Garibaldi, "and that's only because one of them might have to go to the bath-room."

Seeing the young woman's crestfallen face, the chief added, "After we get most of these jokers through their ar-rival and customs, we can free up some people. I'll give you backup as soon as possible."

Baker smiled. "Thanks, Chief."

"One more thing," said Garibaldi, "that *is* a crucial spot, and your people can't leave it for anything. I don't care if they have pee running down their legs, or bug-eyed monsters are eating everyone in sight, they cannot leave that post."

Baker swallowed nervously. "Is it true they can make us see things that aren't there? Put suggestions in our heads?"

Garibaldi nodded glumly. "I imagine they can. We won't have much control over the people at this party—all we can do is keep other people from crashing it. I mean, if some-body from Psi Corps flips out and decides to blow up his buddies, we're in a world of trouble."

That thought was sobering enough to put an end to all conversation in the briefing room. After a moment, Garibaldi waved wearily to the half-dozen subordinates who were still with him. "Go to bed. That's an order."

"Good night, Chief. 'Night," they muttered as they quickly filed out.

The security chief might have sat frozen in the position he was in all night long, just worrying, too tired to move. But the lack of oxygen and sleep made him yawn. That yawn was enough to make him stand up, stretch his arms, and reach for his jacket.

Just when he was about to escape to his own quarters, his link buzzed. "Security," he muttered into the back of his hand.

"Mr. Garibaldi," said a voice. "It's me, Talia."

Oh, Lord, thought the chief, the ice queen. "What can I do for you, Ms. Winters?"

"I'm down in Red-3, with a couple of friends. I was wondering if you could take us on a little tour of the Alien Sector. Maybe Down Below."

"What?" snarled Garibaldi. "Didn't we just agree today that your friends were not supposed to go down there?"

"Aw, come on," said Talia. "The conference hasn't even started yet, and these are real VIPs."

No kidding. VIPs. Garibaldi knew he was going to get tired of hearing that real fast. On the other hand, it was Talia Winters. Late at night, in a party mood. Maybe he would get lucky.

"Red-3, you say?" He yawned and checked the PPG weapon hanging on his belt. "Order me a cup of coffee—I'll be right there."

And so it begins, thought Garibaldi, as he buttoned his collar and slouched out the door.

CHAPTER 4

"THAT'S it for me," said Ivanova with a sigh. "The station is yours, Major Atambe."

Her replacement nodded and assumed the command post in front of the main viewing port of C-and-C. The docking bays were quiet—only two ships were preparing to depart for the jump gate, and the station was secure. Ivanova paused at the doorway and looked back.

"When is the next transport from Earth due in?"

Major Atambe punched up the shipping register. "Oh seven hundred," he replied.

She nodded. "I'll be back then. Wouldn't want to lose any of our VIPs, would we?"

Ivanova strode through the doorway and toward the lift that would take her to her humble quarters. She was thinking about her bed, her most prized possession in the universe. It wasn't a remarkable bed—just a standard-issue single bed, extra firm—but it represented her sanctuary, her escape. No matter what madness was swirling all around her, she could always collapse into that bed and find peace in immediate slumber.

Ivanova began thinking about a remarkable vacation she had planned, if only she could get away with it. In this dream vacation, she would lie in bed as much as she wanted. The link, the alarm clock, the computer, anything that might wake her up would be banished deep into her sock drawer. Perhaps a waiter would come, at her bidding, to bring her bonbons and other snacks, but otherwise she would do nothing but sleep. If she woke up, she would look around to content herself that she was still safely in bed, then she would roll over and go back to sleep.

She chuckled to herself. What had her grandfather always said? "You can get a Jewish woman to do anything in bed but wake up." Her grandmother, she recalled, had never learned to make matzo ball soup in sixty-three years of married life.

Well, thought Ivanova, she had never learned how to make matzo ball soup either. Unfortunately, there was no one around to make it for her.

"Susan," said a voice.

She stopped dead in the deserted corridor, as a feeling of dread crept up her backbone. A figure stepped out of the shadows but made no movement to come closer.

"Hello, Susan," said Mr. Gray, a smile tugging at his thin lips.

"Gray," she snapped. She strode past him.

He ran after her. "Susan, please, I just want to talk to you!"

"I'm not allowed to talk to you. Captain's orders." She pushed the button and waited for the lift.

Gray waved his hands desperately. "Susan, I don't want anything from you, really."

"Then go away." Where was that stupid lift?

The door opened, and she stepped in. To her disgust, Gray followed. Now they were alone in the narrow confines of an elevator car.

"Deck eight," said Ivanova, then she lifted the link to her mouth. "If you persist in harassing me, I will call security."

"Harassing you?" muttered Gray. "All I said was hello!" He stared straight ahead at the door, as if he didn't care to speak to her again either.

"Hello," she said disgruntledly.

"I just wanted to tell you about my new apartment," said Gray. "In Berlin."

Ivanova looked at him. "Berlin. I'm impressed. I didn't pick you as being the avant-garde type."

"You don't know me very well, do you?" asked Gray. "Did you think all telepaths lived in some medieval dungeon somewhere?"

"Yes."

Gray chuckled. "Oh, some of them do. Most of us live out of a suitcase, in army barracks, or metal boxes like this one."

The lift door opened, and Gray waited expectantly. Ivanova stepped out, stopped, and lifted her shoulders in a tremendous sigh.

"Please, Susan," Gray pleaded, "stop thinking of me as the enemy. You know I didn't choose this path—I wanted to be a soldier. I've got a career, and I'm trying to get somewhere in the channels that are open to me, just like you. I'm all alone, just like you."

The young telepath lowered his head. "Maybe it was a mistake trying to see you. I'm sorry I bothered you."

He turned to go, and Ivanova reached out her hand. But she couldn't bring herself to touch him. "Your place in Berlin," she asked, "is it anywhere near the Free University?"

He turned excitedly. "Yes, it is! It's about ten blocks away, and I can take the U-Bahn, or walk. I love walking around Berlin. I know many people find it depressing, because the whole city is like a museum to the destructive power of war. But what can I say, I'm a war buff."

Ivanova shrugged. "Whatever turns you on. I went there on a summer study program to research the dadaists." She headed down the corridor, and Gray scurried along beside her.

"That's a fascinating period," he admitted, "although the dadaists are a bit extreme for my tastes. There are some interesting comparisons between the dadaists and the performance artists of the late twentieth century. Wouldn't you say?"

Ivanova frowned in thought. "I'm not sure. In both cases, their aim was to shock the bourgeoisie and the accepted art establishment. But the dada movement was more of a collective effort, and performance art was very individualistic. I read about one woman who would take a Zima bottle and put it . . ."

Gray suddenly grimaced and put his hands to his head. "What is it?"

He slumped against the wall and motioned for her to look behind them. Ivanova turned to see a small man in a black uniform standing at the end of the corridor. He smiled and strode toward them.

"I knew I would find you here, Mr. Gray," said Bester. "With the Lieutenant Commander."

"Stop that scan on him!" commanded Ivanova.

But Gray was already regaining his composure. "It's all right," he said hoarsely.

"It's *not* all right," snapped Ivanova. The fiery officer glared at Mr. Bester. "None of what you do is all right. You act like telepathy is some giant leap in evolution, but the way you use it is just the same old crap. Control! That's what it's all about.

"Where I come from, we've seen the czars, the Bolsheviks, the secret police, and we know all about you. You just want to tell people what to do with their lives, and to hell with them if they have other ideas!"

Bester took a deep breath and squinted at her. Ivanova braced herself for perhaps a scan, but Harriman Gray stepped between them.

"That's enough, Mr. Bester," said Gray, trembling but jutting his jaw. "As of now, you can forget about me ever being your assistant. I don't like the way you operate. Unannounced scans were not part of the job description."

"My boy," said Bester like a favorite uncle, "don't take it personally. It's just a way we have of shortcut communications. Instead of you briefing me about your whereabouts, I just take a quick peek. I hadn't realized telepaths in the military were so sensitive to these shortcuts."

The Psi Cop looked at Ivanova and smiled like a cobra. "Besides, I see you are attending to personal business. As for that other matter, there's plenty of time to make a decision. I hope you both have a pleasant conference. Good night."

Bester swiveled on his heel and walked briskly down the corridor.

"Some shortcut," sneered Ivanova. "All one-way."

Gray whirled around and stared at her. He was clearly

shaken, but he managed to say, "You were quite magnificent."

Ivanova was too drained to take in any more. "I'm sorry, Mr. Gray, but I've got to get some sleep. And I think the three minutes I promised you are up."

"Please," he begged, "a large favor. Would you call me Harriman and let me call you Susan?"

She stared at him with amazement, then softened and nodded. "All right, but only when we're alone. Around other people, let's be formal."

Gray beamed with pleasure. "Does that mean we're friends?"

"Don't count your luck," she said. Ivanova turned to go, but she halted after one step. "I'm glad to hear you won't be that schmuck's assistant. Good night."

"Good night, Susan," he said softly.

"For humans," said Garibaldi, handing out the breathing masks, "the Alien Sector is always something of a disappointment. You can't see a damn thing, and if you could see, you wouldn't want to. We keep trying to improve it, and the one thing we want to avoid is making it look like a zoo. So, if a bunch of closed doors in murky, unbreathable air is your idea of a good time, let's go."

"Surely, it's got to be more interesting than that," said the tall one, Mr. Malten.

Garibaldi shook his head. "Not really. Most of the folks down here have special food, drink, and atmosphere requirements, so they don't go out much. Ms. Winters can tell you. She's got a regular client in here."

"Yes," said Talia rather proudly. "Ambassador Kosh of the Vorlons. We invited him to the reception tomorrow night, and I hope he'll attend."

Garibaldi added, "But all we ever see of him is his encounter suit. It's up to you if you want to stroll through the sector, but you won't see anything unless we bang on people's doors."

"I hadn't thought of that," said Talia. "I only come down here when I have an appointment."

The small telepath, Emily Crane, looked up at the storklike Mr. Malten. "I don't want to d-disturb the residents."

"Neither do I," answered Malten, placing the breathing mask back on the shelf. "But I don't expect to be short-changed out of our tour of Down Below."

"Of course not," said Garibaldi. "What do you want to see? There's smuggling, stolen gear getting stripped down, a bunch of derelicts nodding out. You name it, we've got it."

"All of it." Arthur Malten smiled.

Talia winced and Emily screwed her eyes shut as a hairless behemoth belted some scaled creature and sent him flying over shipping crates and crashing into broken shelves, long since looted. As the grubby crowd of derelicts screamed their approval, the hairless thing went slobbering after its prey and commenced the beating anew. The babble of the bettors was insane, sounding like quadraphonic bedlam inside Talia's mind, and she would have left if the men hadn't been enjoying it so much.

"What do they bet?" asked Malten.

"Just about anything," shouted Garibaldi over the din, "credits, goats, dust, passage out of here! Passage out of here will settle almost any debt."

"I c-can't stand this," muttered Emily into Talia's shoulder. "It's barbaric."

"I agree!" Talia replied. "We must leave this terrible place at once."

Suddenly, there was a disgusting cracking sound, followed by howls of rage and joy, in equal measures. Talia averted her eyes from the sights on the other side of the room and found herself looking at Garibaldi. Even he was preferable. To her, Garibaldi looked more like a criminal than most of the criminals—crude, shifty, wolfish, a man who prowled instead of walked. On occasion he said something funny, but those occasions were not as numerous as he believed. She would have to be out of her mind to get too friendly with him, yet he obviously liked her. It was hard to hate a guy who drooled whenever he saw you.

The bedlam had died down to a roar, and she was able to hear him say, "This is not a terrible place for Down Below. This is a *nice* place. You see a fight, and they serve you some flavored antifreeze and take your money. What more do you want?"

Then he smiled and rubbed his chin. "Oh, I forgot, you folks can't gamble."

"Isn't that a silly regulation?" asked Malten. "I don't see any way we could determine the outcome of this primitive sport, so what would be the harm in betting on it?"

"It would be wrong," said Emily simply.

Malten smiled. "Yes, I suppose so. But we don't know anything about some of these species, do we? They could be far more telepathic than us, yet no one tells *them* they can't gamble. I think it's a ridiculous rule. Everybody knows who we are, and they can let us play at their own risk."

Garibaldi frowned. "Can't you be horsewhipped by Mr. Bester for saying stuff like that?"

The private telepath snorted a laugh. "I've been saying stuff like that for a long time, only nobody listens. I've worked for thirty years to have telepaths accepted as just another professional class, no different than doctors or pilots. Do you think I like to see Bester and his crowd ruining all my work?"

Talia shifted uncomfortably on the crate where she was sitting. She tried to change the subject. "These fistfights— they can't possibly be legal."

"No," admitted Garibaldi. "We could shut this place down, but the fights would just spring up ten minutes later in a manufacturing bay, or a cargo bay. We haven't got the manpower to patrol all of the station. Down Below was used a lot during the construction of the station. Then funds ran out, and it was left unfinished. People get stranded on B5, or kicked off the crew of their ship, or just dumped here, and there's nowhere else for them to go."

He shook his head in amazement. "I don't understand this

place either, but we've had social engineers through the station who say that Down Below is normal. If it hadn't grown organically from poor planning, we would've had to invent it. If you have order, they say, you also have to have chaos."

The chief looked meaningfully at Talia. "Does that make sense to you?"

"I think chaos can be avoided," she replied.

"It makes sense to me," said Malten. "I want to see more."

Garibaldi led them into a grungy corridor and sniffed the air. "If I'm not mistaken, down this way we have people sifting through garbage. I don't know how they reroute it down here, but they do."

Emily crinkled her nose. "P-people steal garbage?"

"Yes," said Garibaldi with a reassuring smile. "But they don't keep all of it, just the good stuff."

"I think we can pass on that," said Mr. Malten. "What's down this corridor?"

"A shanty camp. Do you want to see it?"

"Yes," answered Malten forcefully.

Talia hung back, but she couldn't hang back too far as Garibaldi led them briskly through a scene of both despair and amazement. Aliens of every description—with jutting jaws, fins, segmented limbs, hairy pelts, or compound eyes—commingled with humans. Adults, children, old people, the dying—they all had a haunted look on their faces as they stared at the visitors. The shanties had been cobbled together from old crates, stolen panels, sheet metal, shelves, and whatever else might stand up.

"We give them fresh oxygen," said Garibaldi. "That's about all they get from us, although the Minbari run a soup kitchen. We can go there next."

Talia couldn't decide which was worse, the sense of despair or the smell of the place. To her surprise, the voices she heard in her head were not demanding, begging, or insistent. Some were resigned and helpless, others were angry at their plight and their well-dressed visitors, and a few were clearly insane. It was a mixture, like any bunch of people, and she knew that some of these unfortunates would scrape their way out of here. Others would sink even deeper until there wasn't a trace of them left.

A thuglike woman stepped in front of Mr. Malten and glared at the telepath. "Hey, buddy, got some chewing gum?"

"No," said Malten, taken aback.

She sneered, "You want to buy some?"

"Beat it, Martha," growled Garibaldi. "You know that chewing gum is illegal on the station."

He hurried his party along.

"Top quality!" the woman called after them. "Real sugar!"

"I doubt that," said Talia.

Emily Crane shuffled along beside her, holding a handkerchief over her nose. "I'd like to leave now," she sniffed.

"So would I," agreed Talia. "We're not going to let the attendees run loose down here, that's for sure."

"All the more reason to see as much as we can," said Malten. "One or two more stops, please."

"It's your play," said Garibaldi. He halted in front of a long tunnel that was rather badly lit. "This way is a shortcut to that Minbari soup kitchen."

Talia looked doubtfully at him. "A dark, deserted tunnel?"

"It's not deserted," said Garibaldi. "I see someone moving around down there. And I can't help it if people keep stealing the light fixtures."

Talia peered into the gloom. There did seem to be vague shapes moving through the passageway. She wished she hadn't asked Garibaldi for this VIP tour, but now she had to trust his instincts.

"Come on," said Malten, stepping into the entrance. "There are four of us, Mr. Garibaldi is armed, and we can always protect ourselves telepathically."

"Only against humans," Talia added.

The foursome started moving down the tunnel, and Garibaldi and Malten had to stoop where smaller ducts crossed overhead. The ducts were seeping a foul-smelling liquid, and Talia dashed under each one. She stumbled, and her hands brushed against the sticky walls. For once she was glad to be wearing gloves for a reason other than to avoid skin contact. When Talia found herself shoving Emily Crane in the back to hurry her along, she told herself to calm down. They were still on Babylon 5, her home base, just in an unfamiliar part of it.

However, Garibaldi's talk about chaos had made her nervous. She didn't like the idea of chaos, and she suspected Mr. Malten wouldn't like it either, if he were actually confronted by it. This was precisely why the control offered by Psi Corps was so important. It could make order out of chaos. She hoped.

Talia noticed that the vague figures at the other end of the tunnel were not at the other end anymore. And they weren't vague anymore. They were three large, hooded figures, and they were rapidly walking toward the party of genteel telepaths and one security officer. There would be a confrontation, Talia could feel it. For one thing, they barely had room to squeeze past each other in the confines of the tunnel.

She didn't want to pry into their minds, but she had to know what the three strangers were thinking as they strode briskly toward them. She could see them clearly now, even in the dim light, and she tried to hear their voices.

Talia gasped. Their minds were cold and alien! They were not human!

"I know," said Malten, hearing the alarm that was sounding in Talia's head.

"Just pay them no mind," Garibaldi suggested, although he didn't sound like his usual, cocky self. Talia noticed that his hand was resting on his PPG weapon.

The security chief quickened his step to get out in front of the others. He waved jauntily as the first hooded figure drew abreast of him. "Top of the mornin'!" he called.

The alien never stopped moving as he slammed his shoulder into Garibaldi and crushed him into the bulkhead. A huge knife flashed under the dark robes, and Emily screamed.

The other hooded thugs rushed toward the telepaths, knives gleaming in their gloved hands!

CHAPTER 5

"UNHAND him!" cried Malten. With a grunt, a hooded alien gave the telepath a right cross to the jaw, and Malten dropped to the grimy floor of the tunnel. Emily threw her body over him, screaming.

Talia did as she had been trained in self-defense classes, which was to attack the vulnerable spots, and she lashed out with a kick to the shin of the nearest attacker. She hit hard armor and nearly broke her toe.

But Garibaldi was fighting back. At least he had grabbed the knife-hand of his attacker and was holding him at bay. "Access tube!" he yelled. "About ten meters down! It'll take you *up!*"

The thug pressed his knife to Garibaldi's throat, but the chief shoved him back with a loud groan and staggered to his feet. The two of them traded blows, and Garibaldi caught one in the stomach. She saw him drop to his knees.

The telepath was still on her feet, so she was the first one to be moving toward the hatchway ten meters away. It was right where Garibaldi said it was, near the floor, and she grabbed the wheel and twisted. Maybe it was her adrenaline, but the hatch sprang open at her touch, and the crawl space beckoned.

"Come on!" she yelled.

The attackers were menacing Malten and Emily with their knives, but the telepaths managed to scramble to their feet and stagger down the corridor. Talia shoved them into the tube, and they scurried like groundhogs into the darkness. She took one glance back at Garibaldi.

A hooded alien had him by the throat and was shaking him like a dog shakes a toy. The other two advanced on him with their knives.

"I'll handle them!" croaked Garibaldi. He was reaching for his PPG.

Talia shook her head and fled in desperation. The hatch clanged shut behind her, and one of the aliens rushed to bolt it behind the fleeing telepaths. The alien holding Garibaldi dropped him and roared a hearty female laugh. She pushed back her hood to reveal her spotted cranium, jutting jaw, and the thick ridge of muscles around her neck.

Na'Toth laughed. "These are the ones who have all of you shaking?"

Garibaldi stood up with a groan and rubbed his jaw. "Hey, Na'Toth, that's not the way it was supposed to work! After you scared the hell out of us, Talia was supposed to rush to my arms, trembling, and I blast my way out of here. You weren't supposed to beat the crap out of me!"

Na'Toth couldn't stop laughing, and her two fellow Narns joined her in the merriment. "I'm sorry," she apologized, trying to restrain herself. "You see, I take favors such as this very seriously. Excellent sport, Garibaldi, thank you for contacting me."

"I do owe you one," the chief admitted. He dabbed his sleeve at his bloody lip. "Do you think that will keep those jokers out of here?"

"Yes," answered the Narn. "They have no stomach for stronger foes. Oh, Ambassador G'Kar and I will be attending the reception. Please inform the captain."

"I will," muttered Garibaldi. "Well, I'd better go after them and at least *describe* how I blasted my way out of here."

"She is attractive," Na'Toth conceded, with a hint of womanly envy.

"Oh, Talia?" Garibaldi shrugged. "She's crazy about me."

"I can see that," the Narn answered drolly.

Garibaldi rubbed his lower back. "I think I'll avoid that rabbit hole and go back the way I came. Maybe I can catch another fight."

"That was a good place to pass signals," Na'Toth remarked. "I will see you in several hours."

Garibaldi limped down the tunnel and waved. "Thanks."

By the time the weary security chief reached the main corridor, stooping under the slimy ducts, he didn't feel like going anywhere but to bed.

He tapped his link. "This is Garibaldi to all on-duty personnel. If anyone reports me as being missing or in trouble, please tell them I am *out* of trouble. I am still Down Below, but the situation is under control. Garibaldi over."

The security chief was strolling back toward the makeshift fight arena, still probing his swollen lips, when a furtive figure bumped into him. The bump caught him in a tender rib, and he groaned and grabbed the little man.

"Ratso, what's the matter with you?"

The grubby derelict glanced around and winced. "Let go of me, Chief! I'm in a hurry!"

Garibaldi tightened his grip on the man's raggedy collar. "If you're in a hurry, then somebody's about to be ripped off or mugged. What's the hurry, Ratso?"

The little man sulked. "I'm not gonna tell you."

"Listen, buddy, don't mess with me. I'm in a real lousy mood. Who's in trouble?"

The little man whispered, "It's me who's in trouble. Deuce is back on the station."

"Deuce?" muttered Garibaldi. That was not good, and the timing was even worse, with Psi Corps squirming all over the place. "Are you sure?"

"Does a packrat have puppies? Of course, I'm sure."

"Why now?" asked Garibaldi. "Doesn't he know we have a warrant out for him? Why would he risk it?"

Ratso winked, or maybe he twitched, it was hard to tell. "We've got 'em all here, don't we? Like, this is the center of the universe. If you were one of those crazy Martians . . ."

Garibaldi nearly lifted the man off his feet. "Deuce is helping the terrorists?"

"Sshhh, sshhh!" cautioned the derelict, pressing his fingers to his lips. "I've told you too much already. I gotta protect myself! Deuce might be settling some old debts while he's here."

"How did he get in? A forged identicard, what?"

But the raggedy man slipped out of his grasp and scurried down the corridor, tossing furtive glances over his shoulder.

Garibaldi scowled. With the attendees due to start arriving in only a few hours, the bulk of his staff were getting their last chunk of sleep before the crush. He had no idea who he could order down here to look for Deuce. Garibaldi would normally do a job like that himself, but he couldn't even assign himself to it. Martian terrorists and the crime king of Down Below—that was a bad combo.

He tried to imagine why the terrorists would need Deuce. Deuce was an expert at smuggling stuff into the station and out again, often in a different form. His loansharking had won him an army of desperate couriers who would do almost anything for a meal and a few credits off their debt. Why did the terrorists want Deuce? What could Deuce get into the station that they couldn't?

A bomb.

But not the kind of bomb that had wiped out earlier Babylon stations, thought the chief, not the big ka-boom that Ivanova joked about so fatalistically. Deuce wouldn't want to blow up his playground and ruin everything. The terrorists would probably settle for some kind of bombing that would be more a symbol than an absolute disaster. But with four hundred psi freaks running around, it wouldn't take much to turn the conference into an absolute disaster.

In fact, thought Garibaldi, if the terrorists had Deuce and his underground network, they wouldn't even need to show up! They could press the button from afar, so to speak. Security would have to look at every single person on the station, not just telepaths and new arrivals, but even the everyday scum.

The security chief looked up from his thoughts and noticed several of the denizens of Down Below watching him. They turned away quickly when he saw them, but that didn't make their scrutiny any less troubling. They knew. Like everyone else in the Alliance, this rowdy crowd of malcontents and misfits had no love lost for Psi Corps. Hell, for all he knew, some of them could be rogue telepaths hiding out down here. His current orders were to protect Psi Corps, and that pretty much pitted him against everyone else in the universe.

Well, so much for the idea of getting any sleep tonight. The captain had been right about one thing—this was your basic nightmare.

"Come in," said Captain Sheridan, wiping the crumbs off his lip with his linen napkin.

The door of his quarters opened, and a crumpled Garibaldi slouched inside. "Good morning, sir."

"Good morning, Mr. Garibaldi. Breakfast?"

"No, thank you, sir. I don't believe in eating breakfast unless I've actually slept." He looked at the captain's sumptuous tray. "Well, maybe a piece of toast."

Sheridan stood and buttoned his jacket. "Feel free to finish it, Mr. Garibaldi. The melon is quite good. I had an urgent message from Ms. Winters last night, and she said that you were in some terrible danger Down Below. Yet when I checked, there was no report of an incident, just a cryptic note from you. I didn't see any report in my download this morning either."

Garibaldi chuckled. "Well, sir, when people ask for a guided tour, you want to liven it up for them. You know, like when you go on a Wild West stagecoach ride, and a couple of bandits rob the stagecoach."

Sheridan frowned. "I didn't know we offered that service, Mr. Garibaldi. Nor was I aware that you were the recreation director of this station. If you would like that job, perhaps it can be arranged."

Garibaldi stuffed a strawberry into his mouth and considered the offer for a moment. "Don't tempt me, sir."

The captain shook his head. "I know this conference presents many problems for you, but we have to go by the regulations whenever possible. I'm pretty sure there's a regulation against mugging visiting dignitaries."

Garibaldi wiped his mouth on the captain's napkin. "Captain, did you happen to see the download of the first issue of the conference newsletter?''

Sheridan rolled his eyes. "Yes, I did."

"That Emily Crane wrote a great editorial, didn't she? In strong language, she warned her friends against going anywhere near Down Below or the Alien Sector. Said their telepathic abilities would be useless if they got into any trouble down there. It even scared me."

"Granted," said Sheridan, "your little stunt worked to our advantage, but no more of that. We'll be under close scrutiny for the way we handle this, and I want it by the book. Is that understood?"

Garibaldi stood to attention. "Yes, sir, understood. I just wanted to show Psi Corps that there are parts of this station beyond their control. The fact is, we do have a major problem Down Below."

"What's that?"

"You've seen a fellow named Deuce mentioned in a number of reports."

"Yes, of course," said Sheridan. "I've read the ombud's list of charges against him. Murder, extortion, smuggling, endangering the station—a nasty character. And a fugitive."

"And he's back. That's not what I'm worried about, because Deuce was bound to come back sometime to check his enterprises. But why now? Could it be because of this conference? Believe me, Deuce wouldn't be against taking money from terrorists."

Sheridan asked, "You're sure he's back?"

"I've got a passenger from a tramp freighter who just sort of disappeared after he came aboard yesterday."

"Can't we find him?" asked the captain.

"With what resources? I've got everyone on my staff committed to the conference. And Deuce is The Man down there. Even if we didn't have this conference to worry about, we might not find him." Garibaldi sighed and rubbed his eyes. "At this point, I don't think I could find anything but a bed."

The captain's link sounded, and he lifted his hand. "This is Captain Sheridan."

"Ivanova here," came the familiar voice. "The *Glenn* is docking in bay six. The manifest says they have fifty-three Psi Corps members aboard, and Mr. Bester has requested that you greet them personally. He also wants Garibaldi to be present to answer questions about security."

Garibaldi winced and grabbed the last piece of toast.

"I'll tell Mr. Garibaldi," said the captain. "We're on our way."

"Oh," said Ivanova, "another transport arrives with twenty-seven VIPs at 8:40, another one with thirty-eight at 9:21. A heavy cruiser with nineteen military telepaths arrives at 10:58, and two transports . . ."

"I will stay in the docking area," Sheridan assured her. "Have the work crews vacated Blue-16?"

"Yes, sir. Although they say the paint is still wet."

Sheridan nodded somberly. "We can take them to the casino for a couple of hours, give them lunch." He looked at Garibaldi and smiled encouragingly. "Very wise to have halted gambling there. We'll get through this, people. Remember, you *love* Psi Corps!"

"We love Psi Corps," Garibaldi muttered with disbelief.

Talia Winters sat down to breakfast in the newly opened cafe on Blue-16, and Arthur Malten sat across from her, looking dapper in a checked suit with patches on the elbow. Befitting its location, the decor was mostly blue, with a bit of burnt orange. It wasn't so bad, thought Talia, except for the faint smell of paint.

"I feel so guilty," said Talia, "leaving Emily with all that work. Are you sure we shouldn't be greeting people as they arrive?"

"And deprive Mr. Bester of all his fun?" Malten smiled and poured some coffee for them. "Don't worry, Talia, we'll have plenty of time to hobnob at the reception, and all weekend.

"Besides," he said cheerfully, "this may be my only opportunity to get to know you, before I get dragged off to breakfast meetings and high-level discussions."

"As for me," said Talia, stirring her coffee, "I'll have plenty of panels to attend, but no high-level discussions."

"That's a pity," answered Malten. He stroked his graying goatee. "Babylon 5 is a backwater, you know. I realized that last night, after that ugly incident. You could do much better than this."

Talia sighed. "Mr. Malten . . ."

"Please call me Arthur."

"Arthur, you should know that I'm only a P5. I'm lucky to have this assignment."

"Nonsense," said Malten angrily. "Your success on B5 has shown that psi ratings are worthless when it comes to judging aptitude for a given job."

He lowered his voice. "That's why I'm against giving so much power to a class of telepaths who have nothing going for them—except that they're P12s and P11s. Being P12 doesn't mean you're well adjusted, have common sense, or good communication skills. In most cases, it means you're neurotic as hell."

Talia shifted in her seat, once again nervous with this sort of talk. All of this was easy for Mr. Malten to say. He was a P10 himself and the founder of the biggest conglomerate of private telepaths in the Earth Alliance. Although the Mix was created under the internal security act of 2156, which meant the corps had technical jurisdiction over it, the Mix was relatively independent; he didn't have to kiss up to Psi Corps for choice assignments.

Malten smiled apologetically. "I know what you're thinking. It's true, I've carved out my own niche. But in the commercial world, we're not so wrapped up in who's got the biggest number. We look at long-term results. Talia, you've got proven interspecies skills which we could use in the Mix."

The young woman blinked at him in amazement. She didn't even see it coming! After all, B5 already was her dream job—to get a chance to leap up another rung so soon was beyond her expectations. And what a rung this was—the top! It seemed too good to be true. There had to be a catch.

"I—I don't know what to say," she answered honestly. "I don't know what Psi Corps will say."

The scholarly telepath patted her hand. It was leather on leather, but his touch tingled her skin for a moment. "Let me worry about Psi Corps," he assured her. "We have a great opportunity ahead of us. We're going to take telepathy into every corner of this universe, not as an object of fear and control, but as a valuable service. We'll say, 'Let telepathy be on *your* side, not just the other guy's.'"

"It sounds wonderful," Talia said truthfully. But she felt a pang of regret over the idea of leaving B5 so soon. It had barely been a year, and she was finally building up her practice. Despite her loyalty to Psi Corps, she was used to being her own boss, a lone operator. Sort of like Garibaldi. She couldn't imagine what it would be like to be one of thousands of telepaths in a gigantic firm with hundreds of branch offices.

"In the meantime," said Malten, reaching into his pocket, "I would appreciate your attendance at one of those high-level discussions I was talking about. It's a secret budget meeting."

He set a data crystal on the table. "Ms. Crane put some information together about the budget. I rely on her, but she's essentially a writer and researcher. She's not at her best when there's a debate, and this could become a fiery one. You and I will have to defend the needs of the civilian sector against Mr. Bester and the military. Will you come?"

Now Talia was afraid her jaw was hanging open. If a job offer had been a shock, the invitation to a high-level budget meeting was a two-by-four to the head. "Why me?" she asked. "I can't argue these points like you can. In fact, I'm not even sure I agree with you."

Malten smiled. "Do you want an honest answer?"

She nodded.

"Because you're beautiful, and you'll be a distraction." He pointed to the crystal. "And I expect you to read what's on there and remember the statistics better than I do. Besides, you're practical proof of what I'm talking about. If you can be a success in this depot for aliens, it just proves that commercial applications can succeed anywhere!''

Talia took a deep breath and pushed a streak of blond hair off her cheek. It still felt as if she had been bludgeoned by a two-by-four, but she picked up the data crystal and put it in her handbag.

''I'll be there,'' she promised.

At that same moment, a hand encased in a grimy glove with the fingers cut off at the knuckles placed a similar data crystal on top of a dented filing cabinet. A cat jumped out of one of the drawers, rocking the cabinet and nearly knocking the crystal to the floor.

Careful! whispered a voice in his head. *If we lose that, we lose all.*

''We're not going to lose it,'' purred Deuce in a jaded Southern twang. ''I just wanted to show it to you, because a deal's a deal.''

It looks like any crystal, the voice said.

Deuce lifted the data crystal to eye level and studied it. ''That's the beauty of it, ain't it? One of a kind. Speaking of crystals, you got the diamonds?''

The voice answered, *Yes,* and Deuce was told to look down at the floor. He saw a black briefcase in the dim light of the storage room and smiled. As soon as he set the crystal back on the beat-up cabinet, a gloved hand snatched it away.

''You'll need this, too,'' said Deuce, pulling a remote control device out of his coat pocket. ''You know how to operate this?''

Yes.

CHAPTER 6

GARIBALDI still hadn't managed to escape from the docking area. He was assaulted from all sides. "Excuse me, Mr. Garibaldi," sneered a cadaverous-looking woman in a black uniform. "These arrangements are simply not acceptable. I can't possibly share a bathroom with somebody!"

"The person in the next room is another woman," explained Garibaldi, checking the manifest and room assignments on a handheld computer. "You see, Blue-16 is crew quarters, and we haven't got unlimited water or space. The only doors that open to the bathroom are from your two rooms. You just lock the other door when you're using it and leave it neat, and . . ." He waved his hands. "Pretend you're at summer camp."

The older Psi Cop batted her eyelashes at him. "It's my security I'm thinking about. I don't know if you know this, young man, but I'm a VIP on the Mars Colony. The terrorists would like my head."

A dozen snappy comebacks competed for attention in Garibaldi's mind, but he didn't use any of them. "Lady," he said slowly, "everybody here is a VIP. A VIP and half a credit will get you a cup of coffee. We threw this shindig together for Psi Corps in two days, and we're not the Ritz-Carlton on our better days—the least you could do is be gracious about it and sleep where we tell you."

The lady Psi Cop snapped to attention. "I see that your overriding concern is for our safety, and that's enough for me. Who is my bathroommate, if I may ask?"

Garibaldi checked his miniature screen. "That would be Ms. Trixie Lee." He blinked at the name in remembrance. "Didn't she used to be a stripper?"

"Yes, she was. It will be good to see her again." The woman smiled slyly. "I was a stripper, too, at one time. It's good training for a Psi Cop. Their minds are rather blank when you're right in front of them, and you can . . .''

Garibaldi laughed nervously. ''Yes, well, enjoy your stay. We are serving refreshments in the casino. Just follow the signs.''

''Casino?'' said the woman, impressed. ''Surely, we wouldn't break the taboo on gambling?''

''Surely not,'' answered Garibaldi. ''The games are shut down.''

The woman lifted a heavily mascaraed eyebrow. ''Mr. Garibaldi, do you consider strip poker to be gambling?''

''Yes,'' he answered, pushing her along. ''Next?''

Before he could prepare himself, Mr. Bester was in his face, oozing niceness. ''Mr. Garibaldi, this is my colleague, Mr. Becvar. He has a security matter he needs to discuss with you, and I would appreciate it if you could accommodate him.''

Garibaldi smiled obsequiously. ''We aim to please.''

With that, Bester left him with a handsome, dark-haired man who spoke with a Spanish accent. ''Mr. Garibaldi,'' he said, lowering his voice, ''have you heard of the Shedraks?''

''Shedraks?'' repeated Garibaldi, shaking his head. ''Sorry, that's a new one on me.''

Mr. Becvar pointed to an air shaft. ''They come in through the air ducts, and they strangle a person in his sleep. I insulted them when I was on Tyrol III, and they have been following me ever since, waiting to get me alone.''

He grabbed Garibaldi by the collar. ''I am not making this up!''

''No, of course not,'' said the security chief, calmly removing Becvar's gloved hands. ''How do we stop these . . . these Shedraks?''

''The air vents,'' the man answered. ''You must plug them up, do you understand?''

The chief consulted his handheld device. ''Let me see what room you're in, Mr. Becvar.'' He paused a moment. ''Oh, that's excellent! You have room 319, which is one of the quarters equipped with special baffles on the air vents. We can close those from central command!''

Mr. Becvar groaned with relief. "Oh, I am so glad.''

"And I'll have my people keep an eye out for Shedraks here at the dock,'' Garibaldi assured him. "Are you okay with sharing a bathroom?''

The man shrugged. "As long as there are no air vents.''

"We'll close them up, too.'' Garibaldi pretended to make a note. "Just follow the signs to the casino, and have a good time, Mr. Becvar.''

The handsome man nodded and shuffled off, glancing worriedly at the air vents over his head.

Bester sidled up to Garibaldi. "Thank you, Mr. Garibaldi. Mr. Becvar had an unfortunate assignment several years ago, and he suffers some aftereffects. If you can believe it, he is a brilliant instructor on blocking techniques. He works at our center at Syria Planum. I understand you know about that facility?''

"Doesn't everybody?'' asked Garibaldi cheerfully.

Bester's face darkened. "No, they do not. I would advise you to keep that information to yourself.''

"I don't know why a training facility on Mars should be such a big deal.''

Bester scowled. "Everything about Mars is a big deal. I need your assurance on this matter.''

"Okay,'' said Garibaldi, "I won't mention it again.''

Bester nodded curtly. "That is wise. Oh, hello, Mr. Pekoe, welcome to the conference!''

Garibaldi breathed a sigh of relief as Bester moved off to greet an Asian contingent of telepaths. Captain Sheridan stepped next to him and smiled.

"How is it going, Chief?''

"I *love* Psi Corps.''

"Have they asked you to do anything you can't handle yet?''

Garibaldi considered the question for a moment. "Actually, they have, but I'm not going to give them the satisfaction of knowing it.''

Sheridan patted him on the back. "You're doing a fine job, Garibaldi. Opening the casino to them was a stroke of genius. I think that's the key to our success, to keep them busy."

"The casino was Ms. Winter's idea," admitted Garibaldi. "I wonder where she is?"

"I hope she's enjoying herself," answered Sheridan. "She's an attendee at this conference, remember that. We're the hired help."

As Talia Winters and Arthur Malten dallied outside Emily Crane's quarters, Talia lifted her mouth to meet his. She worked around his goatee and mustache to give him a kiss that she hoped showed interest, but not too much interest. Malten was divorced, she knew, and he could do more for her career than anyone she had ever met. Nevertheless, she had to go slowly.

Talia decided to detach her mouth before their thoughts started intermingling, and she pushed him away gently. She was blocking for all she was worth, and so was he. That was good. It showed a healthy amount of distrust on both their parts. She wasn't sure she could handle another full-blown relationship with a fellow telepath. The last one had nearly torn her apart.

"I have to get to work," she said. "Don't you have some sort of high-level discussion to go to?"

He smiled boyishly. "I suppose I should go to the casino and see some old friends. Will you be there later?"

"That's my plan," she answered, "after I check out the arrangements on Green-12. If I don't make it, I'll see you at the reception."

"Fine." Malten bent to kiss her again, and the door slid open. Emily Crane peered out, not hiding her shock and disapproval.

"Excuse me," she said, starting to close the door. Her hand fumbled around on the unfamiliar wall panel, trying to find the right button.

"It's all right," Talia assured the woman. "I was just coming to help you. Sorry breakfast dragged on."

"Terrible service," Malten added. "I will have to speak to the captain about it. I'll see you both later."

The dapper telepath started down the corridor, then he turned abruptly. "Oh, Ms. Crane, I won't be needing you to come to the budget meeting with me tomorrow. Ms. Winters will be coming with me. So you can concentrate on scheduling, the newsletter, and such. Thank you."

He walked away with a jaunt to his step, and Talia could feel Emily's eyes drilling into her.

"That was f-fast," said the small woman.

Talia slipped into Emily's guest quarters, where the smell of paint was still strong, and she shut the door behind her. "Hey," she began, "if there's something going on between you and Arthur, just tell me. In fact, I'll listen to anything you want to tell me about him."

Emily Crane went back to her bed, upon which were spread reams of transparencies. She was stacking them together into different combinations of names, panels, and meeting rooms, preparing to run off corrected transparencies.

She swallowed and waved helplessly at one of the piles. "The moderator of the sleep deprivation seminar has c-canceled," she said. "He says that his equipment was lost. Can you think of anyone?"

Talia folded her arms. "Is that all you want to talk about?"

Emily lowered her head and screwed her face into a bitter frown. "I love Arthur. He doesn't think of me . . . in that way. When I heard that the two of us would be c-coming here alone, I hoped, being away from the office, we could . . ." She swallowed and couldn't finish her thought.

Talia felt like putting her arm around the young woman, but she didn't really know her very well. Besides, the answer was—no, they weren't an item. And one awkward, unexpected relationship at a time was more than enough.

"Come on," said Talia, picking up a stack of transparencies. "We've got a show to put on. This kind of conference isn't only about tax laws and penal code—there's a sexual undertow that's difficult to avoid.''

Talia gazed at herself in the small mirror over the vanity, and she saw an attractive woman, flushed by the power she was having over people. Yes, she was only a P5 among P10s and P12s, but let's face it, she was better adjusted and better looking than most of them.

''It's about control,'' said Talia, fluffing her blond hair. ''And what's better for control than sex? You planned to use it, didn't you? I like Arthur, but I would have to think twice about getting involved with another telepath.''

''I'm already involved,'' said Emily.

''I would forget about him, in that way,'' Talia advised. ''Unless I'm totally wrong about him, I would guess he plays the field.''

''Will you be going to the budget meeting with him?''

''Yes. I may never get another chance to meet these people. Arthur calls B5 a backwater, and maybe he's right when it comes to these kind of high-level contacts. So I should meet as many of them as I can, before they go away.''

The small woman gave her a knowing smile. ''Watch yourself.''

''These Minbari,'' said a portly telepath from the military, ''we've got to get all of them off the station. Immediately!'' He looked around at the bustling dock area and lowered his voice. ''They could be spies.''

Garibaldi also looked around and lowered his voice. ''I'm pretty sure some of them are.''

''Then why don't you get them off?'' the telepath demanded.

The chief shrugged. ''We aren't at war with them, for one thing.''

''That's temporary,'' scoffed the military telepath. ''With the Wind Swords and the Sky Riders and their other warrior castes getting the upper hand, it's only a matter of time. I'm an expert in Minbari intelligence, and I tell you we have to get them out of here. They're vicious! They could try to kill us!''

Garibaldi looked at the portly man and sure hoped that he didn't look like that in his similar uniform. "This is your basic free port,'' he explained. "Our charter is that we're diplomatic—we like everyone. Even Psi Corps. The Minbari helped to finance B5, and this is their most important diplomatic mission with the EA. We can't just throw them off B5.''

The telepath muttered, "What a stupid place to hold this conference.''

"I'll drink to that,'' said Garibaldi. "So is there anything else I can do for you?''

The military liaison bumped the security chief with his stomach and glared at him with piggy eyes in a florid face. "I'm serious, Mr. Garibaldi. I won't stay on a station with Minbari present. My life would be worth nothing!''

Garibaldi looked around in desperation and spied a savior. "Lennier! Lennier!'' he called.

The friendly Minbari strolled over in his rustling satin robes. He crossed his arms and smiled angelically, the shell-like crowns on his head looking like a halo.

"Lennier, do you want to kill Mr. . . . What's your name?''

"Barker,'' said the man in shock.

"Why, of course not,'' answered Lennier. "I don't even know Mr. Barker, and I'm sure if I did know him, I would lay down my life for him.''

"I wouldn't doubt it,'' answered Garibaldi. "Mr. Barker, meet Mr. Lennier, who is the aide to Ambassador Delenn and a member of a religious caste, not a warrior caste.''

Lennier smiled beatifically. "Quite pleased to meet you.''

The portly telepath glowered at the Minbari. "I was just telling Mr. Garibaldi that I wanted your people cleared off the station.''

"What a novel idea,'' answered Lennier thoughtfully. "If this would be in the manner of a paid vacation, as you call it, I'm sure we could negotiate it. Would you like to go to the casino and discuss the arrangements? Where would you be willing to send us? Acapulco? Io?''

Mr. Barker looked helplessly at Garibaldi as Lennier led him down the corridor. The security chief gave him a shrug and added, ''He does it with kindness.''

The chief stifled a yawn and tried to unglue his eyes. If he didn't get some sleep soon he would probably say or do something that would start a war.

He handed his computer terminal to a subordinate and told him, ''Just agree to whatever they want, and contact me in an hour to explain it. If it's not too unreasonable, we'll give them whatever we can. But don't contact me before an hour unless it's an emergency.''

''Yes, sir,'' answered the officer.

Garibaldi looked around briefly for Captain Sheridan. Not seeing him in the crush of dignitaries, quadrupled security, and regular traffic, he gave up and wandered off. The simple act of rounding a corner and walking away from those oppressive black uniforms and that holier-than-thou attitude made him feel ten times better.

Just to relax for a few moments, to watch a few old cartoons, and forget all about Psi Corps—it probably wasn't possible, but it would be nice to try. He had done all he could, put all the people he had right where they ought to be, alerted them to all the possibilities. Sure, something could go wrong—it wouldn't be B5 if it didn't—but a major breakdown in security wasn't likely. With a little cooperation and a lot of luck they could get through this. Then Sheridan would owe him one. Big time. There was still an awkwardness between them, born of unfamiliarity. This would go a long way toward easing that.

Garibaldi was feeling pretty good about himself as he got out of the transport tube and headed into the homestretch of the corridor outside his quarters. He didn't even hear the footsteps pounding up behind him until it was too late.

A bearlike body whirled him around and shook him by the shoulders. In his blurred vision it looked like a scarlet mon-

ster, seven feet tall! Garibaldi tried a karate chop, but a brocaded forearm knocked his hand away and gripped his arms.

The alien sputtered as he talked. "How on Centauri Prime
could you close down the gambling! What's the matter with
you? You call yourself a *host?*"

Garibaldi focused on the big spiked hair, the throbbing
dome of a forehead, and the jagged teeth, bared in a snarl.
"Londo," he muttered, "if you knew what kind of day I've
had, you'd have some pity on me."

"And what kind of day do you think I've had?" countered
Ambassador Mollari in his peculiar accent. "First, I come
within a hair of breaking the dice table, but my, er, escort
was getting sleepy and I had to tuck her into bed. Then I go
back to the casino, thinking I will double my jackpot, and
what do I find? Gaming tables shut down, by order of Mr.
Big Shot Garibaldi!"

The Centauri poked Garibaldi in the chest with a stubby
finger. "They cannot even give me my winnings until you—
you personally—open up the tables again! So what is this,
huh? A conspiracy? Did G'Kar put you up to this?"

"Please," Garibaldi begged, "just give us a few days
without gambling. We've got all these Psi Corps telepaths on
board, and they can't gamble."

"Well," scoffed Londo, "they don't have to gamble if
they don't want to! Let them play fish, or old maid, or whatever they do in Psi Corps. In case you hadn't noticed it,
Garibaldi, I am not in Psi Corps. I do not wear those drab,
funereal outfits. I wish to frolic. I wish to gamble. I wish to
do whatever I was doing before they got here!"

"Amen to that," said the chief. "But it's only four days.
I'll tell them to release your winnings to you, and maybe we
can open up the tables for a few hours while they're in their
seminars."

Londo grinned and narrowed his eyes slyly. "You know,
Garibaldi, if these Psi Corps are not allowed to gamble—and
they are in charge of everything else—then gambling is the
one activity they are dying to do. Why don't you arrange it,
and get some compromising visuals on them. Excellent op-

portunity here, Garibaldi, for what you might call a little office politics.''

''I'm too tired to blackmail anybody today,'' yawned Garibaldi, backing to his door. ''But thanks for the idea.''

''I could do it for you,'' offered Londo. ''Might be a bit of fun.''

''Don't mess with these people,'' Garibaldi warned. ''Take that as an order, and a good piece of advice. Humans who are full of themselves—you want to stay away from.''

The Centauri frowned. ''What does that mean? 'Full of themselves'?''

Garibaldi took out his identicard. ''Well, they're people who are pompous, who think the universe revolves around them, who think they're better than everybody, and deserve special treatment.'' He pushed his card into the slot, and the door opened. ''Like nobody you would know.''

''I should hope not,'' said Londo with mock horror.

Before Garibaldi could seek refuge in his dark cave, his link rang. He rolled his eyes, debating what he would do, although he knew he would answer it. ''Garibaldi here.''

''Chief, I'm sorry to bother you, but there's a major incident in the casino.''

''Who? What?'' he snapped.

''It's G'Kar. He's beating the crap out of one of the telepaths. Captain Sheridan just waded in to break it up.''

Londo shouldered past him on his way to the lift. ''Tell the telepath I am on my way to help him!''

CHAPTER 7

THE muscle-bound Narn lifted a squirming, black-suited Psi Cop over his head and bounced him off the bar. He rolled into a glass shelf and brought a row of bottles crashing down all around him.

"That is enough!" barked John Sheridan, stepping in front of G'Kar and pushing him back.

"Unhand me, Captain," snarled the alien, his spotted head pulsating with agitated veins.

"No!" said Sheridan. "This is a public place, and we have guests aboard the station. If you want to fight someone, then how about you and I step outside?"

"Wait, sir!" called Garibaldi, charging into the hushed casino. He pushed his way through the crowd that was pressing around the action.

"G'Kar, what's the matter with you?" he demanded.

Londo peered over the bar at the bloodied Psi Cop and pointed back at G'Kar. "I will help you press charges against this ruffian, if you like."

The Narn shook his head and got flustered. "Well, it . . . it was an overpowering feeling I got from him that he wanted to *kill* me."

"All you got was a thought?" asked Sheridan.

"It was a very clear threat," answered G'Kar.

The security chief snapped his fingers and pointed at his staff. "Get a medteam on that man."

"Already called," the officer replied.

Garibaldi glared around at the blank-faced telepaths surrounding him. "Were any of you with the wounded man before the fight started?"

A young female Psi Cop stepped forward, the black looking good on her. "Hoffman offered to bet us that he could plant a thought in the Narn's mind, as a sort of experiment. I don't know what he mistakenly put there, but the Narn jumped out of his seat and commenced to pulverize him.''

The medteam, led by Dr. Stephen Franklin, rushed into the casino, and this distraction killed the possibility of further interrogation. Captain Sheridan leaned over the bar and noticed that the Psi Cop was bloodied but moving about, even fighting the medics who were waving smelling salts under his nose.

The captain narrowed his eyes at Ambassador G'Kar and was still angry at the Narn for starting this battle. Or did he start it?

"Listen, you hotshots!" called Garibaldi, demanding the attention back. "Even counting all of you, humans are the minority on this station. We also had an incident last night, so be careful!"

"Rest assured, that man will be punished!" crowed a voice from the back. Heads turned as Mr. Bester shouldered his way through the crowd. He peered over the bar at the wounded man with a smile of satisfaction. "He will be stripped of all his rights and duties." Bester smiled. "After a proper hearing, of course."

The Psi Cop turned magnanimously to G'Kar. "My dear Ambassador, please don't allow this incident to spoil your evening. Even telepaths sometimes forget that every gift has a price. Their price is responsibility and discipline. Gambling, abuse of power—these are things we do not tolerate."

Bester bowed and clicked his heels. "Please accept my sincerest apologies, Ambassador G'Kar."

Londo leaned against the bar and muttered, "Oh, brother."

But G'Kar smiled and bowed, looking like he was imitating Bester. "Apologies accepted. Communications are our greatest difficulty, I have always said."

"I hope you're going to attend the reception tonight," said Bester.

"Why, yes, I am."

Dr. Franklin poked his head above the bar and told Sheridan, "He's sedated. He has a broken wrist and a lot of cuts, but his injuries don't appear to be serious."

"Throw him in the brig," suggested Bester.

Franklin frowned. "I think medlab would be better."

"Medlab it is," ordered Sheridan. "With restraints and a guard."

The doctor nodded, and they lifted the unconscious Psi Cop onto a stretcher and took him out. This gave Captain Sheridan a chance to look around at the strange gathering. Garibaldi looked exasperated and exhausted; Londo was eagerly absorbing a description of the fight from the bartender; and Bester and G'Kar acted like old college chums. Strangest of all, thought the captain, he was surrounded by a roomful of humans who seemed more alien and unpredictable than the aliens on the station.

Sheridan realized he had been quite mad to allow this conference on B5. The longer it went on, the more likely something dreadful would happen. There was just too much tinder, too many matches lying around. He heard a voice in his mind, that same little voice that alerts the captain just before his ship hits an iceberg or an asteroid. The danger, said the voice, was just under the surface, waiting for the right moment to rip them apart.

Garibaldi and Ivanova had tried to warn him, thought the captain, but that didn't do them much good now. He had pigheadedly plunged ahead and let Psi Corps bring their conference, and all their baggage, right to his doorstep. Their first site had been bombed, as if that shouldn't be hint enough! Despite all their hard work and dedication, B5 was by design a sieve, a zoo without cages. Whatever was he thinking about?

Well, it was time to make amends and stop depending on his staff to get him out of this mess. "Garibaldi!" he called.

"Yes, sir?" The security chief didn't bother to salute.

"Go back to your quarters and sleep until you have to get dressed for the reception. I figure that will give you almost three hours."

"But, sir," said Garibaldi, "there's so much going on here . . ."

Sheridan lifted his hand. "Link, have all calls for Mr. Garibaldi routed to Officer Lou Welch until twenty-hundred hours. He will assume Garibaldi's duties. Captain Sheridan out." He looked sternly at Garibaldi. "Before you go, is everything all right for the reception on Blue-16?"

"We're shutting down the cafe in about an hour, and we'll reopen with full security."

"Good," answered Sheridan. "Tomorrow I want everyone searched who is going in and out of the conference rooms."

Garibaldi looked thoughtful. "We were going to do a hand-scan on anyone who entered Green-12. Plus, we were going to eyeball for Psi Corps insignias. Did you have something more elaborate in mind?"

"I don't want a strip search," said Sheridan, "but look inside handbags, briefcases, backpacks, handheld stuff. Pat them down, if need be."

"That's fine with me," agreed Garibaldi. "I was going to suggest it, but I didn't think they would let us get away with it."

"As long as it's by the book," said Sheridan, "let's use whatever means are at our disposal. This may discourage them from going in and out of Green-12 too much."

"What are we looking for, sir?"

The captain smiled wistfully. "Some peace of mind. But I don't think we'll find it until they leave."

He hated prowling the corridor waiting for her, but he didn't know how else to approach Susan, without making it look something like a coincidence. Fortunately, Harriman Gray was one of those people who blended in. He didn't blend in very well when he was playing the odious role of the hard-boiled telepath, ready to leaf through a person's mind like a nosy visitor snoops through a person's medicine cabinet; but he could blend in well enough when there were crowds and a swirl of people.

The longer he was around them, the more Gray liked the

alien rhythms and voices of Babylon 5. It made him feel more normal to know that he couldn't read the minds of most of the people here. To them, he was just another alien.

So he circled the corridors where she had to cross, hoping he wouldn't miss her when his back was turned. Perhaps she would get a bite at her favorite restaurant between shifts. She was working a double shift, he was certain, until all the conference attendees were safely aboard the station, where they became somebody else's problem. That was the way Susan worked, making sure there were no lapses on her watch. She hated all of them with a passion, but she would guide their ships to safety as if they were carrying her own mother.

The thought of Susan's mother brought Gray up short. That was the root of her hatred for Psi Corps, and was there anything he could do about it? Would it do any good to apologize? Or to tell Susan how lousy it made him feel to be tarred with the same feather as the Psi Police? Was there anything at all he could say that would erase her years of pain and hatred? No. Not as long as he wore the Psi Corps insignia on his lapel.

What was he doing this for? Why couldn't he come to his senses and forget about Susan? There were plenty of women who would welcome a man with his prestige and career potential, women who would consider him a catch. Well, maybe.

The problem was, Harriman Gray had always wanted the wrong thing, the thing he couldn't have. He had wanted to be a soldier, before his psi abilities had manifested themselves. After that path had been taken away from him, he had wanted to serve the military in a liaison capacity, going home every night to his tidy apartment. Instead, he was shunted from one high-level assignment to another, each one more surreal than the one before it. Now he loved a woman who hated him. Sheesh, thought Gray, maybe he was more neurotic than Bester.

While he considered giving up and joining his colleagues at the casino, he caught a glimpse of a gray uniform dashing into the sweets shop. His heart leaped as quickly as his feet, as he hurried into the shop after her.

"I'll take one of those," said Ivanova, pointing to a dark confection.

"Susan," he said.

Her back stiffened, and she refused to turn around. "Are you following me?"

"Yes," he admitted. "I don't suppose you're going to the reception later on?"

"No."

"That's why I had to follow you."

Susan sighed and finally turned around to look at him. He was reminded of the way his big sister used to look whenever she was annoyed with him.

"You know, Harriman, by the captain's orders, I'm not supposed to be talking to you. Or any of your friends."

"I know," Gray admitted. "I've read all the travel advisories. 'Do not visit Down Below or the Alien Sector. Do not travel alone. And do not speak to Commander Ivanova.' "

She smiled in spite of her herself. "I hope there's a suitable punishment for doing so."

"Speaking of punishment," said Gray excitedly, "did you hear that Ambassador G'Kar beat the stuffing out of a reprehensible Psi Cop named Hoffman? In front of everybody!"

Ivanova smiled. "No, I didn't hear that. We're all doing our part to make this an enjoyable conference."

She grabbed her pastry and waited for Gray to get out of her way. "Excuse me, I've only got about five minutes before the next transport is due."

"Please eat," insisted Gray. He rushed to pull out a chair at an empty table. "It's all right, I'll do all the talking."

Ivanova shrugged resignedly and set her snack on the table. "I can push my own chair in."

"Of course," said Gray, sitting across from her. "I just wanted to tell you—I'm thinking of quitting my job as a military liaison and going into commercial practice."

"That's nice," replied Ivanova with her mouth full of cake.

"Yes, maybe I can even get assigned to Babylon 5."

The officer looked puzzledly at him and swallowed. "We already have a resident telepath."

"Ah," said Gray, "Ms. Winters may be leaving."

Ivanova frowned. "Really? I was just getting to know her. Why would she leave?"

"Better offer."

"How do you know this?" she asked suspiciously.

Gray smiled. "Let's say, a gathering of telepaths is not the best place to keep a secret."

Ivanova set her fork on her plate and just stared at him. "Harriman, if you're trying to get an assignment on B5 just to be close to me, you're wasting your time. Having a strained conversation like this, every now and then, is the best you could ever hope for."

He looked down, deeply wounded. "That's rather cold, isn't it?"

"Yes, it is," she admitted, standing up. "I'm sorry, but I don't want to lead you on."

Gray countered, "There's something else. I *like* being here on Babylon 5! I feel comfortable in this place, like a regular person, not a freak or a snoop."

Susan opened her mouth, as if she were about to say something, but she finally just shook her head and walked off. When she was gone, Gray slammed his fist on the table.

Despite the cruelty and finality of her words, a voice in his head told him that she was still the one for him. Who should he listen to, if not his own heart? If not his own voice?

"Susan," he muttered to himself, "if a strained conversation is all I'll ever get, then I'll take it."

Talia Winters slumped away from the viewer and rubbed her eyes. She had looked at everything on the data crystal ten times, and it still didn't make much sense. It was a lot of bogus figures that didn't add up correctly, a lot of statistics on job creation for telepaths that definitely favored the commercial sector, some pie charts that attacked military spending, and the request for a new research and development center. She didn't know how any of this would coalesce into a convincing argument for the needs of commercial telepathy.

Of course, she told herself, this was just raw data. You had to have it, because sometimes logic alone wouldn't work—there had to be numbers to plug in, charts to pull up. When it came down to it, she felt the strongest argument was that commercial telepaths were the only segment of Psi Corps who managed to pay for themselves. Bester and all his top-secret budgets were a total drain, and so was all the psychic-weapon research the military did. However, she doubted whether either one of them liked to be reminded of this.

And none of these charts or statistics addressed the real problem—that Mr. Bester and his ilk decided who got what in Psi Corps. What kind of argument could overcome that reality?

A knock sounded on her door, and Talia looked up with a start. As she pressed the button to open it, she called out, "Come in."

Emily Crane stumbled into the room. She was wearing high-heeled shoes and a peach evening gown with a single strap. It didn't look half-bad on her, thought Talia. If she could get accustomed to asserting herself, she had promise.

"What are you d-doing?" Emily asked accusingly. "You should be getting ready for the reception."

"Oh, sorry," said Talia, glancing at the clock over her screen. "I've been studying this data crystal you put together about the budget. Now I sort of wish you were going, because I don't think I'll be familiar with this by tomorrow morning."

"Do you think I am?" asked Emily. "You know the things to say. We can back it up later in a memo."

"All right," sighed Talia. "I don't think I can read any more of this crystal tonight, anyway."

"Then g-give it to me," said Emily, stepping carefully toward the viewer. "I have some updates for a few of those charts. I don't think you'll need to show them anything, but I'll give it back to you before the meeting, just in c-case."

She drew the crystal out of its slot and tucked it down her bra. "What we want is the research center. The rest is all smoke and m-mirrors."

"Thanks," said Talia. "I guess I had better get dressed now."

Emily nodded and hobbled out the door. After it shut, Talia thoughtfully pulled off her gloves. It felt good to have her fingers free, and she used them to unzip her skirt and let it fall to the floor. She stretched her fingers and pushed back her hair as she moved languidly toward the shower.

Garibaldi was having a wonderful dream. He was in the shower, with the water cascading all over him. This obviously was not on Babylon 5, he decided, because the water on B5 mostly dribbled. Anyway, he was in the shower, cleansing himself, and he knew that when he stepped out, the four hundred telepaths from Psi Corps would all be gone. It would be just the usual two hundred and fifty thousand dregs of humanity and aliens. He could hardly wait!

He turned off the shower and jumped out, already dry. He liked this shower. And he strode through a dreamworld of laughing, cheerful people, raising glasses and toasting him for ending the horror of the Psi Corps conference. There was Londo, grinning in his snaggletoothed way.

"I got the tape on them!" claimed the Centauri, lifting his glass.

"Excellent," replied Garibaldi with a big grin.

"Well done, Mr. Garibaldi," said Captain Sheridan, patting him on the back. "You're an asset to this station."

"Asset," muttered Garibaldi, thinking he had been insulted.

Then he saw Talia, who was dressed exactly as he was, which was not at all. "I'm taking a shower," she remarked, but her naked body floated past.

He wanted to follow her, but more people were pulling him along, raising their glasses to him. Without warning, the security chief bumped into someone he wanted to see in real life, but not someone he wanted to see in a dream. It was Deuce, the grubby kingpin of Down Below.

"Aw, Garibaldi," drawled Deuce, "you didn't have to get rid of them. I would've done it for you." He laughed and stepped back into the shadows.

Then it was Lennier, underfoot as usual. The peaceful Minbari held up a wad of cash. "We came to an understanding," he explained.

Ivanova walked somberly beside him, deep in thought. "Could you love a telepath?" she asked. "Could you really love one of *them?*"

"I love Psi Corps!" he replied, which seemed to be the right answer. Everybody smiled at him.

And the last being at the end of the line was Kosh, the Vorlon ambassador. The mountain of marble and fabric moved directly into his path and cut off his escape.

"Where have all the Martians gone?" asked the Vorlon in his strange combination of musical notes and synthesized voice. Kosh peered at Garibaldi with a tubelike telescope that issued from his stomach, and added, "Long time passing."

"They are all gone!" cried Captain Sheridan, raising his glass. "Here is to Mr. Garibaldi and his remarkable solution to the problem of Psi Corps."

Since everyone else stopped to look at him and lift their glasses, Garibaldi did likewise. Only he wasn't holding a glass—he was holding a block of wires with globs of dirty plastique. The denotator ticked menacingly!

Garibaldi gasped and tried to throw the bomb away. As it left his hands, it turned into a seering blast of white light and a monstrous *KA-BOOM!*

The last thing Garibaldi saw was Bester howling with laughter—then he mercifully woke up, clutching his blanket in his sweaty hands. Garibaldi's link was blaring, and his personal computer seemed to be shrieking at him, too.

"Okay, okay!" he growled. "I'm up."

"Twenty-hundred hours," said the computer.

He tapped his link, and the captain's voice sounded, "Gar-

ibaldi, this is Sheridan. Everything is under control, but I just
wanted to make sure you didn't oversleep.''

"No danger of that," croaked Garibaldi, smacking his lips
to get the weird taste out of his mouth.

Sheridan answered, "Glad to hear it. I'm at Blue-16 now,
and it's already filling up. We've had some would-be gate-
crashers, but the only outsiders we've invited are the ambassadors and their aides. So access has been fairly easy to
control.''

Garibaldi didn't like hearing the captain sound so nervous,
especially after the dream he had just had. "Fifteen minutes,'' he promised. "Thank you for the rest, Captain, I'm a
new man.''

"We could use some new men," said Sheridan glumly.
"Excuse me, Mr. Bester has arrived.''

Talia Winters took a drink of her Centauri wine and smiled at
Ambassador Delenn. The Minbari female looked as small
and fragile as a porcelain doll, but Talia knew there was a
tough, hard-nosed politician under that demure exterior. A
member of the Grey Council and an early backer of Babylon
5, Delenn understood the importance of the station as few
others did.

"My aide and Mr. Barker seem to have hit it off," remarked Delenn, looking with satisfaction at Lennier and a
stout military man. They were leaning into each other, involved in an animated conversation that excluded all others.

"Well, they should," remarked Talia, "they both hate
your warrior castes.''

Delenn's smile faded only a little as she looked up at the
taller women. "You don't seem yourself tonight, Ms. Winters. Is there something on your mind?''

Talia pushed back a strand of yellow hair, which perfectly
accented her black evening dress. Her white shoulders
gleamed like a spotlight above the black décolletage.

"You're right," she admitted. "I'm agonizing over a decision. In fact, it's a whole bundle of decisions all wrapped up
in one knot.''

Delenn cocked her head. "One should never make a decision hastily. Or alone. I am not much for mingling at parties, and I would be happy to give you my full attention."

Talia swallowed. "All right, I've been offered a new assignment, probably on Earth, with a very big firm. They say they want me for my interspecies experience, but I got that experience working here. In other words, I'd like to take this opportunity, but I don't want to leave B5. Does that make sense?"

"Perfect sense," answered Delenn, taking a demure sip of her tea. "If this firm is who I think it is, there may be a solution. Why don't you open up a branch office for them on B5? Then you can fall under their umbrella while staying with us."

Talia chuckled, then grew somber. "I thought of that. Unfortunately, my physical presence is required for some aspects of this deal."

Delenn smiled knowingly. "Ah, that is often the case. Although you are the one who has to make the decision, my opinion is that B5 will remain a most advantageous base for your career."

Talia looked down at her drink. The greenish liquid seemed to mimic her murky thoughts, and she wanted to throw it out and get something clean.

But a thought touched her mind, a sweet one, and she looked up to see Arthur Malten, now dressed in a very conservative dark-blue suit. Even his eyes were smiling.

"You look lovely tonight, Talia," he said. He turned to Delenn and bowed. "Do I have the pleasure of addressing Ambassador Delenn?"

"You do," she replied.

"Arthur Malten," he announced. "Of the Mix. I have spoken to many of your colleagues."

"Yes," said Delenn, "and we must talk about the proposed branch office you wish to open on Minbar." She smiled at Talia. "But not tonight."

"Yes," said Malten, grabbing Talia's hands through her black velvet gloves. "I'm afraid I must take Ms. Winters away for a moment. Mr. Bester is here, and he's in a very good mood, granting favors left and right.''

''Right this moment?'' asked Talia hesitantly.

''No time like the present,'' Malten replied. ''At least that's what I've always heard.''

''Haste makes waste,'' countered Delenn. ''Isn't that also one of your proverbs?''

Malten glanced at the Minbari. ''I'm very decisive,'' he told the ambassador. ''When I see what I want, I go after it. I'm patient, too, if need be.''

''An admirable trait,'' said Delenn. ''It is easy to be decisive, difficult to be patient.''

But Malten was already whisking Talia Winters away.

CHAPTER 8

TALIA stiffened her back as she strolled across the Blue-16 cafe. Part of it was the touch of Arthur Malten's bare hand on her wrist. Why wasn't he wearing gloves? she wondered. Probably just another example of his well-known penchant for rebellious behavior.

She wanted to tell Arthur that she hadn't made her decision yet—but then she was dazzled by the sights, sounds, and voices of a roomful of influential telepaths. Many of them turned to look at her and Malten, and the attention was alluring in its own right.

Did she really want to bury herself on a station full of alien life-forms and alien concerns? Or was this where she belonged—with her peers, in the midst of important decisions that affected the entire Earth Alliance? These were the people who made the Senate and Earthforce jump, the ones chosen by natural selection to lead.

She put on her most placid smile as Arthur steered her toward Mr. Bester. He was surrounded by his usual black-suited band of sycophants, with a handful of military and commercial telepaths in attendance as well.

When Bester saw Talia and Malten approach, he smiled expectantly, the scorpion waiting for the beetle to come closer.

"Good evening, Mr. Bester," said Talia.

"Good evening, Ms. Winters, you look lovely." He glanced with disinterest at her escort. "Hello, Malten."

"Hello, Mr. Bester," said the tall man. He gestured around at the gayly decorated cafe, jammed with people. "Don't we owe Ms. Winters a debt of gratitude for pulling all of this together so quickly?"

"Yes, we do," agreed Bester.

Talia shook her head politely. "Captain Sheridan, Mr.

Garibaldi, and the entire staff of B5 are the ones who really did it. I merely asked them.''

Bester smiled. ''Don't underestimate your powers of persuasion, Ms. Winters.'' He glanced at Malten. ''I've seen them at work.''

Malten bristled slightly but kept a polite smile on his face. ''I think we all realize how valuable Ms. Winters is. Although Babylon 5 is an important post, it's rather removed from the action. There are many of us who feel that Ms. Winters is being wasted here and could better serve Psi Corps in another capacity. Closer to Earth.''

Bester shrugged. ''She would make a wonderful rogue-hunter, but with a P5 level, what can we do?'' Several of the Psi Cops chuckled.

''We could use her in the Mix,'' said Malten.

Bester continued to smile, but he looked more threatening than friendly as he fixed his dark eyes on the entrepreneur. ''One would almost think, Mr. Malten, that you were trying to get a monopoly on all the talented commercial telepaths.'' His eyes narrowed. ''Getting greedy is not a good idea.''

Well, thought Talia, this conversation was certainly going downhill. ''I see Ambassador G'Kar,'' she said, ''and I wish to hear his side of the incident, which I missed. If you'll both excuse me.''

Walking off, she heard Malten hiss to Bester, ''That was uncalled for!''

Talia took a deep breath and decided not to bother G'Kar after all. He could be a bombastic sort, and she didn't really want to hear a blow-by-blow account of some bar fight. Despite the cheerful dance music that was playing, Mr. Gray looked lonely, standing by himself at the bar. So she headed his way.

''Hello, Mr. Gray,'' she said, grabbing a seat at the counter. As an afterthought, she added, ''Do you mind if I sit here?''

He blinked at her from his dazed reverie. ''Not at all, please have a seat. Are you having a good time?''

Distastefully, she set her glass of wine on the counter. "It'll be better after I get a new drink."

Gray twisted his hands nervously. "Ms. Winters, you've spent more time among aliens and even regular humans than I have. Can I ask you something?"

She smiled at him. "Certainly."

"Can a telepath and a nontelepath love each other?"

Talia smiled, thinking about Garibaldi. "I'm sure it happens all the time, on a superficial level. Whether a telepath and a mundane could stay together for sixty years and watch their grandchildren grow up, I don't know. I would think the odds are against it. On the other hand, I haven't seen many nontelepathic couples stay together for a long time either."

She motioned around the room. "Don't you find it amazing that so many of our kind are either single or divorced? We're all lone wolves."

"Yes," said Gray worriedly. He took a seat beside her and lowered his voice. "When I signed up for Psi Corps, I didn't know it would preclude living a normal life. They told me they would bring out my abilities, not kill everything else." His shoulders slumped. "I suppose, as long as one party is telepathic, there will always be distrust."

"And when both are telepathic," Talia added, "it's too intense to last long."

"So all we have is each other," said Gray, "and we can take very little solace in that."

"None," answered Talia.

She looked up and saw Arthur Malten headed their way, a peeved look on his face. She grabbed Gray's gloved hand. "Would you like to dance?"

He beamed with surprise. "Thank you, I would."

They escaped to the dance floor moments before Malten caught up with them. Talia could see him by the bar, sulking. She guessed that Mr. Bester had turned down his request to have her reassigned. Drawing on her usual optimism, Talia wondered if this wasn't for the best. The conference had barely started, and people were fighting over her. She supposed that was good, although it felt rather vulgar to be fought over like a head of cattle.

Mr. Gray was actually an accomplished dancer; he didn't step on her toes, and he kept a respectful distance. Talia used the roving platform of the dance floor to survey the other attendees at the reception.

Garibaldi and Sheridan, both of whom looked like they were at a wake, gave in to moments of polite laughter followed by long periods of somber realization. Of the ambassadors, G'Kar had the biggest following, and most of them were military telepaths. Apparently, bashing a Psi Cop could make you very popular with the military. Londo had brought an attractive Centauri woman with him, and they had quite a retinue of telepaths following them from one hors d'oeuvre table to another. The Psi Cops gravitated around Bester, and the commercial telepaths had broken up into small groups and couples. Hmmm, thought Talia, if she could find Emily Crane, perhaps she could introduce her to Mr. Gray. But the small woman in the peach dress was not in her line of sight.

On her second pass around the dance floor, Talia was glad to find Arthur Malten talking to Ambassador Delenn. The Minbari would be a good distraction for him, keeping his mind off matters that were up in the air. Up in the air was right where she wanted to leave those matters.

"Thank you for coming," said Captain Sheridan. "It was a pleasure. We are pleased to have you here. Think of us during the appropriations. Have a good conference."

To his credit, thought Talia, he managed to say the same thing a hundred times without sounding like a broken soundchip. She was reduced to a simple smile as the conference attendees filed out of the reception on Blue-16. They'd closed the place down, at the preset hour of 23:00. Almost no one had left early, save for Ambassador Delenn, and the proprietor of the cafe was tallying up the bar tab with a smile on his face.

"Detail two," said Garibaldi, "escort as many of these

folks as you can to their quarters. We don't want them wandering off to other parts of the station."

"Technically, they could go to the casino," said Talia.

Garibaldi scowled. "Do everything but read them bedtime stories," he told his people, "I want them in bed. I'll go with you."

The security chief and his officers took off after a knot of attendees who had halted in the corridor to study their door keycards. Soon those who needed help were taken underwing, and no one was left in the cafe except the workers, tidying up. Talia yawned, and Captain Sheridan looked at her sympathetically.

"I feel the same way," he admitted. "The conference business is not for me—too much conversation. But I think it's been successful, so far."

Talia nodded. "Captain, they are having a grand time. For this group, they were doing handstands they were so happy. Some of these people never feel welcomed anywhere, and you put them at ease. After a few rough spots, the ambassadors fit in very well, too. Although I was disappointed that Ambassador Kosh didn't come."

The captain shrugged. "Well, you know Kosh."

Talia shook her head and laughed, because both of them knew that was a very dumb remark.

"I've got to get to bed," said Sheridan. "My mind is a jumble. I suppose a few hundred telepaths will do that to you. Good night."

"Good night, Captain."

Talia watched the captain go, feeling good about shutting the place down, being the one to turn out the lights. Despite a few personality conflicts, this *was* a successful conference so far. Of course, she reminded herself, this was only the first official function out of two hundred and sixteen panels, seminars, luncheons, and meetings. So there was plenty of time for something to go wrong. But each day without incident was a feather in her cap. Now Psi Corps knew who she was and what kind of territory she had, and B5 was more than an acronym to them.

She stepped down to the corridor level and took a slow stroll toward the exit. All things considered, it was good to know that there was an upward path for her in the commercial sector. But what price did those paths have? It wasn't just the obvious pitfalls that had her worried, but the hidden ones, the ones worked out between Malten and Bester while her back was turned.

And what exactly did they want with her interspecies experience? While it had commercial applications galore, it also had military applications. She didn't want to become an experiment gone awry, like the only man she had ever loved. Nor did she want to become a spy against alien races, such as the Minbari. She had to tread very carefully, eyeball everything, and get it all in writing.

Talia wasn't particularly surprised when she felt his presence waiting for her around a bend in the corridor. He was being sweet again, trying to be apologetic. He would make it up to her, he promised, for those several awkward moments. All his fault, he assured her. Talia smiled and was about to tell him to buzz off for the night, because she really was tired.

"Arthur," she began, rounding the corner. But it wasn't Mr. Malten.

It was Mr. Bester. She glared at him, and he smiled at her.

"That is anatomically impossible," he said. "But a popular sentiment."

Talia sputtered, "You . . . you pretended to be . . ."

"Yes, I know," Bester conceded. "It is very difficult to work around a corner, and the signal is weak—but I can do it, if I know the person. The advantage, as you saw, is that you can pretend to be someone else."

"I don't appreciate that," said Talia.

Bester's smile faded. "Now you sound like your boyfriend, always whining. This is the big leagues the two of you want to play in, so you had better come ready to play ball." He smiled at her. "Do I make myself clear?"

Talia swallowed. "Okay, what do you want to approve my reassignment to the Mix? If that's what I decide to do."

Bester licked his lips. "We shouldn't talk about this out here in the corridor. My room is right down there."

Talia smiled. "I know exactly where your room is, and there's a recreation room even closer. It's perfect for talking. Or a quick game of Ping-Pong."

"Of course," said Bester with a disgruntled expression. "Lead on. I could use some recreation."

The room was empty, and Talia had to wipe her gloved hand over the wall panel to activate the lights. As she had specified, the Ping-Pong table had four new paddles and a package of balls; there was a chess set on one of the card tables, and decks of cards on the other two. In the corner was a compact weight-lifting machine with a video screen for instruction.

"How are you at Ping-Pong?" she asked.

"I react very quickly," answered Bester. "I used to be quite good. But that wasn't the game I had in mind."

Talia sat at one of the card tables and opened up a deck. "Isn't it odd, but everywhere you look there are invitations to gamble. You would think members of Psi Corps would be above temptation, but it comes after us just as much as anyone."

"It is the resistance that makes us strong," answered Bester, making a fist to dramatize his point. He took a seat opposite her and smiled. "Again, that is not the game I had in mind."

"How much will it cost me to work for the Mix?" asked Talia point-blank. "And leave Mr. Malten out of the equation."

"That is wise to leave Mr. Malten out," said Bester with approval. "He started the Mix, but now it has outgrown him. It could perform as well without him as with him."

Talia stared evenly at the Psi Cop. "So it has to be something I can pay for, on my own. How much?"

Bester leaned forward and asked hoarsely, "How badly do you want to go?"

Talia smiled. "Not that badly." She leaned back in her chair. "Is there an economy rate?"

Bester laughed. "You still haven't found the game I want to play yet. I want to play show-and-tell."

"How do you play that?" asked Talia suspiciously.

"It's very simple," said Bester, reaching into his jacket pocket. "I show you a picture of your Uncle Ted—that would be Theodore Hamilton—and you tell me where he is."

Bester tossed a photo of a rakish man with long blond hair onto the table, and Talia was stunned by the juxtaposition of her Uncle Ted and Mr. Bester. One was a ne'er-do-well lady-killer, and the other was, well, Mr. Bester. She laughed with both relief and amazement.

"I can get into the Mix by telling you about my Uncle Ted?" she asked puzzledly.

"You don't have to tell us anything about him, except where he is."

Talia looked helplessly at the Psi Cop. "I think, when I last saw him, I was about fourteen years old. He was just headed for Mars." She peered at Bester. "Oh, I see—this has something to do with Mars."

"You really don't know what he's been doing for the last two years?" asked Bester incredulously.

She shook her head. "I haven't had much contact with Mars." Talia wanted to say that her uncle would never become a Martian revolutionary, but that wasn't true. It probably was something the old romantic would do, especially if there were women involved.

"I would guess that he's been blowing things up on Mars," she said.

"Worse than that, Ms. Winters. Your Uncle Ted has been explaining the separatist position in a very clear way, and people are starting to listen to him. He's popular, and the colonists are hiding him. We've been trying to find him for two years."

Bester leaned urgently across the table. "We want him."

"I haven't a clue where he is," she answered, shaking her head. "And why would *you* want him, Mr. Bester? He's not a telepath, rogue or otherwise."

Bester smiled and answered, "That is on a need-to-know basis, and you don't need to know. But now you know the cost to get into the Mix—on your own terms, without Malten's help. Once you're in there, you can use him or not, as you wish. I believe this is a price you can meet, Ms. Winters, and it won't compromise your high ideals."

"Mr. Bester," she protested, "I haven't seen my Uncle Ted in something like fifteen years. How can I help you?"

"Come now, you're family. You can go to Mars or Earth, ask around, show some concern. Say you only want to say hello to your beloved Uncle Ted before the bad guys get him. Give him a hug for old times' sake."

Bester winked. "Surely, you learned a long time ago to read your mother's mind, without her knowing it. This is her brother we're talking about. Find out where he is."

Talia tried not to throw up, but she did start to gag on the idea of scanning family members without them knowing it. She stood weakly from the table and swallowed down the bile. "I'm not feeling very well, Mr. Bester. I really don't think I can be any help finding Ted Hamilton. Good night."

"The offer won't be on the table forever," warned Bester. "Good night."

Talia Winters slammed the door behind her and leaned against the wall for support. How could it be that talking to Mr. Bester always made her feel dirty? She couldn't avoid him—she would see him at the budget meeting in just ten hours—but she should refuse to discuss anything of a personal nature with him.

Then again, she had asked for it. With ambition and desire came the price. Even in the workaday world of the mundanes, it was no different. Talia had let herself be lured into this insane game, and she shouldn't panic just because the stakes got high. She could always drop out.

And she would. Tomorrow, right after the budget meeting. She'd go back to being the only resident telepath of Babylon 5 so far, and be thrilled with it.

Talia headed for the main checkpoint, and she felt relieved

to see Garibaldi and two of his officers, hanging out, looking edgy but better than they had earlier.

"Good evening," she said.

"Hello, Ms. Winters," the younger one said.

Garibaldi smiled at her. "We took a vote—we all like your outfit. I wouldn't want you to think it was just me."

"Thank you," she said wearily. "I haven't got any witty repartee left. Good night."

"I could walk you home," offered Garibaldi.

"Nope," she said, heading away from Blue-16. Then she stopped. "How did you get away from those aliens last night?"

"Oh, that," answered Garibaldi with a shrug. "I shot one in the foot, and I slugged another one. Then I ran like hell."

"There were three of them," said Talia.

Garibaldi rubbed his nose in thought. "Well, the third one came after you, but I guess you moved pretty fast."

"Yeah," the telepath agreed. "I'm moving fast these days. Good night."

"Good night."

Garibaldi lay in his bed, still thinking about his disturbing dream from earlier that day. His sense of duty kept prodding him to go Down Below and turn over every mattress and garbage can until he found Deuce. But he would have to get really lucky, or Deuce would have to want to be found, for that to work. With four hundred telepaths on the station, Garibaldi didn't feel really lucky, and he didn't think Deuce wanted to be found.

For one thing, Deuce was keeping very quiet. There had been no reports of beatings or murders, no jump in robberies or threats. Nobody had been caught transporting unusual contraband or stolen goods. And Deuce had not been spotted in any of his usual haunts, by any of several informers that Garibaldi had hired. Whatever Deuce's business on B5 was, he was keeping it low-key, just like they were trying to keep the conference low-key. Unfortunately, Deuce was doing a better job of it.

He rolled over in his bed and tried to get comfortable. It was no good. There were too many things around here that should not mix—Deuce, Bester, Martian terrorists, aliens who didn't give a hoot about Psi Corps, telepaths who didn't give a hoot about aliens. Even Captain Sheridan and Talia Winters had looked bagged by the stress, and if it could get to them, it could get to anyone. Come to think of it, neither Bester nor Gray looked too good either, Garibaldi decided. A feeling of paranoia was eating at all of them.

Worst of all, the conference proper didn't really start until tomorrow! He pulled the pillow over his head and tried to go to sleep.

CHAPTER 9

"YES, ma'am," said Garibaldi pleasantly, "we've got to open up your briefcase and look inside."

"I d-don't know why you should," muttered the short, dark-skinned woman. But she started to unlatch her case, anyway.

Garibaldi calmly took the case and set it on the table. As most of the contents were folders of transparencies, brochures, and business cards, he didn't empty it onto one of the bins set aside for that purpose. But he did feel around on the bottom to come up with four smaller objects: her identicard, a creditchit, a dictaphone, and a data crystal.

He held the data crystal out. "What is this?"

The woman put her hands on her hips and gave him a quizzical stare. "Are you saying you don't know what it is?"

"No," said Garibaldi, dropping the crystal and the other objects back into the case. "Just wanted to make sure it was yours. Officer Baker will search your person."

Huffily, the woman stomped on, and a female officer took charge of her.

Garibaldi sighed and looked up to find the cadaverous female Psi Cop.

"Uh, good morning," he said warily. "Did you have a pleasant evening?"

She grinned evilly. "Yes. Trixie and I stayed up all night, talking about the good old days. I never laughed so hard in my life." She winked at him. "We were experimenting a lot in those days."

"I'll bet," admitted Garibaldi. He pointed to her bag. "Can you open it, please?"

"Gladly." Without hesitation, the black-uniformed cop opened her handbag. "You are doing a fine job, Mr. Garibaldi. If anything happens, I know it won't have been your fault."

As he checked her bag, he whispered, "What do you think is going to happen?"

She held her regal chin up and sniffed. "It's just something in their air, isn't it?"

"No, that's fresh paint," said Garibaldi. "Thank you."

"You will pat me down personally, won't you?"

He winked at her. "Maybe the last day."

With a deep-throated laugh, the woman moved on. Garibaldi went through the same routine with dozens of telepaths, all of whom offered various levels of resistance. However, many of them seemed to feign their anger; they secretly welcomed the overt demonstration of security, even if it did suggest that Psi Corps didn't entirely trust its own members.

Garibaldi was just getting into a good rhythm, working the attendees through the main entrance to Green-12. That's when he looked up to see Mr. Bester.

The Psi Cop smiled and held up his hands. "No briefcase or bag." He tapped his head. "I keep everything I need up here."

"That's convenient," said Garibaldi. "I'm going to wave you through. No pat-down."

"How disappointing," said Bester, glancing at Officer Baker. "Is conference room number nine secured?"

"We've swept it twice," answered the Security Chief. "The lock will only open for the attendees on my list." He showed him a transparency of the invited guests for the ten o'clock budget meeting.

"Hmmm," said Bester with interest. "Ms. Winters is coming, too. What a pleasant surprise."

Garibaldi screwed his mouth shut and nodded. "I've got people piling up here, excuse me."

"Go on, go on," said Bester with a wave. He strolled through into the Green Sector, greeting people standing among the potted plants, refreshment tables, and beckoning doorways.

Garibaldi sighed and went back to the next glowering telepath. "Excuse me, sir, you'll have to open up your briefcase."

"By whose authority?" grumbled a black-suited Psi Cop.

The chief smiled. "Security Regulation 13, section 4, sub-paragraph B, Special Circumstance 2."

Talia lifted her arms and let the pat-down conclude as quickly as possible. It was embarrassing. Was Garibaldi doing this just to prove he was in charge? Oh, well, she had too much else on her mind to worry about the games he might be playing. She had come down through a lift entrance from another Green deck, thinking that she might avoid a security check. Fat chance.

"Sorry, Ms. Winters," said a young female security officer, handing her portfolio back. "Just following orders."

She nodded and tried to smile. "How are the attendees taking it?"

"Okay, mostly." The lift opened again, and the officer was distracted. "Excuse me, sir, I'll have to look inside that."

Talia shook her head and moved on. The overzealous searches were a statement, but maybe they were the right statement. Despite the success of the reception the night before, there was a pall hanging over the conference. Of course, that was due mostly to the bombing of the original site, which was symptomatic of the ongoing problems of Mars. Everybody was thinking about Mars, but nobody wanted to talk about it. Mr. Bester had called down early that morning to abruptly cancel two seminars on Mars.

Oh, well, there was still plenty going on. Too much, in fact. She checked her watch to make sure she wasn't running late to what was shaping up to be her most important appointment of the conference.

"There you are," said a warm voice, and Arthur Malten was upon her. He was dressed in a very conservative gray suit this morning. It was almost an Earthforce uniform, except for the fact that it only had one insignia, Psi Corps, the only one that mattered.

"Arthur," she said noncommittally, barely brushing his outstretched hand with hers.

He lowered his voice. "I'm sorry we never got back together last night. You knew, I struck out with Bester."

"That's fine," she said cheerfully. "There was nothing left to talk about. In fact, I'd rather not talk about it this morning."

She started to move away from him, but Malten doggedly followed. "Now don't be discouraged. That was just the opening salvo. I thought we could slip it past him, so to speak, but he understands your worth. He'll want to take something out of my hide for hiring you, I can see that now. But there are other approaches. We'll find the right one."

Talia wondered if she should tell Arthur right this minute that she wasn't interested in leaving B5. No, she decided, this wasn't the time or place to muddy the waters. Concentrate on the job at hand, her inner voice told her.

Malten rubbed his hands together. "At any rate, now we know he's interested in you and your career. This is something good to find out." He quickly added, "For you."

"Of course," she agreed, thinking of her disturbing conversation with Bester last night. Right now, she just wanted to get this budget meeting finished, then move on to the more pleasant aspects of the conference.

"How should we proceed?" she asked.

"Don't attack Bester or the Psi Cops directly," answered Malten. "But it's okay to rake the military over the coals. I believe in being positive, expressing all the good things we're doing."

He guided her down the corridor, which was flowing in both directions with conference attendees trying to find the right room, or the right person, or the right intimate group. Garibaldi's security people were on hand to provide directions and give everyone another dose of suspicious scrutiny. The ebb and flow calmed her nerves for a moment and made her realize that she, Bester, and Malten weren't the only ones in this place. As much as they thought the universe revolved around them, it didn't.

In three short days, Bester, Malten, and all these self-important people would be leaving. Back to their slimepits, as Garibaldi so succinctly put it. And she would be going back to her peaceful life as the resident telepath on B5, none the worse for wear. What was she so nervous about?

Emily Crane nearly bumped into her. "Oh, excuse me," the researcher said sheepishly.

"Hi," said Talia. She looked over her shoulder, but Malten had been waylaid by a band of commercial telepaths who were giving him last-second instructions.

"How's it going this morning?" asked Talia.

Emily made a face and shrugged. "I'm afraid m-most of the panels and seminars will be free-for-all messes. But what can I do about it?"

"Exactly," said the tall, blond telepath. "That's going to be my attitude from now on. What can I do about it?"

"Oh," said Emily, fishing in her briefcase, "here's that d-data crystal. Nobody takes time to look at figures, but you can say we have them."

"Thanks," said Talia. She slipped the crystal into her slim portfolio and sighed. She had to tell somebody. "Emily, I don't think I'll be joining the Mix anytime in the near future."

The small woman smiled. "Well, it's not for everyone."

"But," said Talia, "I would like to talk to someone about opening a branch office someday. Here on B5."

Emily fished in her briefcase for a program. "There's a seminar on that very subject, t-tomorrow at noon. Terrible time, isn't it?"

"I'll be there," Talia promised. "Thanks for everything."

"You've been a help, too," Emily assured her. "Mr. Malten would never ask this, but you might want to sit close to Mr. Bester."

"I will," said Talia. "Since I don't feel comfortable with this material, I'll be as distracting as possible."

"Good-bye," said Emily. She touched her watch. "I've got a d-demonstration to prepare."

"See you later."

The small woman scurried off down the hall and dashed around the corner. Everybody was in a hurry but Talia; she felt as if her feet were in molasses, and her head wasn't much better. This decision not to press Bester, not to push for promotion, had made her calmer, but it had also left her feeling drained. The adrenaline and emotions that had pumped all day yesterday were gone, without much left to replace them. It was just as well she wasn't doing any demonstrations, because she didn't feel as if she would be able to do an accurate scan on a two-year-old.

Suddenly, Talia had a strange image of Ambassador Kosh in her head. It was a flashback to that silly scan of "Invisible Isabel" three days earlier. She could see the Vorlon's mysterious bulk looming over her, the questioning tilt of his massive head-gear, his tubes and orifices probing the air.

The voice which was not there . . .

A little explosion went off in her head, and she staggered for a moment. She caught herself on the wall before falling down completely. Malten rushed over to catch her.

"Are you all right?" he asked with concern.

"Oh, sure," she lied. "Just lost my balance. How much time do we have?"

Malten checked his timepiece. "About ten minutes, although I suppose you could go in and sit down now." He looked worried. "You aren't scared of Bester, are you?"

"No," she continued to lie. "The only control he has over me is what I choose to give him."

"That's a healthy attitude," agreed Malten with a smile. "The commercial sector had such a banner year last year that he has to give us something. Let's just be polite, and keep hammering away."

"Hammering away," Talia repeated, holding her head. She looked around. "I think I will go in and sit down. Number nine, isn't it?"

"Yes," said Malten, glancing over his shoulder. "I'll see you in a few minutes. I have some hand-wringers out here who need to be reassured."

Talia managed a smile. "Go ahead. I can take care of myself."

She walked to the door of conference room nine, expecting

it to open at her touch. But it didn't open. Then she remembered and pulled out her identicard. When she pushed it into the slot, the door slid open, to her relief. Talia slouched into the well-appointed conference room, expecting to find no one there. But she was wrong.

A chair swiveled around at the head of the amber table. Mr. Bester smiled at her and formed his gloved hands into a triangle.

Talia tried not to look surprised. She almost set her portfolio down at the opposite end of the table, but then she remembered what Emily Crane had suggested. So Talia walked slowly to the head of the table and took the seat to the immediate right of Bester, setting her bag on the floor.

The Psi Cop nodded approvingly. "I figured you to be a punctual person, Ms. Winters."

"I try," she remarked.

"You know," said Bester, "before telepaths came along, people used to do studies on body language and spatial relationships—to find out what people were thinking. For example, there were many studies devoted to the way in which people would arrange themselves in a room, when given free choice in seating."

He smiled. "It tells me something that you would take the seat beside me when there are all these empty seats."

"What does it tell you? Besides the fact that I don't want to shout across the room."

"It tells me," said Bester, "that you wish to be close to the seat of power. We need to see if your colleague, Mr. Malten, will take a seat at the foot of the table, thus showing how much he opposes me. That would also demonstrate how much he wishes to keep his distance."

The Psi Cop motioned to the closest seats. "The military will gang up and surround me. They would have taken your seat, so I thank you for taking it first. My own people will sit to my right, and there'll be two people from Corps Administration. You and Malten alone will represent the profiteering side of things. Do you know, Malten could bring more people to this meeting, but he prefers to do everything on his

own. To be honest, Ms. Winters, your presence is just a subterfuge.''

If that wasn't a kick in the teeth, thought Talia, she had
never had one. So she asked him point-blank, ''Do you know
how this meeting is going to turn out? I mean, do you have
an open mind, or is this all a facade?''

Bester narrowed his eyes at her. ''I don't know what will
happen any more than you do. I'm always prepared for the
unexpected.''

The door opened, and three military telepaths entered,
looking very important, grim, and ready for battle. One sat
beside Talia, and the other two sat across from her, taking the
three seats closest to Bester.

The Psi Cop looked at her and smiled.

Mr. Malten, however, did not sit at the foot of the table. He
sat to the left of Bester, about four seats away, and nobody
sat directly opposite Mr. Bester. Despite his nonthreatening
seat, Malten was doing most of the talking in the early part of
the meeting.

''You want long-term?'' he asked. ''Look at what we've
done. We have managed to infiltrate more cities and planets
than you and the military could ever dream about. Bester,
while you try with pathetic results to keep what you're doing
on Mars a secret, I have a dozen offices there. I have nearly
as many people as you have. Because we can work openly,
we will always have the advantage.''

Malten leaned forward. ''Commercial telepaths work
among the people, and they're not afraid of us. When they
receive their first scan in a nonthreatening commercial situation—and it doesn't hurt—then they're more receptive for a
security scan later on. We do a lot of good for Psi Corps. We
want to keep a bigger percentage of what we make, that's all.
We're pulling the load, but we're not getting paid for it.''

One of the military liaison officers began to sputter, but
Bester held up his hand. The Psi Cop wasn't angry, thought
Talia; he seemed to be enjoying the banter with Malten.

''Granted,'' he said, ''our services are not as popular as

yours. But which are more necessary to the safety and security of the alliance? When telepaths go rogue, nobody but us can bring them down. What should we do afterward—stand on streetcorners and pass the hat?''

The other Psi Cops at the table laughed, but Talia felt another white flash in her brain! She screwed her eyes shut to fight the headache and the dizzy sensation. Luckily, no one was paying the slightest attention to her, because Bester was still speaking:

''When you work in secret, Mr. Malten, as we do, you cannot expect support from the public. You and I are like two different fortune-tellers. One of us gives the customer good news, and the other one gives them bad news. You will be paid well, while we work in ignominy. Don't begrudge us a little handout.''

''I'm crying for you,'' Malten scoffed. ''If your budget is too tight, at least look at some of that huge research and development slush fund in the military.''

''One moment!'' blustered a military liaison. ''We must always be ready in the event of war, not to mention the Martian separatists, and one or two new threats. If any of these cold wars become hot, psi weapons may turn the trick. All of our enemies are using them.''

Talia sat up in her chair and blinked to stop the pain. Blast it, she didn't know what was happening to her, but it felt as if her head was becoming unhinged! She kept thinking of Ambassador Kosh and the strange scans she had been performing for him.

''Gone, like the pickled herring,'' came Kosh's words.

Malten had turned his attack on the military. ''While you go out of your way to antagonize other races, including the Minbari, I'm opening up an office on Minbar. Who is in a better position to do intelligence, you or me?''

Bester rapped his fingers on the table and asked, ''You would perform intelligence tasks with your people?''

Malten smiled enigmatically. ''Let's see what we get out of this budget. If you will stop and look, I think you will find that the commercial sector is poised to be very useful. We have the grass-roots organization which both of you lack. We're everywhere, even Babylon 5. If we had the right facilities and support, all of you could be in commercial jobs, purely as cover, and still be doing exactly what you're doing now."

While Bester and the military liaisons digested that one, Talia Winters bolted to her feet. It was overwhelmingly oppressive in the conference room, and she had to get out!

She thought she was quite calm as she said, "Excuse me, I have to go to the bathroom."

Bester looked at her thoughtfully. "Yes," he agreed, "you had better take something for that headache."

"Thank you," she muttered, but Bester had already turned his attention back to Malten.

"I've heard this before," said the Psi Cop, "vague promises that your people would start doing intelligence work for us. But when it comes time to implement it, they're too busy with their regular jobs! Well, let me tell you . . ."

Talia staggered to the door and pressed the panel that opened it. She couldn't get out quickly enough, and she beat on the door to make it open faster. Then she squeezed out before the door had even opened all the way.

Although it was exactly the same remanufactured air in the corridor, it smelled so much better than the air inside the room that she almost skipped with joy. Maybe she was having a reaction to the fresh paint, she thought with a burst of realization. That was probably it. A thing like that might curtail her conference activities.

Just as she was about to stop and catch her breath, a monstrous explosion ripped through the doorway of the conference room, and the concussion hurled her off her feet! The corridor filled with acrid smoke, and alarms and people started shrieking at the same time. It was bedlam in the corridor, and she was nearly trampled by people rushing to see what had happened.

It was finally a security officer who dragged her out of the way and propped her against the wall. "Medical emergency!" he shouted into his link. "Explosion on Green-12, conference room nine! Injuries and possible dead! We need medteams! Bomb squad!''

"The hull is secure!" somebody was yelling. "Everyone just stay calm. This was a localized explosion!"

People ran through the corridor with fire extinguishers, and they shot streams of foam into the smoldering remains of conference room nine. Talia looked down at her sleeve and could see drops of blood, although she wasn't bleeding. It was somebody else's blood! The stench invaded her nostrils, and the sirens and voices of the dead and dying split her senses.

Talia covered her ears and screamed! But that scream was more than her mind could accept, and it shut down. The voices stopped, and she toppled over into oblivion.

CHAPTER 10

TALIA Winters awoke in her own quarters, lying in her own bed. She was even wearing the thick flannel nightgown that she liked to wear when she was feeling cold or ill. With tremendous relief, she realized that the horrible explosion had been a dream. Conference room nine wasn't really in flames, and people weren't dying.

It had been a weird dream, she thought, having Kosh in it, hooded aliens, and a bunch of people she didn't know. But how much was dream, and how much wasn't? Was Babylon 5 crawling with telepaths, or was she the only one? What time was it? Where was she supposed to be? As Talia began looking around her tidy quarters, she began to get a sinking feeling, as if she were slipping back into her nightmare.

For one thing, hanging on the closet door was the dress she had worn to the reception the night before. And if that had been real, maybe the budget meeting on Green-12 was real. And if that had really happened . . . well, it couldn't have, it was too terrible to contemplate! It was just the sort of thing that her fevered imagination would concoct before a stressful day. She was probably late to her own panels.

Talia started to get out of bed; but something else caught her eye, and she gasped!

Standing perfectly still by the door was Commander Ivanova.

"I can't believe it," whispered Ivanova. "I was just about to leave." She lifted her link to her mouth.

"Wait!" demanded Talia. She sat up in bed and wiped errant strands of blond hair off her face. "What's happening? Why are you in my room?"

Ivanova took several strides across the small room and sat on the bed beside her to whisper, "Keep your voice down. You've got two Psi Cops outside your door, and I think they would as soon kill you as look at you. But there are two of

Garibaldi's people to keep an eye on them. Of course, all four of them are out there to make sure you don't go anywhere."

Talia rubbed her eyes and tried to figure out what was happening. She decided to repeat the question until she got an answer. "Ivanova," she said through gritted teeth, "why are you in my room?"

Ivanova cocked her head. "I volunteered to watch you. I had to see the woman who reportedly killed four Psi Cops and a military liaison."

Now Talia buried her face in her hands and cried. She tried desperately to wake up again, to leave this nightmare for anything, anywhere else! But she couldn't conjure up any other visions or memories that would drag her away from this tawdry scene. She was stuck here, and she couldn't change it.

The commander activated her link. "Ivanova to medlab. Ms. Winters is awake now."

"Thank you," said Dr. Franklin. "I'll be right there."

"I didn't kill anyone!" insisted Talia.

"Careful what you say," warned the officer. "You might want to talk to a counsel before you talk to me. I'll have to report anything you say to Garibaldi."

"But I didn't kill anyone!" Talia wailed.

There was immediate pounding on the door, followed by a booming voice, demanding, "We want to see the prisoner!"

Ivanova shook her head glumly. "You're in a load of trouble, Talia."

The telepath slammed her fist into the bed and muttered, "I didn't kill anyone, I didn't." She looked up bleary-eyed. "The people who died . . . was Malten one of them?"

Ivanova shook her head. "Malten came through scot-free. Bombs are weird like that. Everybody who was sitting to the right of Mr. Bester got it. You would've gotten it, too, if you hadn't left the room."

"That's crazy!" moaned Talia. "I didn't take a bomb into that room!"

There was more irate pounding on the door, but Ivanova ignored it. "Actually, the evidence is clear that you *did* take the bomb into the room. It was hidden in that slim handbag of yours.''

''No!'' screamed Talia.

The door banged open, and it was Dr. Franklin fighting his way past two black-suited Psi Cops. ''Stay back!'' he ordered them. ''She's under my care!''

But one of the black-suited cops burst into the room with the doctor before the door shut. He was a muscular lad, still young, with pimples on his face and a scowl of hatred. ''Why did you kill them? Why?''

''Get out of here at once!'' snapped the doctor.

The Psi Cop pointed a black-clad finger at Talia. ''We'll do a deep scan on you. We'll find out why. You know what we do to rogues!''

''Now!'' ordered Franklin, balling his hands into a fist.

The young Psi Cop banged the panel to open the door, then he stepped out into a din of angry voices. Talia held her hands over her ears and tried to shut them out, but the voices wouldn't go away until the door finally shut.

Dr. Franklin knelt in front of the frightened woman and looked into her eyes with a small beam of light. She twisted away, still disoriented and hysterical. Finally Talia took a deep breath and told herself that she had to stay calm and face this. She gripped the sleeve of the doctor's smock, holding it steady so that he could complete his examination.

''I didn't set off a bomb,'' she told the doctor.

''Guess what?'' he replied. ''It's not my job to figure what you did or didn't do. It's my job to get you well. You were in shock after the bombing, so we sedated you. But physically you appear to be fine. Tell me immediately if you feel any pains anywhere. Otherwise, just get lots of rest. Or as much as they let you.''

Franklin stood up and shrugged helplessly. ''Medlab is sort of crazy at the moment, so I had them bring you here. You could go to medlab if you wanted, but you might be more comfortable staying here.''

Talia wrung her hands and looked from Ivanova to the doctor. ''Am I under arrest?''

Franklin looked back at the door and frowned. "I wouldn't expect to be going anywhere real soon."

He turned back to Talia and said sympathetically, "You rest, get something to eat, and we'll give you a thorough exam later. I'll do my best to see that you aren't disturbed too much. I might be able to keep the newspeople out, but I don't know about the rest of them."

Franklin grabbed his bag. "I've got to get back to my prize patient."

"Who is that?" asked Talia.

"Mr. Bester. It's definite—he will live. Whether any of us in medlab will, with him as a patient, I don't know."

Franklin started to the door and turned. "Good luck to you, Ms. Winters. It's been hell for all of us, but that will be over in a few days. Your hell is just starting, I'm afraid."

The angry voices rose a pitch as he opened the door and ducked out, and Talia fought back the temptation to answer them all with a primal scream.

"Wrong," she muttered. "They're wrong."

Ivanova sat on the bed beside her and shook her head in amazement. "I don't know you all that well, Talia, but I never figured you to be a Martian terrorist."

Talia half-laughed and half-cried at the absurdity of it. "Is that what they're saying? I've never even liked Mars—a dusty old place with rabbit warrens for cities. All blue-collar, no decent restaurants."

The telepath suddenly grew very somber. "Listen, I need to talk to the captain or Garibaldi and tell them I'm innocent. I need to clear this up."

"You need to talk to legal counsel," said Ivanova somberly. "You need someone to argue for you, and advise you. You're looking at charges of mass murder, terrorism, and treason. On top of that, the Psi Cops might decide you're a rogue. If they get custody of you . . ." She shuddered and couldn't finish her thought.

Talia started to reach for Ivanova's hands, but she stopped when she realized that neither one of them were wearing gloves. "Help me," she begged. "You be my counsel. Command officers can, in an emergency."

Ivanova leaped to her feet. "I don't think I can. I wish you well, but I don't think I can spend weeks on end talking to *them*. Besides, with charges this serious, defending you could become a career."

"Please," begged Talia. "Just until we see what's going to happen."

"Why me?" asked Ivanova.

"I need somebody who won't be afraid of them."

A firm knock sounded on the door, and the women looked up with a start. "It's Captain Sheridan," called a familiar voice. "And Mr. Garibaldi."

Talia rubbed her eyes and pointed to her closet. "I've got a robe in there. And my gloves."

Before she fetched the robe and the gloves, Ivanova hung up Talia's evening gown from the night before. It seemed like another lifetime ago, thought the telepath, just those few hours. It was amazing how quickly your life could turn to junk.

Ivanova gave Talia her things with a brave smile. "Just stick to the truth."

"That's all I've got," answered Talia, pulling on her gloves. She stood up and pulled off the nightgown, momentarily nude. Ivanova didn't turn away. Talia slipped on the robe, and knotted it. Then she looked at Ivanova and waited for her to open the door.

Captain Sheridan and Mr. Garibaldi entered, both looking as if they had gone through their own set of traumas. Talia could see and hear the commotion outside the door, and a man in a black uniform was shaking his fist.

Garibaldi growled at them, "You'll get your chance!"

"Garibaldi!" snapped Sheridan.

Mercifully, the door closed, ending the angry shouts, for the moment. Sheridan and Garibaldi took deep breaths to try to calm themselves, but their anxiety was more unnerving to Talia than the ridiculous charges against her.

"Thanks for coming," she said, for no particular reason. It was doubtful they had come to rescue her, she told herself.

Sheridan tried to keep his voice even. "Ms. Winters, do you understand what's happened?"

"I didn't do it," she claimed. "I didn't take a bomb into that room."

"Well, then," said Garibaldi, "somebody slipped the bomb into your portfolio. My own forensic people will swear to that. We've got the residue of your handbag all over everything."

"Plus," said Sheridan, "you ran out just before the bomb detonated."

Ivanova stepped between them. "Excuse me, Captain, is this an interrogation, or a trial? You have to let her tell her side of it."

"There's nothing to tell!" shouted Talia. "I was as surprised as anyone when that bomb went off!"

"Why did you get up and leave the room?" asked Sheridan.

"I didn't feel well." Talia frowned, knowing how lame that answer sounded. "It's the truth."

"What did you have in your bag?" asked Garibaldi.

Talia shook her head in desperation. "Just some notes and cards, a conference program, a data crystal—nothing unusual!"

"A bomb is highly unusual," said the captain.

"I didn't know it was there!"

Garibaldi held out his hands, trying to calm everyone and think at the same time. "There are a lot of things wrong with this," he declared. "First of all, it was a very small, very sophisticated incendiary device. We think it was of alien design, because we don't have anything that small that would do that kind of damage, and leave so little trace.

"Secondly," he continued, "just moments after the bombing, that Free Phobos group on Mars was claiming credit for it! We hadn't released a single word about it, yet some jokers on Mars acted like they had won the World

Series. That's the same group who claimed the hotel bombing last week. They must have known about it, but how?''

"I'm not a terrorist," Talia insisted. "I don't even have any connection with Mars!"

Sheridan held up a finger. "Ms. Winters, that's not entirely true. While he was conscious, Mr. Bester gave us the rundown on Ted Hamilton, your uncle.''

"No!" The telepath balled her hands into fists and slumped onto her bed. It didn't matter what she said—fate or some terrible power had beaten her to every signpost, turning every one of them to make her look guilty.

"Please," said Ivanova, "there's got to be some doubt in your minds! Had she died in the blast, you would have figured she was innocent. But since she had the misfortune to live, you think she's guilty?''

The first officer continued, very calmly, "Most of us have worked with Ms. Winters for over a year now—has she ever given any indication that she hated Psi Corps enough to blow up a roomful of them? Now, if it had been Garibaldi or me . . .''

Sheridan cast her a stern glare. "Please, Commander, the well-known animosity of my staff toward Psi Corps isn't helping matters."

"But she's right, Captain," said Garibaldi. "If Ms. Winters had an uncle who was in the Mars resistance, you never would've known it from her. I never heard her talk about Mars." He smiled at Talia. "Except once, when I asked her to do a favor for me.''

Sheridan scowled. "She wouldn't necessarily broadcast the fact that she had an uncle who was a terrorist.''

"Okay," said Garibaldi, "there's one more thing that's really strange. We've been over the conference room a hundred times, and we haven't found any remains of a timer or trigger device. So there must've been a filament or some kind of microscopic fuse inside the charge, and they must've triggered it remotely. But Ms. Winters had only gotten about five meters beyond the room when it blew, and she didn't have any devices on her. In other words, if she pushed the button, where's the button?"

"I didn't push any button!" moaned Talia.

Sheridan shrugged. "If I were the prosecutor on this, I could answer every one of these questions. The fact that this Martian organization already knew about the bombing shows that she had accomplices. So, she planted the bomb, and somebody else detonated it. Or she detonated it, and her accomplice took the device out of her hand while she was lying in the corridor."

"I didn't do it," said Talia firmly. But nobody was listening to her. It was terrible the way they were talking about her as if she weren't there. As if she were already dead!

Of course, five people were dead, she reminded herself. Five fellow telepaths. She should be out in the corridor, demanding for heads to roll, instead of sitting helplessly on her bed, waiting for her own head to roll. Not only was she in danger of being falsely accused and convicted, but the guilty party was getting away!

She jumped to her feet. "You've got to stop them!"

"Who?" asked Sheridan.

"Whoever killed those telepaths!"

"Okay, Ms. Winters," said Sheridan calmly. "I'm getting the distinct impression that you plan to plead not guilty. Which is fine with me."

Talia lifted her chin and asked, "Are you going to arrest me?"

"We have to," answered the captain. "Everybody is fighting over jurisdiction of this case. If we don't arrest you and have the ombuds try you here, then Bester, Earthforce, or somebody will take you away. If you think you'll stand a better chance with them . . ."

"No!" snapped Ivanova. "If Psi Corps declares her to be a rogue telepath, they can deal with her however they please —without a trial. We can't let them have her."

Talia felt weak in the knees, and she sat down again. More than anything, she just wanted to crawl under her bedcovers and go back to sleep. There had to be some way to exit from this nightmare, if only she could think about it. If only she could remember everything. But it was all such a haze. She hadn't felt right the entire morning, and she had barely said ten words to anybody. Her presence at that meeting had been superfluous, as Bester had claimed it was. No, that wasn't it —he had called her a subterfuge.

Apparently, she was a better subterfuge than any of them had imagined. This was what she got for being ambitious and wanting to play with the big boys. She got used. Even now it seemed as if nobody—not her colleagues in the Corps or her neighbors on B5—really wanted to help her. They had their physical evidence and to hell with her! Somebody had to hang for this.

Talia had to flee from Babylon 5, she decided that moment, and find out who really did this.

"All right, it's agreed," said Garibaldi. "We'll have to arrest you, Ms. Winters. But we'll keep looking. I want to find that detonator, I want to know who's on the station from Mars, and I need to talk to all my people who were doing security on Green-12. Maybe you *did* have an accomplice, even if you didn't know about it."

He looked around her crowded quarters. "Sorry, but we can't leave you here, under house arrest. Bester's people are irate about it, plus all they're doing in the corridor is drawing flies. We'll have to take you to the brig, where we have better control over the situation. I'll give you five minutes to get dressed and pack a few things."

"She'll need a hearing before the ombuds to keep her in the brig," said Ivanova.

"I'll arrange it," answered Sheridan. "You sound like her counsel."

Ivanova nodded. "I am. Until I find her somebody better."

Sheridan rolled his eyes toward the heavens. "If you want me to say I was dead wrong about allowing the conference here, I will. I was dead wrong. Dumbest thing I ever did."

Ivanova glanced at Garibaldi and said, "We know that. I'm still her counsel."

The captain looked at the blond woman. "Is that all right with you?"

Talia nodded numbly.

"Come on, Ivanova," said the captain, "and let's get the paperwork started."

They opened the door, and Sheridan and Ivanova battled their way into an angry crowd, filled with floating video recorders. Garibaldi stared at them until the door closed, and the muscles around his neck tightened.

"Oh, brother," he moaned, "now the press has found us. Talia, what is this mess about? What happened?"

She shrugged and wearily shook her head.

"Who did you screw with?" he asked.

"Go away," she said in a husky voice. "I don't trust any of you. You know I didn't do this, but you're going to put me on trial!"

"That's to keep you on the station, until we find out who did it!"

She sniffed and untied her robe. "Right, you can tell me that when I'm convicted of five murders. Or tell me that when you turn me over to Bester. Or maybe you think I want to spend the rest of my life as the most famous prisoner in the brig of Babylon 5. You can sell tickets—there she is, the Psi Cop Bomber."

Garibaldi pointed at her and promised, "I'm going to find out who did this. You can bank on it."

"Get the hell out of here and let me find my clothes." The blond woman stood up and started to take off her robe, and Garibaldi hurried out.

"Doctor!" screamed a little man lying in the recovery room of a busy medlab. He started to thrash around in his bed, and then he winced and gasped from the pain.

"Doctor!" he cried through clenched teeth.

Dozing in the corner, Mr. Gray bolted to his feet and was the first one to the man's side. "Please be calm, Mr. Bester. It's wonderful to see you looking so . . . so awake, but you must remember your injuries." He rearranged some of the tubes and sheets that covered Mr. Bester.

The Psi Cop slumped back onto the bed, grumbling.

"Yes," said Gray, "your buttocks area was apparently very badly mangled, and the burns on your leg and arm—most unfortunate. Altogether, you were lucky."

"I don't feel so lucky," muttered Bester.

Gray swallowed. "Yes, but look at the alternatives."

Bester laughed sourly. "They can't get *me* so easily. Have they arrested Talia Winters yet?"

"Yes," answered Gray, "the last I heard, they were taking her to the brig. You know, she never struck me as being the violent type. I would have thought she was on a career track. I wonder if she really . . ."

"Don't wonder," said Bester, followed by a coughing fit. "She brought that bomb into the room, I know it! It was no accident that she ran out when she did. But who put her up to it? I don't know that."

"The Free Phobos group is claiming responsibility."

"I know," growled Bester, "but who are *they?*"

Gray looked down apologetically. "The conference has officially disbanded. Transports are taking most of the attendees out tonight."

"Damn," muttered Bester. "They'll get away."

"Who will get away?"

"Whoever put Ms. Winters up to it!" snapped the Psi Cop. "She couldn't have managed this by herself. Who *is* Free Phobos, and why do they want me out of the way?"

Gray cleared his throat. He wasn't about to say what he was thinking, that the number of people who wanted Bester out of the way was too numerous to investigate.

"You've never heard of Free Phobos?" asked the young telepath.

"Not before the first bombing. And not again until this second one. I've had plenty of people looking for them, too."

Bester grimaced in pain and tried to get comfortable in his hospital bed.

"Can I get anything for you, sir?" asked Gray with concern.

Through clenched teeth, Bester grunted, "Yes! Catch the bastards who did this to me! The ones who killed our people. You're still attached to my office—that's a direct order."

"Sir," said Gray, taken aback, "what about your own Psi Cops?"

Bester smiled with satisfaction. "We have Ms. Winters, or soon will have her. She's our dirty laundry, and we will wash it ourselves. We'll find out as much as there is to know from her, but there may be other leads. Follow them, Gray. Get to the bottom of it."

The young telepath felt a grip on his forearm, and he looked down to see burnt fingers wrapped in bandages, smearing blood on his sleeve.

"Promise me," rasped Bester.

"I'll find them," said Gray, removing his arm.

Garibaldi pulled open the door in slow motion, but the lights and the voices struck her in high-speed, strobelike bursts. Garibaldi grabbed her arm and dragged her out of her quarters, because she couldn't make herself move. Talia felt like she was staring at an oncoming train, the rush of people was so intense. The lights blinded her, the hands pushed in, while Garibaldi's security people pushed out. The black-suited ones stood on their tiptoes and shook their fists, shouting:

"Murderer!"

"Traitor!"

"Back!" snapped Garibaldi, like a lion tamer.

She could see a wedge of gray-suited backs forming before her and leading the way down the corridor. Garibaldi wrapped his arms around her like armor and steered her behind the wedge. People stood in doorways and clung like flies to the wall to get a look at her. The same people would have only given her a glance the day before.

The flying wedge swept through a bulkhead and down a ramp, and the crowd of people vanished. She was surprised to see only Garibaldi and his gray-suited security people. As they weren't needed to spearhead the charge anymore, the officers fell back to rear-guard positions. Soon it was just her and Garibaldi, followed by a man holding a PPG rifle.

Irrationally, she thought for a split second, *Can I get that rifle away from him?* But where would she go? How would she get off the station? Talia had to think about it—she just had to think.

Her inner voice was telling her to escape. It wasn't right or wrong, or even logical, but she had to listen. There was only one thing Talia Winters knew for sure—she had to get off Babylon 5 and exit from this nightmare!

CHAPTER 11

GARIBALDI pounded his knuckles together and looked at the bulk of his security staff, most of whom had been on duty the morning before in Green-12. He prowled around the briefing room, peering at their dour expressions.

"I know we're pretty down now," said Garibaldi, "but that assignment is over. Let's move on to the next one, which is to find out who had anything to do with that bombing. Now, who inspected Ms. Winters when she entered Green-12 that morning?"

"I did, sir," said Molly Tunder, a young woman who looked mostly Asian.

"What did you find in her bag?"

Tunder shrugged. "Nothing that struck me as odd. Cards, a conference program, notes on a transparency."

"And a data crystal," Garibaldi put in.

The young officer shook her head. "No, sir, I don't recall a data crystal."

"But she told me she had one," the chief insisted.

"I suppose," said the officer, "she could've been holding it in her hand."

"How did she appear to you?" asked Garibaldi.

"Out of sorts, distracted. But then, it was a stressful situation—the searches and pat-downs. And I couldn't spend much time with her."

Garibaldi knew the feeling. He would rather be down in the brig now talking to Talia, but he couldn't hold her hand and find the real culprits at the same time. There were a million things he wanted to do at once, but he had to calmly step through them.

"Detail one, you're at the beginning of your shift," he said. "As soon as we're finished here, you head Down Below and shake the trees. See if anybody knows anything about anything. And see if you can find Deuce, although I suspect he's already left the station. Deuce has the good sense not to get caught in a bombing.''

His link buzzed, and the chief answered curtly, "Garibaldi.''

"This is Rupel in the brig. Ms. Winters has a visitor, and she's demanding to see him.''

"Who is it?''

"Ambassador Kosh,'' came the answer.

"Kosh,'' muttered Garibaldi. Relationships between humans and aliens were hard to explain, but he knew there was one between Talia and Kosh. Maybe the ambassador could help her get good legal counsel. On the other hand, the Vorlon often lived by his own rules, and who knew what they were?

"It's okay,'' he said. "But have someone present. I'm going to be down there in a few minutes to talk to Ms. Winters. Out.''

He turned off his link and looked at the expectant faces. "I've already got Jenkins's report about finding Ms. Winters in the corridor after the blast. Did anybody else see anything?''

There were several seconds of uncomfortable silence before Garibaldi realized that even the professional observers hadn't seen anything. They were as mystified, sickened, guilt-ridden, and angry as he was.

"All right,'' he concluded, "you've got your assignments. We're looking for Martians, the forensic team is at the scene, and some of us are going Down Below. The good news is that all the telepaths are either gone or on their way off the station, except for the Psi Cops. There are still about fifty of them on B5, so stay away from them. Don't argue legalities with them. If they try to provoke anything, send them to me or Captain Sheridan.''

Garibaldi nodded grimly to each of them in turn. "Dismissed.''

The word "brig,'' decided Talia Winters, must have been a euphemism for a kennel. That was the way it felt to her—an airy, roomy, and bare cage for a person, with as much personality as a slab of concrete. She had lots of privacy due to the fact that there was nobody else in B5's neglected brig. Had the place been crowded and the dozen-or-so cells full— she didn't want to think of the bedlam.

Talia prowled her cell like a panther, ever moving, watchful, and ready to spring. At what? The cells were protected by a double cardkey system—first mechanical locks on each individual cell, then a barred doorway operated by cardkey. She didn't know how many guards waited outside the barred door, but she had seen several already.

Suddenly the door opened, and a massive figure filled it. Talia's heart pounded with hope, although this figure was a very strange savior. A bundle of exotic fabrics and armor as smooth as porcelain, Ambassador Kosh glided into the room and stopped a few meters in front of her cell. The head-gear nodded, and little tubes and orifices sniffed the air.

"It is the Hour of Longing," said Kosh in his twinkling, synthesized voice.

Talia snorted a derisive laugh. "You've got that right, Ambassador Kosh." She shook her head in amazement. "Everything going fine, and somebody lowers the boom on you. But I'm glad to see you. I've been thinking a lot about you, including a time just before the bomb went off."

She could see the guard edging closer to overhear them.

"Excuse me," she said, "can we have some privacy?"

"I'm afraid not," the guard answered politely. "Mr. Garibaldi's orders."

"Oh, is that right?" she seethed. "Bless Mr. Garibaldi for keeping the deranged terrorist under a close watch!"

"Anger is a blue sea," said Kosh.

Talia blinked at him, suddenly realizing that she could try to talk to Kosh in that cryptic language of allusions that he often employed. If only she understood it. Well, there was no time like the present to give it a try.

"This pickled herring would join the other ones," she said.

Kosh's bulk leaned forward. "The wings fly at midnight."

"I want to see the World Series," Talia remarked.

The guard squinted at both of them and leaned forward curiously.

"Apple pie," said Kosh, "and hush puppies."

"Inna Babylon, do you know Babylon?" she asked in a Jamaican accent.

"Gone, like the pickled herring."

"The eagle flies on Friday."

"Invisible Isabel," answered Kosh. He turned to the guard and bowed. "Our business is concluded."

The guard stopped scratching his head long enough to go back and open the door to the outer chamber. Ambassador Kosh swept out with grandeur, even in this place.

The guard gave Talia a quizzical look and said, "I don't know what happened there, but Garibaldi is on his way down. He wants to talk to you."

"I refuse to see him," she declared.

"I'll let you tell him that," said the guard.

"Tell me what?" asked Garibaldi, sweeping into the detention center.

"I refuse to talk to you without my counsel present," Talia claimed.

"Not even if it's to clear your name?" he asked incredulously.

She crossed her arms and regarded him warily. "If it's not, I'm going to clam up. I'm tired of talking, because nobody listens. What is it?"

"You told me you had a data crystal in your bag. Is that correct?"

She sighed. "Yes."

"Was it a real crystal, one you had accessed before?"

"Yes, it was," answered Talia. "It had statistics for the meeting, and I was studying it the day before."

Garibaldi frowned, as if he didn't want to hear that. He continued, "The officer who checked you in didn't find a data crystal in your bag. Did you have it in your hand, or a pocket that we might have missed?"

Talia frowned, trying to remember bits and pieces of that

terrible morning. "Oh, yes," she answered slowly. "Somebody had borrowed it and then given it back to me."

Garibaldi leaned forward. "Who?"

Talia started to speak but paused. After what she had gone through, she was reluctant to give out Emily Crane's name and put the poor woman through the same thing. Besides, she was certain that Emily Crane wasn't a terrorist bomber. In fact, the blast had nearly killed her beloved Authur Malten, and that let Emily out of the equation completely.

"I'll remind you," said Garibaldi, "whoever put that bomb in your bag meant for you to die, too."

Talia screwed her eyes shut and tried to keep from losing it. "Are you sure the data crystal was a bomb?" she asked.

"No," admitted the chief. "But it's an object that we know somebody else gave you. Since that's what you say happened . . ."

"It *is* what happened," she insisted.

"Okay, then," said Garibaldi, "this is information *you* need, for your defense."

"Listen," said Talia, "I don't want to unleash Bester and his people, plus all of Earthforce on this poor woman. I really believe she couldn't have anything to do with it."

"Maybe," conceded Garibaldi. "We think the same way about you, but . . ." He didn't finish the thought.

Talia nodded bitterly. "That's why I'm not going to put this woman through what I'm going through."

"Come on," begged Garibaldi. "I promise, I'll check her out personally. Listen, you'll need to talk to her, anyway, for your own defense. I won't give her name out until I've checked her out first."

"You really promise that?" asked Talia. "Because if I see her in this cell next door, and we're both innocent, I'm coming after you."

"I promise," said Garibaldi with a lopsided smile.

Hoarsely, the blond woman said, "Her name is Emily Crane. All I know about her is that she works in the Mix with Mr. Malten."

Garibaldi pressed his link. "Ivanova, it's me. Can you tell

me if Emily Crane has left the station? She was one of our recent guests, a commercial telepath.''

''Hang on,'' said the second-in-command. Several long seconds ticked off before Ivanova reported, ''She left in the first transport out. Her boss, Malten, was shaken up, and she was taking him home.''

''And where might home be?'' asked Garibaldi.

''The destination of the transport is Earth. That's as specific as it gets. They should be there in a day or so.''

''Thanks. Out.'' Garibaldi shook his head. ''Earth. Not much chance of me going there real soon.''

Talia laughed nervously. ''Me either.''

''I'll look up her branch office,'' said Garibaldi. He leaned against the bars of her cell, looking like a sad basset hound. ''I'd love to get you out of here, but we're in enough hot water already. Besides, you're safe here. So, is there anything I can get for you?''

''A hacksaw.''

Garibaldi had a pained expression on his face. ''How about some reading materials?''

She slumped onto her bed and yawned. ''Not tonight, okay? I had my dinner, and I think I just need to sleep.''

''I'll bring you some books in the morning,'' said the chief. He started out and turned. ''I'm sorry about this. We'll find some way to get your life back to normal.''

''Or what passes for normal,'' said Talia. She stretched out on a thin mattress resting atop a metal frame that was welded to the deck.

''Say, what time is it?'' she asked.

Garibaldi checked his link. ''Let's see, twenty-three forty.''

''Thanks.''

''Did you have a nice visit with Ambassador Kosh?''

''Good night.''

She rolled away from him, and her eyes darted about frightenedly as she waited for him to leave. Finally, she heard the door ooze shut. She sat up in bed, looking around. There was a surveillance camera in each corner of the room, with its own area to cover, but otherwise, she was alone.

Or was she alone? What had Kosh meant by Invisible Isabel? That had been a game, right? A practical joke. There were no invisible people, really. Although who knew what there was in the Vorlons' advanced culture? She knew she had picked up the trace of a voice on Red-3, after she had eliminated all the visible people in the cafe. Whatever it was, it had been real to Kosh, too.

There were only twenty minutes left, she remembered, before Kosh was going to make his move. But what was his move? What was her part in it? How could she get off the station, even with the Vorlon's help? She had to calm down, Talia told herself, and stop asking questions for which there were no answers. If indeed Kosh had agreed to help her escape in twenty minutes, then he would. If she had misinterpreted his signals and he didn't help her, she was no worse off. One way she was a fugitive, but in the other way she was a prisoner with a celebrated murder trial ahead of her.

She half-expected some calm voice of reason and responsibility to take her aside and tell her that escape from Babylon 5 was crazy. Not only that, but it would make her look guilty. Even the people who defended her now would stop defending her, and probably chase her. But for some unfathomable reason, Talia knew that she could get off B5, and that she *had* to get off, if she wanted to stay alive. Moreover, she had to go to Earth if she wanted to clear her name. It was mad, but she had to do it.

In the clear light of madness, Talia stopped to think about Emily Crane. What did she really know about the small woman who stuttered? She was a licensed telepath specializing in the ad business, but maybe she had deep roots to Mars and the separatist movement. Maybe, in fact, the dark-skinned woman had actually tried to kill her, plus Bester, Malten, and the ones she had succeeded in killing.

What was that old expression, "the banality of evil." Ms. Crane was a banal person, a cipher among the rampant egotism of Psi Corps. Maybe that was just the sort of person a terrorist agency depended upon to infiltrate and do its dirtiest work.

Talia rubbed her eyes and plucked at the white jumpsuit and white gloves she was wearing. It had seemed a logical choice in clothing when she had put it on in her quarters—something comfortable for lounging about the cell—but now it seemed too flimsy and insignificant to get her all the way to Earth. What had she been thinking?

Without really knowing the time, Talia looked up, knowing that something was about to happen. If, she asked herself, there was an invisible being name Isabel in this detention center, what should Isabel be doing? That was easy—she should be unlocking the cell door.

The lock was on a box about two meters beyond the door, and it was operated by an electronic cardkey. In addition to the electronics, a mechanical bolt held the door shut. Talia concentrated on the bolt. Although she wasn't a locksmith, part of her espionage training at Psi Corps had involved the picking of locks and a few other counter-intelligence measures. She knew how a lock ought to work and how it ought to look inside. She couldn't get her hands inside the lock—but that was okay, she had Invisible Isabel. She was beginning to suspect that Isabel was tied to the telekinetic powers given her by Ironheart.

Concentrating very hard, Talia thought about being an invisible person who could slip into a small place and turn the tumblers. She could see her tiny hands running over the miniature components, bypassing the electronics to go directly to the mechanism. When the tumblers tripped, the bolt would spring back. *Move the tumblers, pull the bolt,* she told herself, *just the way you move your lucky penny.*

She ignored the sweat running down her face, slicking strands of blond hair to her pale cheeks. Talia thought only about Invisible Isabel and her tiny fingers. She was real, the telepath told herself; she was real, and she could move those small tumblers. She could, she could . . .

When the click sounded, it was like waking up from a dream. Talia heard her cell door creak open before she could even focus her eyes on it. She stood and pushed it wide open. There was no overwhelming sense of freedom as Talia stepped out of her cell, only terrible fear of what she was about to become. All her life, she had toed the line, done the right thing—a good daughter, a good student, a willing recruit to Psi Corps, and a hard worker ever since. There had been one or two romantic lapses, but youth had to be served. Since then, she had trod the straight and narrow.

She told herself that she was already considered a terrorist, a murderer, and a traitor, and she was about to add fugitive to the list. And rogue telepath. Of all the terrible labels, that one frightened her the most. Maybe she could clear herself of the other charges, but once a rogue telepath . . .

Talia had wandered to the front of the outer door, wondering if she was supposed to open it the same way. There was a small window in the door, and one of the guards jumped up and looked at her in amazement. She didn't hide from his startled gaze. What was the point?

The guard ran to his desk and started to pick up his PPG pistol and a cardkey, but he suddenly did a very strange thing. He started to move like a man who thought he was weightless, like a man who couldn't decide how to put his feet down. A second later he staggered and collapsed to the floor.

Talia pressed her face against the small window and could see two more guards lying unconscious on the anteroom floor. She looked instinctively at the air vents—if there was a gas, it was invisible. Just like her friend.

The seconds seemed to drag on, and there was nothing to do but stand there and wait for the next act of this surreal drama. In a few moments, the door on the other side of the anteroom—the one to freedom—opened, and Ambassador Kosh glided in. If the Vorlon was surprised by the sight of three guards lying unconscious on the floor, it didn't show in his movements. He went straightaway to the desk. When he stopped, a small mechanical claw issued from his ornate robe and picked up the cardkey. Then it extended over a meter to insert the card into the slot, and the door opened.

Talia walked into the anteroom. When she didn't faint, she knew the gas had dispersed even if its effects remained in force. She looked at Kosh, wondering what he would do next. The Vorlon's robe opened, and a little shelf slid out.

Upon the shelf was a Minbari robe and hood. She took the hood and put it over her head. It not only hid her face, but it hid the fact that her head didn't look like the hairless, crested dome of a Minbari.

"I'll be tall for a Minbari," said Talia with a humorless smile.

Mr. Bester was sitting up in his bed. He still looked terrible, thought Mr. Gray, and his mood was even worse. Gray almost felt sorry for the man who stood in front of him, getting a dressing-down.

"Captain Sheridan," growled Bester, "how dare you defy me! You cannot delay justice forever. I will get that woman in my custody—it is inevitable. If you persist in blocking me, it will mean the end of your career! After that pathetic show of security, I wouldn't be surprised if the Senate was already picking your replacement. And if you defy me, and the will of the Senate, by letting Talia Winters elude justice—nobody in the Earth Alliance will be able to save you!"

Sheridan's lips thinned. "Are you done?"

"No!" shrieked Bester. "I'm just beginning. By tomorrow morning, my people will have talked to the senators on the judicial committee. We will have a reversal of your foolish policy so fast that you won't know what hit you!"

"As a matter of fact," said Sheridan, "I've already heard from several Senators. They are putting the pressure on me, and so is Earthforce. But I told them exactly the same thing I'm telling you—this crime was committed on Babylon 5, and that's where we'll try it. We won't rush to trial either. Our investigation isn't complete, and Ms. Winters deserves the best legal counsel we can find. It may take weeks, or months."

Bester twisted in anger and followed it up with a grimace

and a howl of pain. Dr. Franklin, who had been hovering nearby, stepped between them.

"Captain Sheridan," said the doctor, "this man is due to receive artificial skin grafts in one hour. If you can't talk to him without aggravating him, I'm going to have to ask you to leave."

"But *he* summoned *me!*" protested Sheridan.

"That doesn't matter," said the doctor. "He's the one who's lying in bed, wounded."

Bester croaked, "It's okay, it's okay. I'm calm. Sheridan is fighting a losing battle here, and he knows it. If he wants to go down fighting, that's his business. I'll be happy to take him down."

There was some commotion in another part of the medlab, and Gray looked up to see Garibaldi and another security guard rush into the room. Garibaldi had been looking terrible for days, thought Gray, and now he looked worse than Mr. Bester.

"Captain," said the security chief, "we have a major breach in security."

Sheridan visibly blanched. "What's happened now?"

Garibaldi sighed and looked at Bester. "I guess we can't keep it a secret." He turned to the security guard who accompanied him. "Tell them what happened, Rupel."

The guard shook his head, as if he still wasn't sure. "It was peaceful at the brig, nothing was going on. And I looked up and saw Ms. Winters standing on the other side of the door, out of her cell!"

"What did you do?" asked Sheridan.

The man shook his head. "I started to go for my weapon and the cardkey and . . . that's all I remember. The next thing I know, I wake up on the floor, and the other two guards are out cold, too. She got clean away."

With horror, Gray glanced down to see if Mr. Bester had been seized by fits of anger, but the Psi Cop was unaccountably smiling. In fact, he looked pleased with the shocked expressions all around him.

"Thank you so much, Mr. Garibaldi," said Bester. "Your

incompetence has just ended a lot of pointless debate. A telepath who is fleeing prosecution is automatically classified as rogue.''

Bester smiled with the delicious irony of it. ''Now that Talia Winters is a rogue telepath, we don't need anybody's permission to go after her. Mr. Gray, call my subordinates in. We're going to bring down a rogue.''

CHAPTER 12

"SIR," said Garibaldi desperately, "let me go after her."

Captain Sheridan and the security chief regarded each other with a mixture of confidence and uncertainty. They hadn't worked together very long, but they had been forced into a level of faith reserved for old comrades. Despite the way things had gone so far, thought Garibaldi, there had to be a way to pull this out of the fire. The captain had to trust him.

"How do you know she's left the station?" asked the captain.

"We're looking for her," explained Garibaldi. "My people are all over the docks, but we've been so backed up with the conference—and the mass exodus after the bombing—that we've got transports taking off every five minutes! We're eyeballing everything that goes out, but we could be missing something. In fact, we may already be too late."

Garibaldi rubbed his jaw. "To escape like this, she must've had help. I have a hunch about who helped her, and I have a hunch about where she went. There's a lead that only she and I know about—she might try to follow it up."

From his hospital bed, Bester was leaning forward with interest. "I'm a great believer in hunches, Mr. Garibaldi. Tell me, where is she going?" He cocked his head, as if listening, then he smiled. "You don't have to tell me. It's Earth."

The chief looked at the Psi Cop with disgust. "Your people are the ones who spooked her. They're the ones who made her run."

"I don't agree with that," said Bester. "I think fear made her run. But I agree that she had help. She's had help from the beginning, and just like you, I want to find out who's bankrolling this. So let's make a deal."

Bester grimaced as he shifted around to get a bit more height in his bed. "I will hold back my Psi Cops for a few days. Instead, let's send Mr. Garibaldi and Mr. Gray to Earth to find her. And her accomplices.''

Garibaldi turned his attention to the pasty-faced Gray. ''I don't want him coming with me.''

''Okay, Mr. Gray,'' said Bester. ''Let's alert my people on Earth—they can bring her down as soon as she steps off the transport.''

''Wait,'' said Sheridan, holding up a weathered hand. ''Mr. Bester is right about one thing—as soon as he calls the Psi Cops on her, it becomes an assassination. The local police will be after her, too. If we're going to find out anything, we want her investigated. We want all the leads followed up. Garibaldi, if you think you know where she's going, go there. And take Mr. Gray with you.''

Garibaldi shook his head, as if he couldn't believe what he was hearing. ''I work better alone.''

Bester smiled. ''I think you will find Mr. Gray is very little trouble. And he's *not* a Psi Cop—he's not authorized to take her out. He's just an investigator, like yourself.''

Garibaldi looked at Mr. Gray, who gave him an encouraging but nervous smile. He doesn't really want to go, thought Garibaldi; he just wants to get away from Bester, and I can't blame him for that. The security chief decided he would agree for the time being to take the telepath, and ditch him as soon as possible.

He scowled at Gray. ''All right. The last transport for Earth is leaving in an hour, docking bay five. Let's be on it.''

''Absolutely,'' agreed Gray. ''I have some theories of my own about this matter.''

Garibaldi started to tell him where to put his theories, but he decided to tell him after they were safely away.

Captain Sheridan took a deep breath and turned toward Dr. Franklin. ''Why don't you sedate your patient and get started.''

''Not a bad idea,'' said Franklin. ''Nurse, hypo!''

''Wait a minute,'' protested Bester, thrashing around in his bed. ''I need to report in! I need to call the president . . .''

Franklin administered the hypo.

Still scowling, Bester lay back in his bed. "Do a good job, you two," he murmured. "You don't want me to have to get out of this bed and come after you. . . ." His voice trailed off as he fell asleep.

"Mr. Garibaldi," said the doctor, "before you leave, we could use some extra security on the door."

"All right," scowled the security chief, "but having extra people hasn't solved any problems so far."

"We need to think like these terrorists," suggested Harriman Gray. "I have a lead of my own to follow up. I'll tell you about it on the flight. See you later, Mr. Garibaldi."

The slim telepath dashed off to follow his lead, and Garibaldi rolled his eyes at Captain Sheridan. "Sorry, sir, but why are you making me bring him?"

"Just like you said," answered Sheridan, "by ourselves, we haven't done much good so far. Maybe if we join forces with them—I don't know, it's worth a try. And I want to say, I know how you feel about Ms. Winters, but she's a fugitive. Bring her in, if you get the chance."

"I will," agreed Garibaldi. He lowered his voice. "I think it was Ambassador Kosh who helped her. I haven't got any proof, but he went to visit her half an hour before she escaped. Rupel, who's a linguist, listened to their conversation and couldn't understand a word of it."

"All right," said Sheridan grimly, "leave Kosh to me."

Talia sat in total darkness, wondering if she was going to her death, to her freedom, or just going mad. Under Kosh's orders, and against her screaming better judgment, she had ditched her Minbari outfit and crawled into a reinforced cargo box. And that's where she had remained for the better part of an hour now. There had been no instructions from Kosh, except to show her how the pins could be removed from the inside to let the straps work themselves free. Not even a proper good-bye from Kosh or anyone else, and she had been sealed up in this box. Even though Talia knew she could get out by pulling the pins, she had no idea where she would find herself.

She presumed she was on a vessel and that her rescuers had left Bablyon 5, because she had been knocked around by some pretty good g-forces. Or maybe somebody had simply tossed the crate down a stairwell—it was impossible to tell! In the absence of instructions or guidance, what was she supposed to do, stay in the box forever? Or until customs sold it for unclaimed surplus?

Worse yet, she had started to hear scuffling sounds outside in the—wherever she was. The sound was too heavy and massive to be rats, she hoped, but that didn't explain what it was. Could it be somebody moving the crates around? Or a heavy person just passing through? She had heard no voices, which for some reason made her think that it wasn't the crew. And if it wasn't the crew, who was it?

She had reached the level of endurance for breathing foul air and listening to strange noises in the darkness, while hunched in a terrible position. She had to find out where she was, or go crazy. So Talia reached for the pins that held the straps closed from inside. She already knew they would slide out easily, because she had been toying with them in the dark for the better part of an hour.

She felt the smooth sticks come out in her hands, and she knew the straps were now just lying across the top of the crate. All she would need was a swift push to be out of that stifling darkness. But once out, the secret of the box would be revealed. As with many boxes, there would be no putting back the surprise after it popped out. Whoever was shuffling around out there might view her as a stowaway and kill her. Or they might know Mr. Bester, who had to be looking for her by now.

It was the unknown either way, decided Talia, and she would rather die with light in her eyes, fresh air in her lungs, and her back straight. She pushed open the top and stretched.

A creature in rags gasped with fright and fell over a similar crate. Talia jumped out of her own crate and scrambled behind it. They peered at each other with fear and curiosity.

He had long, scraggly hair and a grubby beard, but he was at least human. She was about to welcome him with a big smile, when she saw his hand ease out from behind the box, and it was holding a PPG pistol.

"Suppose you just put your hands up," he said in a Southern drawl. "I didn't know I had company."

"Me neither," gulped Talia, raising her hands. She was instantly afraid she might be better off with aliens or Bester than this seedy character. She didn't want to tick him off by scanning him, and she had a feeling he'd been scanned before and would know it.

She wanted to get a good look at the place where she might die, so she glanced around. To her surprise, she was in another, much larger cargo crate with alien lettering running all around the top. It reminded her of a Dumpster she used to play in as a kid. But there was a naked lightbulb and some sort of ventilation system supplying them oxygen.

"I've seen you somewhere," said the man suspiciously.

She tried to smile. "Well, it's obvious we frequent the same places."

"Keep your hands up," he snarled. He didn't wave the weapon around like a maniac. In fact, he held it very steadily, as if it were an extension of his arm.

Talia looked around again, trying to see if there was any obvious way out of the Dumpster. There seemed to be a lid to the thing, and she could see what looked like a switch box amidst the alien lettering. But it didn't look promising.

Conversationally, she remarked, "I think we have more in common than a lot of people who have just met."

The man gave her a lopsided grin. "Well, maybe we do have some mutual friends. The question is—are you a plant put here to get me, or am I a plant put here to get you?"

He scratched his stubbly chin. "Since I know I'm up to no good, you must be a plant." He lifted the weapon and aimed it at her breastbone.

"I'm running away!" she shouted. "I'm a fugitive!" She put her hands over her face in case he blasted her anyway.

But he lowered the weapon and smiled. "Yeah, now I remember—you're B5's resident telepath. They got you for the bombing!"

He howled with laughter, and she thought for a second about making a lunge for his weapon. She figured a second would be as long as she lived, if she didn't make it.

He laughed so hard that he had to dab his eyes with his dirty sleeve. "I guess you're in too much trouble to turn anybody in. My name is Deuce."

"Deuce," she breathed. "The one from Down Below?"

He bowed mockingly. "One and the same. I see my reputation precedes me even in the hallowed halls of Psi Corps."

"I didn't do that bombing," she said, as if that made any difference to a man like him.

"I know," he said, dabbing his eyes. "You were in the wrong place at the wrong time."

"You know who did it?" she asked accusingly.

Deuce leveled the weapon at her again. "Lady, you were in the wrong place yesterday, and you're still in the wrong place. Ask me no questions, and I'll tell you no lies."

Talia was fairly certain that Deuce was going to kill her, just as soon as she stopped being amusing. But they weren't alone—wherever they were. Somebody was piloting this ship, and somebody had made a deal with Kosh to take her and deliver her somewhere. She and Deuce were not in a vacuum.

Irrationally, Talia made a lunge for the switch box, trying to get out. Deuce leaped to his feet right behind her and knocked her down with a vicious punch to the shoulder.

"Stupid bitch!" he muttered. "Don't you know what those signs say?"

Talia lay crumpled between the two crates, holding her throbbing shoulder. She just stared at him, waiting to see if he would kill her.

"I guess you don't know," he muttered, jerking his thumb at the strange letters. "This here is a methane-breathers' ship. We're in a self-contained cargo container with its own atmosphere. In this case, it's set for oxygen. If you had opened that hatch, we'd be rolling on the floor, bug-eyed and suffocating, in about a minute."

"I'm sorry," said Talia, sitting up. "I've never been a fugitive before. I guess I'm not too good at it."

Deuce shook his head, as if he couldn't believe what he had gotten himself saddled with. He sat on the edge of a crate and just looked at her.

"Lady, the problem is, you can't do nothin' for me, and I can't do nothin' for you. You're poison, all the way around."

"That's not true," Talia insisted, shifting around to see him. "I won't ask you any more about the bombing—I don't care what you had to do with it. But I know you can get me a fake identicard and a new name, and some clothes. Maybe that's why my friend put me here with you."

Deuce rubbed the stubble under his chin. "Your friend must be awfully well connected to know my comings and goings. Yeah, I could arrange those things." He smiled at her. "What could you do for me in return?"

Talia wiped her face with her forearm and tried to think. "Isn't there something in your line of work that could use a telepath?"

The criminal leaned back and considered the offer. "There might be. But that doesn't change the fact that you're poison. By now you have Psi Cops, Earthforce, regular cops, and all the school crossing–guards looking for you. I'm small potatoes compared to you."

"Okay," she promised, "I'll leave whenever you say you want me to go." She couldn't believe she was making promises to a petty gangster, who had in some way arranged the bombing. What could she find out from him? She didn't want to think what it would take to gain his confidence.

"I'm going to regret it if I don't plug you now," said Deuce with all sincerity.

"Commander?" said the communications officer at the command center. "A Mr. Gray wishes to speak to you. He says it's the last time, and it will only take a moment."

Ivanova looked down from her station with a sour expression. As there was nothing pressing her for perhaps the next thirty seconds, she picked up a headset and put it on.

"Patch him through," she ordered.

"Is this Susan?" asked an uncertain voice.

"It is, Harriman. What do you want?"

"To say good-bye. I'm leaving on a transport for Earth in fifteen minutes with Mr. Garibaldi."

"So I heard," said Ivanova. "I don't know whether to wish you luck or not. I don't believe Talia Winters is guilty."

Gray replied somberly, "Whether she is or not, it's better we find her than Mr. Bester. This escape of hers doesn't look good, but we all know there's more to this affair than meets the eye. Garibaldi and I will get to the bottom of it. And, Susan . . ."

"Yes?"

"I'm determined to do something that will win you over."

Ivanova finally smiled. "That I would like to see. Take care of yourself, and Garibaldi."

"Thank you, Susan. Good-bye."

Ivanova took off the headset and laid it on the console. Garibaldi and Gray were such an odd pair, she thought to herself, maybe they really would do something useful. The way it was going, they couldn't mess things up much more than they already were.

"I'm sorry," said a synthesized voice, "Ambassador Kosh is indisposed."

"Well, you get him disposed right now!" growled Captain Sheridan.

"I'm sorry," said the voice, "Ambassador Kosh is indisposed. Please contact the ambassador at a later time."

Sheridan banged on the intercom outside the Alien Sector and cursed. Yelling at a computer voice wouldn't really do much good, he told himself, and he had no desire to storm Kosh's inner sanctum. Mainly, he had no desire to see the squidlike Vorlon warships come out of the jump gate and turn Babylon 5 into dust.

Everyone had warned him that Ambassador Kosh marched to his own drummer, but everyone had also said that contact with the advanced Vorlons was worth the occasional misunderstanding. However, in some of Kosh's actions there was no misunderstanding, just a willful disregard for convention. Of course, being unconventional meant being alien, thought Sheridan, and there was no doubt that Ambassador Kosh was alien.

He turned to go, and he nearly bumped into Lennier, Delenn's aide. The Minbari jumped sprightly to get out of the way.

"Excuse me, Mr. Lennier," said Sheridan, "I'm sorry. Did I step on your foot?"

"It's fine," said Lennier. "I keep forgetting, human hearing is not very good, and I should clear my throat when I approach."

"Well, if you're waiting to see Kosh, he's not receiving visitors."

"No," answered the Minbari, "I was waiting to see you, Captain Sheridan."

The captain shrugged. "I have a few minutes. But I warn you, it hasn't been a good week. So I hope you or the ambassador don't have some terrible problem."

They walked slowly down the corridor, and Lennier replied, "We have no complaints, but I'm very aware of your problem. This propensity toward violence is most regrettable."

Sheridan bristled slightly, knowing that was a gibe. He had seen the Minbari in warfare, close up, and he knew they could be as violent as anyone.

"Can you get to the point?" he asked bluntly.

Lennier stopped and gazed at him. "I may have some information for you."

"If it's about the bombing," said Sheridan, "I'm listening."

Lennier grimaced with minor embarrassment. "I became rather well acquainted with one of the attendees, a Mr. Barker. I gather he is a well-placed military liaison." The Minbari smiled. "He considers himself an expert on Minbari affairs, and he is indeed a wealth of information. Most of it over a decade old."

Sheridan waited patiently. He had learned a few things in his life, and one of them was that the Minbari could not be hurried. Whether you were listening to a story or setting up a counterattack against them, they would take their time doing whatever they were doing.

"At the reception," said Lennier, "Mr. Barker had a considerable number of refreshments, and he took me into his confidence. At the time, what he said to me sounded bizarre, but considering the events of yesterday, his remarks were eerily precognitive."

"What did he say?" Sheridan almost screamed.

"He said that he wasn't worried much about Mr. Bester and the Psi Cops, because they were going to be aced out. That was the exact phrase he used, 'aced out.' I asked him who would take their place in the pantheon of Psi Corps, and he said the commercial sector would come out on top, because they had the money behind them. Mr. Barker wasn't too happy about this one way or another, you understand. He envisioned the military getting the short end of the stick either way."

Lennier cocked his head and frowned. "He said that Bester was history, which at the time seemed mere wishful thinking. But the next day, Bester was almost history, wasn't he? And the suspected bomber is from the commercial sector."

"Yes," said Sheridan thoughtfully. "Everybody wants to blame Martian terrorists, but what is B5 to them? That's been bothering me this whole time. Thank you, Mr. Lennier, you've given me something to think about."

"Can I ask one thing in return?"

"Sure," said the captain, fearing the worst.

"Can you explain to me what that means, 'getting the short end of the stick.' A stick has only two ends and is joined at the middle—how can one end be shorter than the other?"

Sheridan sighed. "Actually, it means getting the short end when you draw sticks—I think. Why don't you walk with me to my office, and we'll figure it out."

* * *

Garibaldi gave a pained grin and held out his hand. "After you, Mr. Gray."

The slim telepath nodded his thanks and hoisted his flight bag onto his shoulder. Garibaldi followed several paces behind him on their way through the air-lock and onto the transport *Starfish*. It was the essential red-eye flight with about half the seats empty, and most of the other seats occupied by people who would soon be dozing.

The only passengers who looked wide awake were six black-suited Psi Cops sitting in the first row. They gave Garibaldi a look of unbridled malice as he walked past them with Gray, and he tried not to look their way.

The telepath stopped in the middle of the passenger cabin and asked, "Is this one all right?"

"No," growled Garibaldi, "in the back." He almost asked Gray if they had to sit together, but that would have been a churlish thing to ask in a half-filled cabin. Later on, he would claim to be tired, then he would head off in search of some privacy and elbow room.

They sat in the next-to-last row. Behind them a Centauri was already snoring, his hair sticking up from his pillow like a row of porcupine quills.

Gray opened up his briefcase and took out a stack of transparencies, dossiers, and photographs. Garibaldi couldn't help but watch the telepath arrange these materials in meticulous order. Then the telepath looked expectantly at Garibaldi and asked, "What have you found out?"

The security chief smiled smugly. "I haven't got a stack of files, but I've got one name. And that should be enough."

Gray pursed his lips. "The name is?"

The security chief smiled. "First, you tell me what you've got."

"All of these files," said Gray proudly, "are a record of the bombing at the Royal Tharsis Lodge on Mars."

"Mars?" mused Garibaldi. "I thought we were trying to solve the bombing on B5?"

"But they are related. The Free Phobos group claimed

responsibility for both bombings, and Mr. Bester and myself were present at both.''

''You saw the bombing on Mars?''

''Thankfully, at a distance,'' answered Gray. ''Although if it hadn't have been for Mr. Bester's quick reactions, both of us might have been casualties. Do you see why I think they're related?''

''Yeah,'' said Garibaldi thoughtfully, ''unless it's some kind of conspiracy against the places themselves. What if somebody had a thing against this hotel on Mars, and they also had a thing against Babylon 5. So they picked the two places just to wreak havoc there. What I'm saying is, whoever the idiot was who picked B5 may have also had something to do with the bombing of the hotel.''

''No,'' said Gray, chuckling. ''That was *me*. I suggested Babylon 5.''

Garibaldi jerked up in his seat. *''You* brought them here!''

His hands were reaching for the telepath's throat when a feminine computer voice made an announcement: ''Welcome to Earth Transport *Starfish,* serving the routes between Babylon 5, Earth, and Centauri Prime. The first leg of our journey —Babylon 5 to Earth—will have a duration of forty-eight standard hours. Please settle back in your seats, and relax. A robotic cart with food and drink will appear in the center aisle after departure. You may signal for it by pushing the service button on your armrest. Credits are accepted. Enjoy your flight.''

Still seething, Garibaldi slumped back in his chair. Forty-eight hours was too long to sit next to a dead body, and that thought was the only thing that kept him from throttling Mr. Gray.

The little man looked embarrassed. ''In retrospect, it was a mistake bringing the conference to B5. At the time, it seemed a logical choice. Removed from Mars, good security, a new place for most of them. I was very surprised when the violence followed us from Mars. This makes me believe even more strongly that the two bombings are related, and not just by the claims of a mystery group. I don't see how we can solve the second bombing without starting with the first.''

Garibaldi muttered, "But Talia Winters was nowhere near Mars when the hotel bombing happened.''

"Precisely," answered Gray, "which is an indication of her innocence, or the possibility that she was used as a dupe. Now tell me about that lead you have?''

Garibaldi smiled and closed his eyes. "When you show me something really good, I'll show you mine.''

"Prepare for departure to Earth," purred the synthesized voice.

CHAPTER 13

TALIA screamed new nodules on her vocal cords as she felt the sudden sensation of weightlessness. At first she thought the ship had stopped until she heard the whistling of wind all around them. Deuce cut forth with a litany of swear words, and their voices were quickly drowned out by a rush of air against the Dumpster-like cargo container. They weren't just weightless—they were plunging through planetary atmosphere! Massive gravity had its grip on them.

Then the naked bulb burst, showering them with glass fragments, and the air ventilators stopped working—and both of them were screaming! Talia hardly noticed the way the cargo boxes banged against her, threatening to crush her in the free-fall. She just spun around in the darkness, her body a rubber ball cascading from one wall into another, swiping Deuce and the boxes in the process.

When she realized she might as well die calmly, Talia wrapped her arms around her head, tucked her legs in, and tried to still her galloping heart. Then the floor of the container abruptly rose up and crashed into her! She lay sprawling, gasping for air, as the big crate righted itself and shifted around. Now she heard groanings and creakings of a weirder sort, and air roared around the exterior of their strange vehicle.

"Damn," muttered Deuce in the darkness, "I wish they'd warn us before they cut us loose."

Still gulping air, Talia wheezed, "You *expected* that?"

"Old smugglers' trick. They plot their trajectory over the desert in North America and slow down just enough to push us out. With a parachute. It's not very accurate, but the *federales* are none the wiser that they dropped something."

Talia listened to the air whizzing past them, and she marveled at the fact that she was taking a parachute jump, albeit inside a box with bruises and welts all over her body. Blood was running through the hair on her scalp from a nasty cut.

"The chute is open?" she croaked.

"It had better be," mused Deuce, "or we'll be coyote dinner. But what if they would never find our bodies. We could be legends! Everyone would think we ran off together, you and me, and are living the good life on Betelgeuse 6."

"Yeah," said Talia with a gulp. "So where are we, anyway?" For all she knew, it could be Betelgeuse 6.

"You'll see," answered Deuce. "Brace yourself. I hear the wind changin'."

She had a second or two to curl up in a ball before the giant crate hammered onto something solid. She caught her breath, thinking they were safe, when the Dumpster began to move again. This time it tilted radically to one side and slid down an incline like a house on skis. She tried to scream, but her voice was too raw; she could only stare into the darkness and feel the rattling bumps beneath her. They thudded to another abrupt stop, and this one held, at least until Talia could start breathing again.

"Are we alive?" she rasped.

"Yeah," answered Deuce. "Cover your head—I'm gonna shoot my way out of here. Sometimes the metal starts to melt."

She didn't know Deuce very well, but she had learned to heed his warnings. Talia covered her head, but she kept one eye open to see what he was doing. She gasped when several plasm streaks shot through the darkness and punched holes in the lid of the container. Using the light from the discharge to aim, Deuce worked the smaller holes into a jagged hole about half a meter in diameter, or just big enough for a smallish person to climb out.

Talia squinted her eyes, expecting blinding sunlight to flood through the hole. Instead, soothing darkness greeted her eyes, plus the sight of nearly as many stars as a person saw in space. A city girl, she wasn't sure what all this meant.

"Where are we?" she asked.

"I told you," muttered Deuce, "you're gonna die here

real soon if you don't stop asking me questions. If you're going to be useful to me, you've just got to obey me, and that's it.''

"Sorry," she answered. Talia knew she had a secret weapon in her ability to scan him, but she had a feeling that Deuce had been scanned before and would know it. Behind the rough exterior was a cagey and cool intellect, and she had every reason to believe that Deuce was as ruthless as he claimed to be. He would kill her for a slight provocation. So she opted to lie low and pick the time and place to scan him, knowing she might only get one chance.

In the dim starlight, she could just see Deuce scrounging around in his crate, the one in which he had been smuggled aboard the methane-breathers' ship. He finally pulled out a black briefcase and a dirty duffel bag. He opened the duffel bag and took out a crowbar, which he used to pound down the ragged edges of the hole he had shot open. His pounding turned the crate into a tin drum, and Talia had to cover her ears. Deuce finally stopped and took a flashlight out of his bag to study his handiwork.

"There," he drawled, "at least we'll have air. Want to go out and take a look around?''

Talia shook her head worriedly. She was beginning to feel that terrible panic she had felt upon waking up after the bombing—the shock, the disorientation, the feeling that she was stuck in a nightmare.

In fact, she told herself, she *was* stuck in a nightmare of the worst sort—reality. There was no waking up, so she might as well deal with it. She was in a shot-up Dumpster in the middle of the desert, chased by everyone, in the company of a murderer. No matter where they were, she was dependent upon this criminal for the time being, and it might get worse before it got better.

One thing Talia knew would never be the same—she would never again be smug about her life. Right now, being the lone human telepath on an out-of-the-way depot for aliens sounded just fine, the dream job. She would never again knock it or quest after anything higher. And if she

could get back to that life, she would be eternally grateful.
Right now, she wondered if it was even possible to recapture
any shred of that past.

While she was musing in the dim light given off by a
holeful of stars, Deuce turned on his flashlight again and
began searching for something else in his duffel bag. He
drew out a small electronic device, checked to see that it
hadn't been damaged, then pulled out its antenna. He pressed
a button on the device, and a red light began to blink on and
off.

Talia was about to ask him what it was, but then she remembered: No more questions. Perhaps she should just stop
talking altogether. Hobnobbing, being charming and gregari-
ous, had only gotten her into trouble in the last few days. And
when it had mattered, when she kept telling everybody the
truth, nobody would listen to her. Maybe she should adopt
Deuce's motto: Ask me no questions, and I'll tell you no lies.
If she said nothing at all, she couldn't say anything wrong.

She was startled by a thud as Deuce turned one of the
crates on end. Then he proceeded to climb up and peer out
the hole. He made a low whistle.

"We are really in the middle of nowhere. I hope my boys
have some decent coordinates."

Talia started to ask if this was really Earth, then she remembered not to talk. That device was some kind of homing
beacon, it was clear, so somebody was out there, looking for
them. She suddenly had a strong instinct to get out of the
crate, and she pounded on Deuce's calf.

"Hey!" he shouted down. "What's the deal?"

She tried an experiment and told him telepathically to get
off the crate.

He blinked at her and smiled. "All you had to do was
ask."

Deuce climbed down and Talia climbed up. By standing
on her tiptoes, she could just get her head, the top of her
shoulders, and one arm out through the hole, but she was
glad she had made the effort. Their little vessel was parked at
an angle at the bottom of a dry wash, buried halfway under

the sand, and surrounded by scrubby desert. Trailing behind them like a tattered bridal veil was the parachute that had saved their lives. It was ripped and streaked with dirt from the tumble down the wash.

In the blue starlight she couldn't see very far, but she could see gnarled trees at the rim of the wash and other ghostly shapes. Mesquite trees, Joshua trees, chollas, yuccas, prickly pears—she tried to remember all the spiny, weirdly shaped flora that grew in places like this. She was glad this desert wasn't just sand dunes but had some vegetation to it, even if the plants did appear stunted and misshapen.

She suddenly had an overwhelming desire to stand on the ground. After the nightmarish events of the last three days, she just had to get out and stand on firm ground. She began to squirm out, and Deuce put a hand underneath her foot to give her all the leverage she needed to get her hips through.

Talia screamed as she slid down the tilted side of the crate and plummeted into the sand. It got into her mouth and hair, but its grittiness felt wonderfully real, and the air smelled like perfume after that stifling container. After her scream, the desert was silent, but as she sat without moving for a few minutes, the twitters and chirps came back. She heard a distant howl. Unaccountably, Talia felt relaxed and unafraid for the first time since that awful morning of the conference.

The telepath was startled a moment later when a black briefcase landed in the sand not far from her. She reached over to open it, but the clasps were locked; it was a solidly built case. She pushed the briefcase away and ducked when the dirty duffel bag came flying out of the hole a moment later. The bags were followed by Deuce himself, squirming through the small opening. Like Kosh, he was an unlikely savior, she thought, but if she would ever end this nightmare and get her previous life back, she needed him. She would leave him his blood money in the briefcase. He had probably earned it.

She scrambled out of the way as she saw Deuce getting ready to slide down the crate and hit the sand. He rolled athletically off the edge of the crate and landed on his feet, never losing his grip on his PPG.

"Ah," said Deuce, "that's better. If we haven't been found by midday, we're going to regret getting out of there. But maybe we can crawl under it for shade."

He plopped down in the sand and fished a hat out of his duffel bag. "So," he drawled, "know any good jokes?"

She looked at him intently for several seconds, and he nodded. "You're not going to talk anymore, huh? Are you, like, suffering from some kind of trauma?"

Talia nodded, and it was the truth.

"So, when my friends show up, you're a mute, right? And you ain't no telepath."

She nodded again. "Not a bad cover," agreed Deuce, "because you can still communicate if you want to, with certain people. This ain't new to me, you know. I've had experience with telepaths before."

Talia nodded. She was almost certain of that.

Despite his best intentions to ignore the telepath, Garibaldi found himself peering over Gray's shoulder at his stack of files. As the transport *Starfish* made its way to Earth, Gray began to explain his documents in a conversational tone that the security chief found he could tolerate.

"These are the photos and dossiers of all the people who died in the hotel bombing. Twenty-seven of them, according to the reports, although not all the bodies were recovered."

"That's not uncommon on Mars," said Garibaldi. "In that atmosphere, an unprotected body can get desiccated very quickly. And the winds are strong enough to blow a body clean away, or it could fall into a crevice and disappear. Not to mention the difficulties of mounting a real search outside."

"At any rate," said Gray, "the police didn't investigate these people too thoroughly, because they think they're victims. They also found tracks outside the hotel, so they assumed the bomber came overland. This plays into the stereotype of the usual Martian terrorist, a madman who lives in the wilds and would be spotted immediately in polite company. But what if it was an *inside* job, like the bombing on B5?''

''You mean, the bomber is one of the missing employees?'' asked Garibaldi doubtfully. ''That's pretty farfetched, without some evidence.''

''I've got some evidence. Remember, Mr. Bester and I were at the site when it happened. When a person is going through a psychic trauma, their mind sends out a sort of SOS —a telepath can hear it for miles. And these people were dying as they were being sucked out of the hole in the side of that hotel. We could hear their voices, screaming for help, just as well as I can hear your voice now.

''Mr. Bester told me that he counted twenty-six voices, and I think he's right. But the reports list twenty-seven deaths, or should we say, dead and missing. I trust Mr. Bester's talents, and I think one of those people lived.''

Gray leaned forward in his seat and eagerly explained, ''All they had to do was to carry a suit and a breathing mask with them when the blast went off, and they could just walk away! Maybe they would leave one or two footprints going in both directions to fool the police. It was night, and somebody could've had a rover waiting for them.''

Garibaldi rubbed his chin thoughtfully. ''I can see the advantages,'' he admitted. ''You're working inside, and you have your leisure to plan it all, get the bomb in, and detonate it. They don't investigate you, because everyone thinks you're one of the victims.''

''There is a modus operandi match, too,'' said Gray. ''Ms. Winters would have been a victim, too, if she hadn't walked out when she did. Plus, that bombing on Mars made everyone take the Free Phobos group seriously, even though nobody knows anything about them. It was a setup for the B5 bombing.''

Garibaldi smiled and asked, ''Can I take a look at the photos of those hotel employees?''

''Certainly,'' said Gray, looking pleased with himself.

He handed over a stack of colored transparencies, and Garibaldi studied them intently. Most of them were what you would expect hotel waiters, cooks, and buspersons to look like—young, disadvantaged, with the pale pallor and surly expressions that typified people born on Mars. It was a hard place to live, and a lot of Martians resented having to bow and stoop to wealthy tourists to bring home a few credits. None of the employees' photos showed smiling faces, eager to prove themselves.

On his second pass through the photos, Garibaldi stopped. There was a young, dark-skinned woman in a hairnet, an assistant cook. He looked at her eyes. They were not sullen eyes like the others, but they were guarded, as if she were trying not to reveal anything. But she didn't fully succeed, because he knew he had seen her somewhere before.

More importantly, she had worked at the hotel for only a week when the bombing occurred.

"This is a possibility," said Garibaldi. "Do you recognize her?"

Gray turned the photo several different angles. "I'm not definite, but she bears some resemblance to the woman we flew to B5 with, the one who accompanied Mr. Malten."

"Do you know her name?"

Gray shook his head. "She was a mousy type—didn't stick in the brain too well."

Garibaldi sat forward and whispered, "If she's the one who flew in with him, then she's probably the one who flew out with him. I think her name, as a telepath, is Emily Crane."

Gray gave him a sidelong glance. "Is that the name you have?"

Garibaldi nodded. "Yep. She borrowed a data crystal from Talia Winters, and she returned it to her the morning of the bombing."

"Does anybody else know about her?"

The security chief shook his head. "No one."

"Uh-oh," said Gray with wide eyes.

"We can find her," said Garibaldi. "I promised Talia I would check her out myself. Besides, we don't want the regular cops or the Psi Cops shooting her, or spooking her, before she can clear our suspect.''

"No, that's not what I meant." Gray pointed down the aisle.

Garibaldi followed his finger and saw the six Psi Cops slouching their way down the aisle. In their black uniforms, they looked like a motorcycle gang from twentieth-century visuals Garibaldi had seen. Before he even had a chance to unfasten his seat belt, the six were leaning over him and Gray.

"You let our people get killed," snarled one. "And then you let that murderin' bitch get away."

"Leave Mr. Garibaldi alone," ordered Gray huffily. "He did the best he could."

"Shut up, worm," snapped another. "We don't think he did the best he could. If you know what's good for you, you'll stay out of our way."

One of them grabbed Garibaldi's collar and tried to hoist him out of his seat, but his seat belt held him fast. So instead he slapped the security chief hard across the face.

As Gray stared at him with concern, Garibaldi massaged his inflamed cheek. "Is it going to take the six of you to beat me up?"

"Yep," said another one. He put his foot on Garibaldi's toes and tried to grind them into the deck.

This time, the security chief yelped with pain and jerked his foot back. Gray was still staring at him, wondering what he would do.

"Keep your belt on," he whispered to Gray, "and hang on to your papers." The little man did as he was told.

"You're hot stuff on your own turf," said one of the Psi Cops, "but off it, you're nothin'. You're yellow."

"No," said Garibaldi, "I'm just smart. For example, did you fellows know that there's an emergency pull cord under the seats of this kind of transport? If you didn't know, there's a little sign over on the bulkhead that explains it."

But they weren't listening. A brutish Psi Cop gripped his collar again. "Now it's time to send *you* to the medlab."

Garibaldi reached under his seat and yanked on the emergency cord. At once, alarms went off inside the cabin, and another thing happened. The ship began to slow to a stop. With the absence of acceleration, the simulated gravity inside the cabin stopped also. The six Psi Cops, and anyone else who had been moving around the cabin, began to float weightlessly.

"Help!" screamed one, as he floated past Garibaldi, who was still strapped safely in his seat.

"Let me help you," said Garibaldi. As the man floated helplessly past him, the lanky security chief reached up and grabbed his collar. Holding him steady, he smashed him in the nose. Globules of blood went floating out of his nostrils. Clutching his documents, Mr. Gray watched all of this in amazement.

When the man tried to retaliate by swinging his fists, Garibaldi just gave him a shove, which sent him spinning into the bulkhead. There was a loud clang as his head hit the metal. The chief then calmly grabbed the leg of another Psi Cop who was floating past and pulled him down just far enough to punch him in a very sensitive spot. The man howled with pain, and Garibaldi sent him crashing into the ceiling.

By now the other four Psi Cops were trying desperately to get away from Garibaldi, but all they could do was float. They were saved by the captain's voice on the intercom.

"What's the matter back there?" she asked. "Who pulled the emergency stop?"

"I did, Michael Garibaldi, Security Chief of Babylon 5," he reported. "There was an altercation, and this was the simplest way to end it."

"I hope it's over," said the pilot. "Because you've cost us at least half an hour. That's the time it will take to get us back up to speed. Anybody floating will just have to keep floating until then."

"Too bad," said Garibaldi. A Psi Cop floated overhead, and Garibaldi flicked a long arm up and punched the man in the stomach. The Psi Cop groaned and rolled over.

The chief smiled at Mr. Gray. "There's a lesson in this—it's not good to be overconfident."

"I never am," Gray replied somberly.

The first rays of sunlight brought the slate-colored clouds to life, and they looked like the underbellies of a herd of buffaloes, slowly stampeding across the sky. Talia could see their woolly heads, their massive horns, their hooves, and the steam which shot from their nostrils. The crest of rugged mountains to the north was like a fence that penned them in, with the sun chasing them from behind.

Talia watched, fascinated, as the fiery dome of the sun rose over the desert floor. The vast desolation of this land was both frightening and soothing. It reminded her too much of her present life—drained and shot to hell, but filled with a strange promise of light that could chase away the darkness.

Deuce was asleep in the sand of the dry wash, clutching his briefcase and his PPG pistol across his chest. She could easily wrench one or both away from him now, but what good would that do her? Where could she go without Deuce and his friends, whoever they were? She did steal a few sips of his water, though, after she found a canteen hidden in his duffel bag. With Deuce's well-developed sense of self-preservation, he had failed to mention that he had any water.

Talia climbed out of the wash and watched the sun thaw the dew off the flat leaves and thistles of the plants which grew along the wash. It had been a long time since she had seen a sunrise on Earth, and the woman couldn't help but to feel a bit sad and homesick. She fought the temptation even to think about going to see her family. They would be watched. They would be hounded by newspeople, police, and the curious. Her family was undoubtedly going through hell, and that was just more incentive, if she needed any, to clear her name.

The distant mountains were taking on a reddish hue, and they reminded her of all the lakes, plains, and forests of this magnificent planet. Talia wondered if she would ever see those natural wonders again. She had thrived on an artificial satellite in a distant part of space, so maybe she could thrive anywhere, without her friends and family. Maybe she could be an expatriot of Earth. In truth, Talia wanted to join the migration of clouds across the sky, just a nebulous being who never had to worry about people, death, or detention cells.

She didn't know how long she stood there, watching the ragged horizon, before she saw them. At first, it seemed they were just another copse of misshapen trees in the distance, but the black specks kept coming closer. It was their unerring march through the wilderness that made her certain they were coming for her and Deuce. But who were they? What were they?

As the specks drew closer, she decided they were Hovercraft. She counted four of them, small ones. Talia supposed that a Hovercraft was a good vehicle for this type of terrain, which was treacherous but mostly flat. She heard some footsteps crunching the sand behind her, and she turned to see Deuce. He was drinking from his canteen, and he offered it to her without comment. She took a long drink this time. They were saved, so to speak, and there was no reason for Deuce to hoard his water any longer.

Talia glanced at the criminal, and he shook his head. "No, they're not like me. And they're not like you. Unless you lived about five hundred years ago, they're unlike anybody you've ever met. This is their home. Don't make fun of them, okay?"

Talia shook her head. She was not in any position to make fun of anybody, especially people who would consider this wilderness their home.

With reluctance, she removed her white linen gloves and folded them in the pocket of her jumpsuit.

CHAPTER 14

From his duffel bag, Deuce took out a pair of banged-up but good binoculars and handed them to Talia. She nodded her thanks and put the lenses to her eyes to study the approaching party. The four Hovercraft were clipping along at a good rate of speed, spewing up dust clouds behind them, and she realized with a shock that the pilots were all women!

As she looked closer with the binoculars, Talia decided that they weren't necessarily women but people with very long hair that whipped in the wind. Two of them were bare-chested, and she could see their bronze skin glistening in a halo effect created by the morning sun at their backs. It wasn't until she saw the stylized eagles painted on the noses of the Hovercraft, and the feathers flapping from the roll bars, that she felt certain who they were. In this wilderness, it made sense.

Indians, she thought aloud.

Deuce chuckled. "Well, real Indians wouldn't think so. Those are Bilagaani, as they call themselves. White Indians."

Talia nodded. She had heard of the White Indians, people who had forsaken their own culture to emulate the culture of another race that had flourished five hundred years earlier. They were shunned as pariahs by actual Native Americans, at least those who were trying to maintain their culture. Many Native American tribes had gotten rich and conservative from gambling enterprises around the turn of the millennium, and they had given up any effort to maintain their culture. The White Indians had picked up where they left off, often moving into deserted Indian villages.

"Don't be fooled," said Deuce. "This ain't a game to them. They take it real seriously, especially the religious parts. Some of them were born and raised this way, so they don't know any different. Others have come along, bringing their big-city skills with them." Deuce smiled. "Those are the ones I like."

The grubby criminal motioned at the vast desert. "They live out here where nobody else will live, and nobody pays them much mind. So they do little favors for people like me." He smiled at Talia. "People like *us,* I should say. You're a much bigger criminal than I am."

She glared at him, and the man laughed. "I won't tell them who you are. But there should be a big reward for you by now. Better watch your step."

Talia nodded somberly. After another twenty minutes, the four Hovercraft came shooting out of a gully, skimming over the crusty sand. She could hear the hiss of their powerful propellers. Unlike wheeled vehicles, thought Talia, these did little to disrupt the ecosystem, other than blowing the sand around. The Hovercraft looked like blunt-nosed racecars, with roll bars and a combination spoiler/solar panel in the rear of each vehicle. The fanciful eagles and coyotes painted on the craft did much to make them look authentic, but the people driving them only succeeded in looking strange.

The Bilagaani stopped their vehicles and turned off their engines, and the Hovercraft settled into the sand. One by one, the drivers got out, stretching their legs. There were no cries of greeting, no rush to shake hands with Deuce and Talia. In fact, there was a deliberate reserve in their actions, as if a rushed greeting would be unseemly. Their hair, driven into ratty knots by their journey, hung to their waists. They were wearing moccasins and thick flannel pants tied with drawstrings; two of them wore crudely sewn shirts made from the same material. From their necks hung leather pouches, and there were short knives strapped to their arms.

One of the bare-chested Bilagaani was a tall, muscular man with chestnut-brown hair. He was the kind of character, thought Talia, who existed mainly in fiction—romantic, handsome, although caked with dirt and sweat. The other bare-chested Bilagaani was a middle-aged woman with brown hair, and her breasts were as tanned as the rest of her.

The third one was an older man with white hair, and the fourth one looked like a boy.

Finally, it was the man with white hair and a creased face who approached them and held up his hand in greeting. "Brother Deuce," he said, "I hope all goes well."

"Brother Sky," said the gangster, "it is well to see you again."

Talia felt the others staring at her, and she stared right back. After her adventures of late, she was certain she was just as grungy and disreputable-looking as the rest of them. She could feel the caked blood in her scalp and on her forehead. And she felt bare without her gloves.

"What is your name, child?" asked Brother Sky.

Deuce shrugged. "She don't talk, and I don't know what her name is. But I would like to make some arrangements for her."

Sky smiled benignly, showing several missing teeth. "We will double your fee."

"What?" squawked Deuce. "You had to come out here, anyway! How can you double it?"

"Very well," said Sky, "we can leave her here, to feed Brother Coyote."

"All right," muttered the gangster. "But she needs everything I'm getting—new identicard, passage east."

Sky held up his hands in a token of peace. "The Creator will provide." He turned to the handsome one. "Make our peace with the land for this intrusion."

The young man leaped down into the wash and took only a few strides to reach the half-buried cargo container. He gathered up the parachute and stuffed it into the hole in the top of the container. Reverently, he took his pouch off his neck, opened it, and faced the east. As he spoke words in a language which Talia didn't recognize, he took bits of dried vegetable matter from his bag and tossed them into the wind. Everyone watched silently as he repeated this procedure facing the south, the west, and the north. Then he returned the pouch to his neck and climbed out of the wash.

"Father," he said, "we should return here and break down this container. There are things we can use."

Sky nodded. "Yes, my son. That is well." The old man motioned toward his Hovercraft. "Deuce, you will ride with the boy, as he is lighter. Your friend will ride with me."

The old Bilagaani studied Talia for a moment. "You will need a name, at least for the period you stay with us. Since you come from the sky, I will call you Rain."

Talia nodded and smiled. She liked the name Rain.

Boston was a strange city, thought Garibaldi, as he and Harriman Gray rode an autotaxi through the financial district. Mixed among the gleaming skyscrapers with mirrored surfaces were these old gray buildings with bay windows and skylights. The autotaxi shuddered up a steep hill, and they got a glimpse of the sparkling ocean and a sleek ocean liner at the dock. Then they plummeted down the other side of the hill and entered a grimy tunnel that looked as if it had been built at the dawn of time. The whole city seemed a dichotomy, thought Garibaldi, both modern and ancient, clean and dirty, with the usual big-city feature of way too many people.

They emerged from the tunnel, and the robotic car jerked sharply around a corner, following an invisible track in the street. Gray was thrown against Garibaldi by the centrifugal force.

"Sorry," said the telepath, straightening his shoulders.

"Why are you sorry?" asked the security chief. "You're not driving. We did tell this thing to go double-time."

Gray sighed and flicked on the viewer on the dashboard. He flipped stations until he found some news, and Garibaldi wasn't surprised to see a photo of Talia Winters.

". . . whose whereabouts are still unknown," said the newscaster. "The commercial telepath has been implicated in the recent bombing on station Babylon 5. She made good her escape three days ago and has not been sighted since. In addition to being wanted by authorities for the bombing on Babylon 5, Talia Winters has been declared a rogue telepath by the governing body of telepaths, Psi Corps."

"What?" growled Garibaldi. "I thought Bester was going to lay off for several days!"

Gray shrugged. "Maybe he woke up from his surgery in a bad mood."

"If you have any knowledge of the whereabouts of Talia Winters, please contact your local police or Psi Corps office."

Garibaldi flicked off the viewer. "Sheesh," he muttered. "If she lives through this, it'll be a miracle."

"I don't believe our chances of finding her first are very good."

"Yeah, but we're the only ones who know that she might be coming after Emily Crane. It's a long shot, but it's worth a try."

The vehicle came to an abrupt stop in front of one of the behemoth skyscrapers, not one of the charming stone buildings. Gray and Garibaldi looked at one another to see who would be the first to draw his creditchit.

"Your expense account has got to be better than mine," observed Garibaldi.

The telepath sighed and ran his card through the slot. "Thank you," said a synthesized voice. The doors opened, and they stepped out.

"Floor thirty-eight," said Garibaldi, looking at his electronic address keeper.

Garibaldi's Earthforce uniform and Gray's Psi Corps insignia got them past the security guards in the lobby without any problem, even though they didn't have an appointment. Garibaldi and Gray had agreed not to alert Emily Crane that they were coming; they wanted to surprise her and judge her reactions for themselves. Even though the rest of the universe thought Talia Winters was guilty, Garibaldi was going to prove them wrong. He just hoped he could do it before Bester and his goons got ahold of her.

The receptionist of the Mix office on floor thirty-eight was a dour-looking older man. At least he looked dourly at the two uniformed men as they approached his desk. His nameplate read: "Ronald Trishman."

"Hello, officers, what can I do for you?" he asked, while grabbing a keypad and trying to look busy.

Garibaldi tried to be charming but businesslike. "Does Emily Crane work here?"

"Who are you gentlemen?"

"I'm Michael Garibaldi, Security Chief of Babylon 5, and this is Mr. Gray, Psi Corps military liaison, currently under assignment to Mr. Bester. You've heard of him, right? We would like to see Emily Crane."

"Do you have an appointment?" asked Ronald Trishman, showing his displeasure.

"No."

"I'm afraid you'll need an appointment."

"That's a nice try," said Garibaldi. "Tell her she can talk to us or the Psi Cops. It's her choice."

The receptionist swallowed and touched a commlink panel on his desk. "Ms. Crane, there are two gentlemen here to see you. One is the security chief of Babylon 5, and the other is a telepath working for Mr. Bester. They say you can talk to them or to the Psi Cops."

"Please send them b-back," came the answer.

"Room two twelve," said the man. He buzzed open the door to the inner chamber, and Garibaldi was there in two strides, with Gray rushing to keep up.

When they found room 212, Emily Crane stood waiting for them in the doorway, a look of concern on her plain face. She was wearing a brown suit that was too long for her diminutive height, and it didn't do much to enliven her personality either.

"Hello," she said simply. "Come in."

She ushered them into an office that was a considerable contrast to her appearance. It had striking furnishings of a Frank Lloyd Wright influence, with ornate fractals carved into her Mayan-styled desk, conference table, and bureau. Emily Crane seated them in comfortable chairs decorated with a Mayan pattern in blood red.

Gray managed a smile and was the first to speak. "We're

sorry we have to bother you, Ms. Crane, but there's a matter we have to clear up.''

Garibaldi crossed his legs and smiled benignly. They had decided in advance that Gray would do the questioning, because he was a fellow telepath. She might open up more for him. If he faltered, Garibaldi would step in and play good cop/bad cop. He was looking forward to being the bad cop.

Ms. Crane said nothing and waited for Gray to go on. Garibaldi realized that talking was not her strong suit, and she was going to do as little of it as possible.

"I'm assigned to Mr. Bester," said Gray, "and he is convinced that Talia Winters is guilty of the bombing on Babylon 5. She claimed to have certain items in her handbag, but her recollection does not match the recollection of the security officer who searched her on the way in."

Gray smiled rather charmingly. "This may seem like a trivial matter, but we need this information for the sake of completeness—to know exactly what was in her bag. Did you give Ms. Winters a data crystal sometime that morning?"

"Which morning?" asked Emily Crane. "We were passing a data crystal back and forth—m-myself to Mr. Malten and Ms. Winters. It was a very hectic t-two days."

Good dodge, thought Garibaldi. It wouldn't be easy to tie Emily Crane to this, especially with Talia on the loose, unable to testify and looking more guilty every minute. He had to remind himself that he was the only one in the entire universe Talia had told about Emily Crane.

"We're talking about the morning of the bombing," answered Gray. "After you had passed through security."

Garibaldi sat up with a start. He knew that he had seen Emily Crane before, but he hadn't remembered exactly when. Now he knew! He had checked her through himself that morning—in fact, he had held the bomb in his hand! That was twice he had held the bomb, if you counted his dream.

When he turned back, he found Emily looking at him in a strange way. She was scanning him!

"Stop it!" he barked. "You just answer the question, all right. Did you hand her that data crystal, the one I let you take through security?"

"No," she answered haughtily. "If you want to try to prove I did, good luck."

Garibaldi lost it and jumped to his feet. Leaning over her desk, he shouted at her, "You killed *five* of your own kind! And now you're going to let an innocent woman hang for it! I thought I had seen every kind of monster in Psi Corps, but, sister, you take the cake!"

Gray was holding his shoulders, restraining him more in symbol than reality. "We'll get her for it," he said with a sidelong glance at Emily Crane. "Remember, we can place her at the hotel bombing, too. We'll get her for that one, if not this one."

Now Emily jumped to her feet and pointed toward the door. "Get out!" she demanded.

While he was leaning over her desk, Garibaldi made a point of studying everything on it. Amid the billing statements, electronic gadgets, and printouts was one thing that caught his eye—a disposable transparency, the kind that self-destroyed after a brief period. It bore the logo of the Senate and several warnings of a classified nature. It seemed to be from the chairperson of the armed forces committee, a strange thing for a commercial telepath to be concerned about. He couldn't read more than that, but he did catch the number of a bill that was apparently under consideration.

"Out," she said, "or I will call security and my lawyer!"

Garibaldi pointed a finger in her face. "You get that lawyer, because you're going to need him."

"Come on," said Gray, pushing Garibaldi toward the door.

Once outside on the street, the agitated chief took a few deep breaths and looked at a morbid Mr. Gray. He felt pretty bad about it, as if they had blown the interrogation, but he couldn't think of another way they could've handled it.

Garibaldi shrugged. "Hey, at least we know who the bomber is."

"But we're the only ones who know," complained Gray, "and everybody else is looking for the wrong person. I suppose we could tell Mr. Bester, who would make Ms. Crane's life miserable, but somehow that's not the same as bringing her to justice."

"That's the last resort," said Garibaldi. "What do you think Crane will do? Will she fly?"

"As long as Ms. Winters is a fugitive, Ms. Crane is basically safe. If Ms. Winters gets killed, which is altogether probable, then Ms. Crane has nothing to worry about."

Garibaldi groaned. "We know *who,* but we don't know *why.* Who was she really trying to kill? Bester? Malten? Too bad for her, because she missed on both counts."

"If it's not personal," said Gray, "is it actually tied into the Martian revolution?"

"Listen, do you know anybody in the Senate?"

"A senator?" Gray asked doubtfully.

"It doesn't have to be a senator, it could be a clerk or an aide, maybe even a lobbyist. Somebody in the know. I saw a confidential memo on her desk, and it was from the Senate. I think it was about some pending bill. Maybe there's a connection with Mars."

The telepath pouted for a moment. "I would rather follow up my lead on the hotel bombing."

"Think about it, Gray. You would have to go to Mars to do that. You'd have to track down all the personnel data she gave when she was pretending to be a Martian domestic worker. If this thing takes us to Mars, I promise we'll do it."

Garibaldi patted the telepath on the back. "We're here in the East Coast metropolis. Let's check on stuff we can check out here. Also, we have to keep an eye on her in case she flies. You know, Gray, you have surprised me. You are doing a helluva job. We arrived here from two different paths, but we both got to Emily Crane."

Mr. Gray nodded somberly and made a fist. "We work well together. I say, let's nail whoever did this."

* * *

It seemed like a mirage, shimmering in the desert heat, a pile
of adobe cubes; they looked like loaves of bread baking in
the sun. After the long haul over the rugged terrain in the
Hovercraft, without seeing anything except endless tracts of
desolation, even these humble abodes looked miraculous.
Talia rubbed her eyes, both to get a better look and to get the
sand out. No, it really was a village, a low-level form of
civilization to be sure, but Talia didn't think she had ever
seen anything so beautiful.

"Bilagaani Pueblo!" shouted the old man into the wind,
which ate most of his words.

Talia nodded and gripped the sides of the roll bar tighter.
The sensation of metal against her bare hands felt strange.
There really wasn't a second seat in the small Hovercraft,
and she was hanging on for all she was worth.

As they drew closer, she decided the adobes looked like a
pile of children's blocks, a smaller block piled on top of a
larger block to form rudimentary second stories. The extra
space also allowed walkways between various structures on
the second story, and wooden ladders stretched to every roof
in the pueblo, untilizing all the space. There were rounded
wooden beams sticking straight out of the adobes at irregular
intervals, and smoke curled from a chimney on the topmost
structure.

Gathered around the pueblo were pens for animals—goats
and chickens seemed to be the most popular—and there were
several low-slung lodges, little more than a meter high. Some
of these low lodges were skeletal structures, nothing but
twigs with colorful bits of cloth tied to them. Near each
lodge was an immense fire pit filled with gray rocks, and
Talia wondered what so many fire pits were used for. Colorful feathers and handmade pennants decorated staffs and
poles all over the village.

The dogs were the first ones to come running to greet the
Hovercraft, and they were yapping and wagging their tails
happily. They were followed by children, who were also yapping but had no tails to wag. Undaunted, they twirled clack-
ing noisemakers over their heads, causing the chickens to

scurry. Adults began to emerge from the adobes, and they exhibited only a mild interest in the new arrivals.

Talia now saw that the village was nestled against a small plateau barely taller than the tallest adobe and exactly the same color. This must make it difficult to spot from the ground, she thought. Atop the plateau was the incongruous sight of solar panels, microwave antennae, and satellite dishes, and in the distance were white windmills, churning in the breeze. She imagined that the solar panels and windmills generated all the power the pueblo could ever need. Maybe there would be a hot bath tonight, she thought hopefully.

Then she saw the muddy stream, barely a meter wide, skirting both the plateau and the pueblo as if it were trying to avoid them. She saw no other signs of water, and her hopes sank.

The strange caravan swerved to a halt near the other parked Hovercraft, and the pilots killed the engines. She gasped as the vehicle dropped to the ground. A moment later, Brother Sky was offering his hand to her.

"Come, Sister Rain," he said. "Do you need food?"

She nodded and got out of the Hovercraft. The dogs sniffed her, and the children ran around her in circles, giggling. Talia looked over and saw Deuce getting out of the boy's Hovercraft. The gangster managed to greet several people while keeping his black briefcase clutched to his chest. His duffel bag was slung over his shoulder.

She turned to see the bare-chested young man with the chestnut-colored hair. By himself he pushed the Hovercraft close enough together to loop a length of steel cable through their rings and chain them together. He glanced up at her and smiled, and she was instantly embarrassed about watching him. When she turned away, she found the middle-aged woman staring at her. The woman gave her a toothless grin and walked away, and she could see skin lesions and ruined skin on the woman's naked shoulders.

The people of the pueblo looked healthy enough, but many of them had the kind of simple ailments that come from living primitively: bad skin, bad teeth, limps, injuries, and one case of cataracts. Had they been in a city or a space station, they could have been cured of most of those ailments over the weekend. Those who weren't nude were dressed in similar dirty clothes and wore similar waist-length ratty hair. It was disconcerting to see all these Earthlings living in such primitive conditions, and Talia was glad when Sky escorted her inside a ground-floor adobe.

She had to duck her head to fit through the doorway, and she was surprised to find a tasteful electric floor lamp giving off a subdued bit of light. She was even more surprised to see a table, upon which sat a sprawling machine; it had various spools and feeds and looked like it was intended for small manufacturing. The smells of the room were also a strange mixture of industrial solvents and chile, cilantro, and onions.

"I will be right back," said Sky. He disappeared into the adjoining room, which Talia assumed was the kitchen. She could see no cooking utensils in the outer room.

A moment later, Deuce entered and slumped onto one of the mats on the floor. He kicked off his boots and groaned with relief. His feet added another odd smell to the room.

"Ever see anything like this?" he asked.

She shook her head in an honest answer.

Deuce grinned. "They bend the laws, but they're good people. They're on the edge, like you and me."

Talia nodded. Unfortunately, she couldn't argue with that generalization, given her present circumstances. The young man with the chestnut hair came in, and he was carrying a mangled pad of paper, a stubby pencil, and a measuring tape.

"Stand up, Brother Deuce," he said, motioning to the gangster.

Deuce complied, and the young man measured his height, as if he were fitting him for a suit. When he was done, he wrote his findings on his pad of paper.

"I'm going to guess on your weight," he said. "Our scale broke. But I'm pretty accurate." He tapped his pencil on his chin until he came up with a guess, which he also wrote on his pad. "Sister Rain," he said, "it's your turn."

She pointed to him and gave him a quizzical expression. "You want to know my name?" he asked. "It's Lizard."

At her startled expression, the young man chuckled. "It is our custom to name a child after the first thing the father sees. Sometimes this works out well, sometimes not. But we praise our grandparents and the Creator for giving us life, and we accept our name with their blessings. Turn around."

She obeyed, and Lizard ran the measuring tape from the crown of her head to the heels of her feet. In doing so, his fingers touched the bare skin at the nape of her neck, and it gave her a shock. For that split second, she glimpsed involuntarily into his mind and saw that his life out here was lonely. Painfully lonely, but he couldn't leave.

"Fine," he said, jotting down her measurements. "You look about the same weight as my sister—I'll use that. Thank you. I need to go back to my house and get on the microwave link. In maybe an hour, I'll have some matches for identicards. It's gotten too hard to do real forgeries, so I'll have to match you with a living person and download their data. You're just going to travel around with these cards, right? You're not going to apply for a job or a security clearance, are you?"

Deuce laughed hoarsely. "I don't think so."

Talia shook her head.

Lizard brushed his unruly hair back and gripped it in a ponytail. He waved to them and walked out, and Talia found herself watching his finely chiseled backbone and shoulders.

Deuce grinned. "You heard the rule against messing around with the chief's daughter? Well, that's the chief's son. Same rule."

Talia flashed him an angry look, but he ignored it. Nevertheless, she told herself, it was very good advice. The last thing she needed was to settle down out here in the wilderness, with a bunch of misfits who had stolen somebody else's culture. What did she really know about these people? She could wake up one morning and find Psi Cops staring down at her, while Lizard and Sky pocketed a nice reward. No, she was a shark now—she had to keep moving. She had to search out her prey, the same ones who had preyed on her.

That thought brought her back to Emily Crane. Ever since Garibaldi had elicited that name from her, Talia had wondered whether Emily actually had something to do with the bombing. If the bomb had been hidden in the data crystal—and she didn't know how likely or unlikely that was—then Emily had indeed not only tried to kill her, Bester, and Malten, but she had succeeded in killing five telepaths and casting the suspicions onto an innocent person! In other words, Emily Crane was an extremely dangerous and ruthless person. She had to be stopped.

Talia sat on the packed-dirt floor and wrapped her arms around herself. Having an identicard would make traveling possible, but it didn't mean she could travel with impunity. It didn't mean anything, except that she could risk her neck a dozen other places.

Sky came back into the room holding a handmade ceramic bowl. Its contents smelled good, and Talia sat up eagerly. The old man put the bowl in her lap, with no spoon, and she tried to ignore the strange things she found in it. There was a base of some sort of gruel, some vegetables which might've been bits of cactus, and some meat and black things.

Talia looked at Sky, and he smiled encouragingly. "Go ahead. It's all yours."

She apparently wasn't going to get a spoon, so she dipped her fingers into the potpourri and grabbed a glob of it. After her first hesitant taste, the weary fugitive was soon scraping the sides of the bowl with her fingertips.

"I'm glad you like it," said Sky, grinning. "You want some, Brother Deuce?"

"No, thanks," said the grubby criminal, stretching out on the mat. "But I could use a nap." He put his briefcase under his head as a pillow.

"Make yourselves at home," said Sky. "I have some crops to attend to."

He strode out through the low opening in the adobe hut,

leaving her alone with Deuce, who was quickly snoring. Taking a hint, Talia lay back on the hard-packed earth, thinking she could never get comfortable on bare dirt.

She was asleep in a matter of seconds.

CHAPTER 15

GARIBALDI stood on the concourse of Boston's Travel Center, staring at a blank viewer and waiting to link up with Babylon 5, as hundreds of commuters rushed behind him, headed toward bullet trains that would take them up and down the eastern seaboard. Gray stood to his left, fidgeting.

Finally, there was a chime and Captain John Sheridan's handsome face appeared on the viewer. Garibaldi sighed with relief. "Captain, I wasn't sure I'd be able to get through, but I thought I'd better report in."

"That's fine," answered the captain. "Have you turned up anything?"

Garibaldi glanced around to make sure nobody but Gray was eavesdropping. "Yeah, I think we found the bomber. But I don't know how we're going to prove it without having Talia Winters to testify. Her name is Emily Crane, and she works for the Mix in Boston. She handed Talia a data crystal just before they all went into that conference room."

"Interesting," mused Sheridan. "She's a commercial telepath, and that corresponds with some information that Mr. Lennier gave me. At the reception, he was talking to a military liaison named Barker."

Gray interjected, "He's high up."

"I gather that," said Sheridan. "He told Lennier that Bester would soon be history, and that the commercial sector was going to make a grab to control Psi Corps. I can't imagine how they would go about doing that, but it ties together."

Garibaldi frowned. "Unfortunately, it doesn't clear Talia, because she's also in the commercial sector. But it does let us concentrate our search."

The captain's link buzzed, and he lifted his hand to answer it. "Excuse me," he said. Over the long-distance connection, Garibaldi couldn't make out every word of the captain's conversation, but he clearly heard "Mr. Bester" mentioned several times.

"Out," said Sheridan. He turned back to the viewer and shook his head. "I've got to go. Our prize patient is making life difficult for everyone again. Now he's demanding to have his own doctor flown in! Dr. Franklin is about ready to walk. Keep me posted."

"Right, sir." Garibaldi pushed the button to sign off, then he nodded to Mr. Gray. "Time to call your friend."

"But he's only a clerk in the Senate," Gray protested.

"That's good enough. Those guys do all the work, and they know everything. Call him up, and ask him about Senate bill 22991."

Reluctantly, Gray pushed his creditchit into the slot and dialed some numbers on the commlink. After a few moments, a clean-cut, bookish-looking man about Gray's age came on the viewer.

"This is Senator Donaldson's office."

"Marlon, it's me—Harriman! How are you?"

"Harriman, what a surprise! My gosh, how long has it been? Was it the frat reunion in Montreal? Was that the last time I saw you?"

"I believe so," answered Gray. "You're an old hand now —five years working for the senator."

"And you look great," Marlon replied. "Where are you living these days?"

Garibaldi sighed and gave Gray a hand signal to hurry up.

"Berlin," answered Gray. "Listen, Marlon, I need some information about a Senate bill. I believe it's still in committee and hasn't gone to the floor yet."

Marlon smiled helpfully. "Whatever you need."

"I think the bill has something to do with telepaths. It's number 22991."

A pall fell over Marlon's face, and he looked as if he had been struck by a severe case of gastrointestinitis. He glanced around nervously and lowered his voice. "How do you know about that? I can't talk about it."

Garibaldi stepped into the picture. "Oh, I think you can,

Marlon, or we're going to come down to the senator's office
and ask everyone who goes in and out until somebody tells
us.''

"Who are you?''

Gray rolled his eyes with embarrassment. "This is Michael Garibaldi, Chief of Security for Babylon 5. We're
working on a case together.''

"Is he serious about what he just said?''

"Yes,'' answered Gray with a sidelong glance at Garibaldi. "He's impatient, rude, and has very little tact.''

"None,'' agreed Garibaldi.

The Senate clerk was still shaken. "I can't talk about this
on a public comm. Do you still have my address? It hasn't
changed since I've been in Washington.''

"Yes,'' said Gray, consulting a small electronic device.

"I'll be home by six tonight. Why don't you meet me
there? And don't go asking anybody else. I'll tell you what I
know.''

"Great,'' said Garibaldi, "we'll buy you dinner.''

Looking very glum, Marlon signed off.

"Well done,'' said the security chief, slapping Gray on the
back. "You just have time to buy me lunch before we hop the
rails to Washington. Let's go.''

Talia Winters felt somebody toying with her hair, and she
woke up with a start to find a teenage girl leaning over her.
The girl jumped away.

"I'm sorry,'' she said, "you have such beautiful hair.
We're not allowed to cut our hair short like that. I wish we
could.''

Talia sat up, disoriented, and looked around the humble
adobe hut, with the strange machine in one corner and the
smells of cooking wafting from the other room. Once again
she thought about how her life had taken on such a surreal
quality that her dreams seemed normal by comparison. In her
dream, she had been back on Babylon 5, conversing with
tentacled aliens. Awake, she was a fugitive from the law, a

rogue telepath, reduced to hiding out in the desert with a group of neo-primitives.

"My name is Rain," said the girl, stroking her honey-blond hair over her naked shoulder.

Talia almost answered the girl in spoken words, saying she was Rain, too. But she didn't have to say it. The girl laughed in a lilting voice.

"Yes, I know, you are Rain. When Brother Sky names the girls, they are almost always Rain. Some of the people place great significance in this, others say he is misogynistic, but I say he just doesn't like to remember names."

The teenager stroked her hair again, and her green eyes drilled into Talia's. "I think we should call you by your real name. It suits you so much better."

Talia almost cried out, but she forced her tongue back into her mouth as she stared into those vibrant green eyes.

"Winters," said the girl. "Sister Winters is so perfect."

The telepath fought back questions that tried to stampede out of her mouth. She shook her head vehemently, and the young Rain surprised her by nodding in sympathy.

"Yes, I know, you have to be Rain like all the rest of us. It's not fair, when Winters is better for you. I'm sorry." She shrugged and scrambled to her feet. As she dashed out the doorway, she whispered, "I'll see you later."

Talia tried to still her initial impulse to bolt from the pueblo and keep running. Where would she go? she asked herself. It's not surprising for the Bilagaani to know her real identity, she reasoned. They weren't as cut off out here as they seemed, not with that battery of antennae and dishes on the plateau. Lizard was out there now, stealing data off a secured link. It wasn't panic time yet, Talia assured herself, although it wouldn't take much to push her to it.

Young Rain had been so innocent about knowing her real name, and threatening at the same time. Talia couldn't believe they were scheming to do her harm. Would an adolescent be allowed to blurt something like that out, if the tribe was planning to turn her in? The Bilagaani simply knew who she was, and they didn't care if she knew it.

Hey, she reminded herself, these people were breaking serious laws themselves. They didn't want Psi Cops around. By running, she had naturally fallen in with people like Deuce and this weird offshoot of the underground. These were the people who lived in the cracks in the sidewalk, who lived in places like B5's Down Below. Like it or not, she was part of their world now, and she might visit more way stations in the underground before her journey was through.

If she didn't clear her name, she would have to live in the cracks forever.

No! she told herself. She wasn't going to let that happen. Talia wanted her real life back, and she resolved anew to keep her mouth shut, to keep to herself, and to keep moving. She wouldn't admit to anything. But she desperately needed to dye her hair or get a wig to go along with her new indenti-card. Hell, she thought, these people had enough hair to make her a hundred wigs! She wondered if they could impro-vise a wig or a dye-job for Sister Winters.

Talia glanced at the mat where Deuce had been sleeping and wondered where he was. She wanted to know how soon they would be getting out of the pueblo, and by what method. She might opt to make her own travel arrangements if what Deuce had in mind was too dangerous. Of course, she thought glumly, she didn't have any money. She could get Emily Crane's business address at any public terminal, and then she would at least know her destination. She figured she could play it by ear after she confronted Emily Crane, but first things first—where was Deuce?

She got to her feet and shuffled out the doorway. Shielding her eyes from the intense sunlight, Talia peered into the courtyard formed by the crude semicircle of stacked adobes. The courtyard looked brown and dusty, like an old coin, and nobody was visible. Even the chickens and goats were sleep-ing under mat lean-tos. It was hot, but it was the kind of dry heat that didn't leave her sweating so much as parched and enervated.

Talia sidled around the corner of Sky's adobe and saw a ladder leaning on the wall and leading up to the next level.

She heard some muted voices coming from above, so she decided to climb the ladder and try her luck. It was either that or sit around and go crazy, waiting for something terrible to happen.

The handmade wooden ladder creaked under her weight, but it was just the leather stretching; it never felt as if it was about to give way. She climbed up quickly to the next floor, which was the top of Sky's roof, and saw several scattered wooden toys—crude wagons, blocks, and noisemakers. Through an open door, she saw three children asleep, as she had been until a few minutes ago. It was siesta time, she concluded, the hottest part of the day when anyone with any sense would be sleeping. It was amazing how cool the adobes stayed compared to the outside temperatures.

"We build the adobe walls with bales of hay in the center," said Lizard.

She whirled around to see the handsome Bilagaani poking his head out of the low doorway of the neighboring adobe. His chestnut hair framed his face in sweaty ringlets.

"You were wondering how they stay so cool," he explained. "Everyone wonders that. Come inside before you roast."

Was Lizard a rogue telepath? wondered Talia. This would be the place for a rogue to hide out, she supposed, if there was such a place. She ducked into his cool adobe and was struck by a blast of air from a powerful fan; it blew her hair and clothes back and made her stagger. Lizard reached out a hand to pull her in.

"Keeps the dust out," he explained, as he motioned around the cramped collection of electronic equipment, most of it in no order that she could discern. He went back to his desk and looked at one of his four viewers, this one filled with data.

"Can you be thirty-two years old?" he asked. "I don't think you look that old, but this is the closest match. Height, weight, family background . . ."

She yanked at her blond hair, and he nodded.

"So you want to change your hair color, make it darker? I

thought you might. Then I've got one that will match even closer. I'll format that data, and we'll run you a card on the machine downstairs. Now, listen, these identicards are good for maybe four uses, about a week of traveling, and by then"—he looked at the screen—"Frieda Nelson should be retired. You'll have to become someone else, because the system will eventually realize that Frieda Nelson can't be in two places at once."

He crossed his brawny arms and stared at the screen. "She's twenty-nine and hails from Eugene, Oregon. Remember, if you use it more than four times, you're taking a chance."

Talia nodded and tried to give him an encouraging smile. It was too bad that she couldn't stay and chat with this exotic young man, but she had to get organized. She had to get out of here—she could feel something already closing in, even if it was just her paranoia. Talia held up two fingers and shrugged.

"Deuce?" asked Lizard.

She nodded eagerly and shrugged again, as if to ask where he was.

Lizard chuckled and turned back to his screens. "I don't think you want to talk to Deuce at the moment. He is lying with one of the women of the tribe, Sister Morning. She's the one who came with us to get you."

Talia blinked at him, wishing she hadn't asked.

"Morning is a widow, and she took an interest in Deuce the last time he was here. She thinks she has a chance to convince him to stay, but I don't think so. Deuce likes a faster pace than Bilagaani Pueblo, I'm afraid."

Talia looked desperately around the little room with the huge fan, and her eyes lit upon Lizard's pad of paper and stubby pencil. She grabbed them, flipped to a clean page, and began to write. Lizard watched her with interest, a quiet mirth in his blue eyes.

After a few seconds, she handed him a sheet of paper bearing the scrawled words: "I need address for Emily Crane, works at the Mix."

Lizard rubbed his angular chin. "The Mix? Then she's a telepath, right? Are you sure you know what you're doing? Listen, you don't have to be in a hurry to leave. This is not a bad place to hang out, and we could get to know each other."

Would she get the same recruiting inducements as Deuce was getting? wondered Talia. She supposed there had to be some incentive to get people to live way the hell out here in this wilderness, and that might work with some people. But Talia couldn't imagine a life of nothing but sand, gruel, and Lizard. She had a life that she already enjoyed, and she longed to get back to it. The telepath pointed inflexibly at the sheet of paper bearing Emily's name.

"Okay," said the Bilagaani, punching in a few commands. "To get her business address will only take a moment."

Talia paced the cramped office. She didn't know why she was angry at Deuce for stopping to enjoy the local recreation. It was stupid to think that she had won that gangster's allegiance or loyalty. He was a cutthroat, pure and simple, and he would help her only as long as it didn't hurt him. Like the canteen he had hidden from her, Deuce would always save the best for himself. He had gotten her this far, but she would have to get the rest of the way on her own.

"Does Boston sound right for Emily Crane?" asked Lizard.

She nodded, and the young man printed Emily Crane's address onto a clear address card. When he went to hand it to her, his hand caught hers, as if to steady it, and their thoughts mingled disconcertingly. He told her, *It doesn't matter who you are.* She gripped his hand in return and told him telepathically, *It does matter! I am a hunted terrorist, and I will destroy you all if I stay. I have a life, and a purpose. Only death will stop me from clearing my name.*

Talia yanked the address card out of his hand and studied it. She memorized it all, including floor 38, and tucked the card into a zippered pocket of her jumpsuit.

"All right," said Lizard with resignation. "You'll need clothes, a disguise. Come with me."

He took her back out into the sunlight. Despite the heat, they climbed down the ladder and walked completely around the pueblo and toward the plateau that protected it. Talia wanted to ask where they were going, but she didn't dare. She saw the crops that Sky had talked about—neat rows of squash, corn, and various herbs she didn't recognize, all irrigated from the muddy stream. Tied to wooden stakes in the garden were colorful bits of cloth and miniature windmills; she supposed the purpose of the adornments was to frighten away the birds.

She also saw modern equipment connected to a concrete building. That had to be the collection center for their power transformer, Talia deduced, because of all the wires stretching from the building to the solar panels on the plateau and the windmills beyond. This was quite an operation they had here. Although the Bilagaani lived primitively by twenty-third-century standards, they weren't exactly nomads or monks who had taken a vow of poverty. They couldn't just get up and leave this pueblo. She wondered how it happened that they never got raided. Did they pay people off? Maybe they paid them off with information.

Before she could fully worry about such a prospect, Talia's attention was drawn to the extraordinary erosion on the plateau. Close up, it looked pockmarked and pitted, not the smooth rose-colored monument it had seemed from afar. Even Lizard appeared subdued by this sight, as if he could remember the plateau a million years ago, when it had been young and tall, a budding mountain. Now it seemed to mirror the tribe—a ghost of a grandeur long past, something more depressing than beautiful.

True to his name, the young man darted among the pockmarked cavities in the rock face and promptly disappeared. Talia hurried after him, and she almost cracked her resolve by calling his name. When she finally saw the low entrance to the cave, barely a meter high, she stopped. Ever since she was a little girl, she had been afraid of caves. Fortunately, she had never had much cause to come into contact with caves, growing up in a succession of urban areas. But here was one now. It had swallowed Lizard, and now it beckoned her.

Was he waiting inside to jump her? Talia thought fretfully. If he was the type to do so, she decided, she might as well confront him here and now. There was certainly something inside the cave he wanted her to see, and there was no time like the present to see it. Talia got down on her hands and knees in the caked sand and crawled into the hole.

The telepath was surprised to see a glimmer of light just ahead of her, but she didn't dare get to her feet until she saw how low the ceiling was. Then she rounded a corner and saw Lizard, standing upright and lighting an old lantern with some liquid floating in a glass bulb. She didn't know how it burned, but it gave off an amazing amount of light. She assumed that if the tall Bilagaani could stand upright in the cave, then so could she.

As she walked toward him, she saw the remarkable treasure hidden in the cavern. There were dozens of trunks, suitcases, and boxes filled to overflowing with clothes, hats, coats, belts, umbrellas, and other accessories. She moved from one box of treasure to another, surveying ancient things like fox stoles and brocaded bolo jackets. She remembered when those had been popular about a dozen years ago. This cave was like the world's largest emporium of antique clothing!

"The desert keeps these things very well," observed Lizard. "When people come to join us, they bring goods they cannot use anymore, and we store them here. We keep thinking we will burn them, but every now and then something turns out to be useful. You are welcome to anything you find here."

Talia nodded her thanks, although she felt a bit overwhelmed. She wanted a clean suit of nondescript civilian clothes, not trunkfuls of dirty, exotic, antique clothing.

"There is a mirror over there," said Lizard, pointing to what looked like a narrow doorway containing more people and another lantern. Talia jumped before she realized it was just their reflection.

"I will go finish your identicard," said the muscular young man. "Take your time."

Talia nodded her thanks and looked around with dismay at aged trunks full of dusty clothes.

Mr. Gray leaned forward in the autotaxi. "That's him," he said, pointing to a slim man walking down the sidewalk."

"He's late," muttered Garibaldi.

"Marlon has a very responsible job," countered Gray. He ran his chit through the slot on the dashboard, settling their debt with the robotic vehicle, and the doors opened to let them out.

Once they reached the sidewalk, Marlon glanced back at them, but he exhibited no inclination to greet them. It was cloak-and-dagger stuff all the way, thought Garibaldi, as they followed the man through the wrought-iron gate and into the courtyard of his apartment complex. This was one of those pseudo-Roman places, thought Garibaldi, with lots of chintzy columns and porticos. The pièce de résistance was a lighted swimming pool with a fake mosaic portrait of Neptune on its bottom.

Without saying anything, they followed Marlon to his apartment on the first floor, poolside. Garibaldi looked around as Marlon unlocked his door, figuring that if anybody was watching them they would assume that the guy was about to be mugged. But this strange procession had taken only a few seconds, and they were all safely ensconced in his apartment a moment later.

Marlon and Harriman Gray hugged each other like the old friends they were.

"Thank you for seeing us," said Gray.

Marlon gave Garibaldi an annoyed glance. "You didn't give me much of a choice, did you? How did you find out about bill 22991?"

"It's connected to the bombing on Babylon 5," explained Garibaldi. "So tell us about it." The chief sat down on the silk sofa, crossed his long legs, and waited.

The clerk sighed and went to his well-stocked bar. "I need some sustenance first. You want one?"

"Sure," said Gray.

"I gave up sustenance," answered Garibaldi.

Marlon collected his thoughts while he mixed the two drinks. He looked very serious as he delivered Gray's drink and took a seat beside Garibaldi on the sofa.

"It's like this," he began, "a lot of people hate Psi Corps."

"That's not exactly a news flash," said Garibaldi.

"Yes, but they *really* hate them, especially the Psi Cops and the intelligence groups. Only they're too afraid to say anything. I'm talking about senators here! You should see some of the things Psi Corps does to them—blackmail, intimidation, threats—it's terrible!"

Marlon took a gulp of his drink. It smelled like a martini to Garibaldi, a strong one, too. The clerk continued, "It's a secret proposal so far, but there's a bill under consideration that would privatize Psi Corps. Under the guise of saving money, this bill would take Psi Corps out of the military—which doesn't control it, anyway—and make the governing body of telepaths a completely civilian office."

He took another drink and went on, "Even though a lot of the same telepaths would still be around, the Senate hopes this will cut their ties to their allies, kill all their secret intelligence gathering, and basically neutralize them. All the good stuff they're doing, they can keep doing as a civilian entity that answers directly to the Senate. As far as the public is concerned, nothing changes—Psi Corps just becomes private instead of military. In reality, a lot changes."

Gray interjected a question. "This sounds like quite a windfall for somebody. Who would take over Psi Corps once it's privatized?"

Marlon shrugged. "Who else? There's only one firm of private telepaths that's big enough—the Mix."

Garibaldi and Gray looked at one another. They didn't need to be reminded who Emily Crane's employer was—the Mix.

"Does Arthur Malten know about this?" asked Garibaldi.

"Are you kidding?" scoffed Marlon. "He's been lining this up for years, going to all the senators who have been harassed by Psi Corps and making secret deals. When he has enough votes, and that may be soon, this bill will miraculously jump out of committee and go to the floor in the dead of night. It will be passed immediately, before Psi Corps has a chance to stop it. The president will sign it in his pajamas. When Psi Corps wakes up the next morning, Malten will be in charge."

"Does this mean that Malten's a good guy?" asked Garibaldi.

Marlon laughed cynically. "Hell no, he's doing it for the money. With the Psi Corps budget to play with, he stands to make a fortune! It's risky for Malten, but the Mix is already as big as it's going to get under Psi Corps. This is Malten's chance to grab everything." The young clerk drained his martini.

Gray cleared his throat and asked, "If you wanted to get away with this, would it be a good idea to kill Mr. Bester?"

"Well," answered Marlon, "they say the only way to kill a rattlesnake is to cut off its head. As long as Bester and his cops have carte blanche to deal with the telepaths as they want, he's in charge."

The clerk stood and went to the bar. "Harriman, would you like another one?"

"No, thank you," said the somber telepath. Garibaldi felt sorry for him. No one ever liked to hear about internecine warfare in their own ranks. This was telepath killing telepath for personal gain and power. Garibaldi might be content to let them kill each other off, but they were killing innocent people in the crossfire—twenty-six of them at the Royal Tharsis Lodge—and they were casting the blame on Mars separatists, who didn't need more grief.

Gray turned to Garibaldi and said puzzledly, "But Mr. Malten was in the explosion."

"He could've been wearing body armor. As I recall, he

didn't have a scratch on him, but his nerves were so shot that
he had to leave B5 right away.''

With determination, Harriman Gray rose to his feet. ''I'm
sorry, Marlon, we'd like to stay, but we should really see Mr.
Malten as soon as possible.''

''No need to rush off, then,'' said the clerk. ''Malten is on
Mars.''

''How do you know that?'' asked Garibaldi.

''He sent the senator a message from there just this afternoon. He's been letting us know his whereabouts in case we
have to move fast on the privatization bill. These bombings
are making everyone nervous, and that's actually playing into
his hands. They're afraid that Bester is going to mount a real
crackdown when he gets back on his feet. Say, you don't
really think Malten is behind the bombings?''

''Keep that under your hat,'' ordered Gray. ''We're following up leads, that's all.''

''But I thought you had the bomber. What's her name, the
blond woman who's been all over the news. They say her
uncle is a terrorist.''

Garibaldi shook his head with frustration. They had no
shortage of suspects anymore, but they still had a shortage of
evidence, and a more serious shortage of official cooperation.
If only Talia hadn't run for it, all of this could've added up to
some kind of a defense for her.

Where are you, Talia? he asked himself. *What are you
doing to get yourself out of this mess?*

CHAPTER 16

TALIA Winters squealed with delight when she pulled the curly brown wig out of the hat box. She glanced behind her in the wavering lamplight of the cave to make sure that no one had heard her. It was a quality wig made from very good synthetic hair, and the hat box had kept it in decent condition. She put the wig on, tucking her blond tresses out of sight, and admired herself in the mirror. She saw that the wig was long and curled down her back, and she decided she would leave it that length. To complete the effect, Talia grabbed a beret and pulled it down on her head. Not only did the beret help to hold the wig in place, it gave her a slightly Bohemian look that went with the unruly hair and the old clothes.

Talia had chosen the most expensive outfit she could find to wear, even though it was ten years out of date, on the theory that expensive clothes always showed their quality. Better for a stranger she met in her travels to think she once had money, and didn't have it any longer, than to think that she had never had money. It was a designer pantsuit in navy blue, and she had found a plain black jacket to go with it. To see how the ensemble looked with the hair, she stripped off her white jumpsuit and tried everything on.

The effect was dramatic. Talia no longer looked her sophisticated, elegant self but more like . . . like Emily Crane. That is, she looked a bit mousy and frumpy. Was this the way Emily had mastered her deception, by trying on mismatched hair and outfits until she had achieved the requisite dowdiness? It depressed Talia to think that she had been fooled so easily, but more and more she couldn't think of any other explanation for a bomb being in her bag. Garibaldi was right—Emily was the only one who could have given it to her.

She could get confirmation about Emily from Deuce, but

she could also get shot between the eyes for asking him. She would just have to ask Emily herself. Damn, she wished Boston weren't so far away.

The telepath tried to imagine what kind of person Frieda Nelson of Eugene, Oregon, was. With these clothes, Frieda was probably an artist of some sort, maybe a person who wrote plays, painted pictures, or constructed homey crafts out of gingham and wood. She might even be the sort of person who would like hanging around at Bilagaani Pueblo with persons named Rain and Lizard. She was not Talia Winters, that was for sure.

"Knock, knock," drawled a voice. "Are you decent?"

She said nothing; she just waited for Deuce to crawl into the cave, carrying his ever-present briefcase and duffel bag. As soon as he got an eyeful of her, he burst out laughing.

"I'm sorry," he said. "You look like a teacher I once had. I didn't like her much, and I put a firecracker in her wastebasket. That was the last bit of official education I ever had."

When Talia said nothing, he reached into his pocket and pulled out an identicard. "Here's yours," he said. "I want you to know that this card and your transportation cost me a one-carat diamond. I don't know when you're going to pay me back, but I always remember my debtors. And I charge interest."

She snatched the card out of his hand but didn't promise him anything. At least now she knew what he carried in that black briefcase, and why he guarded it so closely.

"Lizard told me he already explained to you about these cards. They're okay to use a couple of times, but you're pushing it after that. We're supposed to be leaving at midnight, after their sweat."

She gave him a quizzical look.

"Sweat lodge," he explained. "Those small lodges out there—they heat up a bunch of stones, beat the drums, sing songs, and pray to their grandparents. And sweat. We'd be welcome to join them, I'm sure."

Talia shook her head.

"Deuce! Rain!" called a frightened voice.

They whirled around to see Rain, the teenager with the green eyes, come crawling into the cave. She looked worried, and she pointed to the sky.

"A black shuttlecraft just flew over," she said, panting. "Very high up. Brother Sky says it's Psi Cops!"

Talia felt as if she had been stabbed, the grip of panic was so strong on her chest. Deuce just looked disgusted.

"Bastards always spoil everything," he muttered. "If they find that cargo container out in the desert, we're pretty much had."

Talia suddenly realized that she was not going to change her clothes. She was going to make a run for it dressed like this—Cinderella before the ball. But where? How? There were voices in the narrow tunnel leading into the cave, and she waited tensely to see who it was. Nervously, she balled her hands into fists.

Sky entered, followed by Lizard, and both men looked equally grim. "We saw them," said the old man. "The buzzards are circling. You must leave now."

"How?" growled Deuce. "Do you want us to walk?"

"We'll sell you a Hovercraft," said the old man. "Two stones."

"Whoa!" the gangster wailed. "That's highway robbery! What the hell do I need a Hovercraft for? Just get me to a town, and I'll be all right." He pointed rudely at Talia. "I don't care what you do with *her.*"

Lizard stepped forward, the muscles on his chest tight with anger, and he grabbed Deuce by the neck and shook him. "You came down with her, and you have to look after her! Remember, we could take all the diamonds and show the cops where your body burned up. There would be just enough left to identify."

When Deuce reached for his PPG, the old chief was quicker and grabbed his wrist. Talia also attacked Deuce, whirling around and punching him in the stomach.

"Okay, okay," croaked the petty crook. "Two stones it is!"

The Bilagaani dropped him to the floor of the cave, and he

scrambled for his briefcase. "I want a fast one, and I'm gonna pick it out myself."

Eyeing everyone suspiciously, Deuce extracted two diamonds from his briefcase and gave them to Brother Sky. The old man pointed toward the hole leading out of the cave and nearly pushed him through it.

Talia started to follow, and she felt Lizard grab her arm. She wrenched it away from him and glared at him. She wasn't in a mood to be friendly, especially to a guy who would kick her out into the midday desert with Psi Cops patrolling the air. She glanced around the graveyard of ancient clothes and decided it was more like a tomb.

Lizard shrugged helplessly. "We've got to get you out of the pueblo, that's all. Too many people's lives would be in jeopardy. Personally, I would like you to stay."

She nodded, softening a bit. It really wasn't his fault or the tribe's fault that she was a fugitive. It was her own damn ambition and foolishness. She touched Lizard's bare chest once, briefly, before she crawled out of the cave, and she hoped that would give him a strong enough impression to remember her by.

The sun was brutal, baking the pueblo and the plateau to a dusky brown. But she noticed that it had slipped substantially toward the west, and she guessed that it was about four in the afternoon. Talia didn't know much about fleeing across a desert, but she figured that nighttime was the right time. Well, it would be dark in a few hours, and maybe they could elude capture until then. She didn't want to count on her luck, because she hadn't had any lately.

Talia didn't know whether Deuce had picked the fastest Hovercraft, but he had picked the one with the loudest, brightest paintings on its hood. She guessed there was some logic in that—if they were spotted from above, it would be assumed they were Bilagaani. She was glad now that she had the long hair to fit the image of a Bilagaani plainswoman.

As Deuce was already in his seat, she climbed aboard without another word. The tribe was gathering around to see them off, and they were silent and noncommittal. Morning, the middle-aged woman who had comforted Deuce, was the only one who was crying. What a strange place this speck of North America was, thought Talia, odder than anything she had seen on Babylon 5.

"They were traveling west," said Brother Sky, pointing toward the sky. "If you travel northeast, you will find the town of Clement. Beware the salt flats."

"Thanks," muttered Deuce, not sounding like he meant it.

Lizard suddenly handed Talia a waterskin, and she gripped it for dear life. "Peace," he said somberly.

She nodded and tried to give him a smile. Deuce started the engine and gunned it, but the solar-powered turbine didn't make much noise. The Hovercraft lifted into the air a few centimeters and blew sand all over Lizard, Sky, and the others, but they stood their ground. A few even lifted their hands in a gesture of parting. Talia gripped the roll bars as they rocketed out of the Hovercraft pen and headed for the mountains to the northeast.

The crabcakes and sirloin tasted great, but they didn't sit very well in Garibaldi's stomach. He kept thinking about all the things he should be doing and all the places he should be running. The sedate Washington restaurant wasn't distracting him enough. The conversation of Marlon and Harriman wasn't doing him any good either, as they kept reliving fraternity pranks and trips to Fort Lauderdale. Then Gray launched into a description of his apartment in Berlin, and soon they were both discussing decorating ideas. Garibaldi wanted to climb the drapes.

"Excuse me," he said, rising from the table. "I need to take a little walk. We don't get rich food like that on Babylon 5, and my system is staging a revolution. Maybe I'll find a commlink and check in."

Gray gave him a quick look of concern, and Marlon paid no attention as the security chief slipped away from the table. He shot through the French doors and lacy curtains and found himself on the patio. He took a flight of curving stairs down to a meandering garden.

The out-of-doors smelled wonderful, and it began to lift his spirits immediately. There were gardens and open spaces on Babylon 5, but you had to seek them out. He seldom had time. The air of Babylon 5 was the best money could buy, but it couldn't compete with the pine aroma of the trees and the genuine steer manure on the lawn. It made him wonder how he could spend his days on a space station, revolving around a spooky, half-dead planet, when there was this planet, perfectly designed for the habitation of humans.

He thought about having to go back to Boston tonight, or first thing in the morning, and he realized what he missed about B5. It was self-contained. No running around in funny little vehicles trying to see people—everyone on B5 was a twenty-minute walk, or closer. And a quarter of a million people was considerably more manageable than four billion. Yes, the air smelled good on Earth, but it wasn't home.

After a few more sniffs of the real thing, Garibaldi went around to the front of the converted mansion. He thought he had seen a public commlink by the bathroom. Yes, he was right.

The commlink wasn't busy, and Garibaldi ran his chit through and punched in his commands. Then he leaned against the wall to wait, knowing it could take a few minutes. Some very elegant women were arriving with their dates, and they reminded him of Talia—thoroughbreds, smart, fast, gorgeous. He didn't know whether he would ever see Talia again, and that was beginning to depress him. Not that she had ever given him much more than the time of day, but she had been so assertive, confident, and proud of her accomplishments. It pained him to think she had been reduced to running like an animal, scared of every shadow.

He didn't know how it would be possible to find Talia before the others, but he had to try. There was always the possibility that she hadn't fled to Earth and had hitched a ride to the far ends of the galaxy. But he felt certain she had come to Earth. Not only was Emily Crane here, but this was familiar territory for her. People usually ran from the strange and to the familiar, not the other way around. Garibaldi often thought that if he ever had to run from B5, he would go back to Mars. He figured Talia would come here.

Earth was logical for another reason. If you were a human and you wanted to hide, you didn't go where humans were rare—you went where there were a lot of humans. Unfortunately, that just made his job more difficult, and nothing short of finding her would help her now.

A synthesized voice startled him. "Hang on for your link to Babylon 5."

"I'm hangin', I'm hangin'," he assured the computer.

An empty chair appeared on the screen, but presently Captain Sheridan dropped into it. "Garibaldi," he frowned, "we've had a development here."

"Yes, sir."

"Mr. Bester has flown the coop. His supposedly private doctor arrived, but they were really just a bunch of Psi Cops who whisked him onto their ship. We never saw a doctor, but we did see some orders that made it all official. Dr. Franklin doesn't know whether to be angry or relieved."

"Can Bester get around?" asked Garibaldi.

"Not well. The doctor said that in a few days he could get around on crutches or a cane. Since he's refused all medication, he won't be in a very good mood."

"What do you think his plans are?"

"To get Ms. Winters," answered the captain. "That's all he could talk about. How are you coming along?"

Garibaldi glanced around and lowered his voice. "We've got strong leads on both Arthur Malten and Emily Crane. It's good stuff, but we can't pin them without Talia."

"That is a problem," conceded Sheridan. "We've got some happy people now that the last of Psi Corps is gone, but everyone feels badly about Ms. Winters. I wish we could have handled it differently. What's done is done."

"Don't bet against me," declared Garibaldi. "I'm going to bring her back, alive and free. Good-bye, sir."

"Good luck. Sheridan out."

Garibaldi signed off and paced around the foyer for a few seconds. He had to do something! Go somewhere! After all, they had learned everything they came to Washington to learn. Maybe he would go back to Boston right now and hang out in Emily Crane's front room. Was the woman from the Mix so confident that she wouldn't make a run for it? She and Malten had strong motives to stage these bombings, and that might inspire them to do something crazy.

Garibaldi tried to imagine a Psi Corps without the military trappings, threats, and overbearing nastiness, and he liked it. He liked it a lot. That thought made him realize that, philosophically, he was on the side of the bombers! Geez, why couldn't things be white and black, good guys and bad guys?

The main thing was that he couldn't sit around talking about Berlin, debutante balls, or frat parties. He had to ditch Gray right away. The telepath had been of surprising usefulness, being right about the Mars bombing fitting in with the B5 bombing. He had saved them a great deal of time by calling Marlon, but his usefulness was at an end. They knew everything they were likely to know without collaring either Emily Crane or Arthur Malten. For that they needed a bloodhound, which Garibaldi was. It could get rough, and Gray would just get in the way.

Garibaldi started out the front door of the restaurant, prepared to jog to the corner to catch an autotaxi, when he heard a loud, "Harrumph!"

He turned to see Gray, standing in the shadows with his arms crossed. "I wondered when you would run out," the telepath said accusingly.

Garibaldi shrugged. "Listen, I just heard that your boss, Bester, is on the prowl again. I thought maybe you might want to connect up with him, make a report or something."

"I thought we were a team," said Gray, clearly wounded. "My orders were to get to the bottom of this, and working together we were getting to the bottom of it. I'm sorry that you don't think our partnership is worthwhile."

"Aw, look," said Garibaldi with a smile, "I'm just antsy. I've got to do something. Tell you what, I'll meet you back at Emily Crane's office tomorrow morning at nine hundred hours. You can finish your dinner with your friend."

"You'll meet me tomorrow morning?" asked Gray doubt-fully.

"Didn't I just say I would?"

"All right," said Gray. "Really, we're the only ones who know what's going on. We need to back each other up."

"Yeah, yeah," muttered Garibaldi, hurrying off. "See you tomorrow."

"What about your part of the check?"

"Thanks!" hollered Garibaldi, disappearing down the driveway.

Talia Winters peered out the rear of the Hovercraft with Deuce's beat-up binoculars. She wondered if she could spot the shuttlecraft before they spotted the Hovercraft. Probably not. Even if they did, that was only half the battle, because then they would still have to hide. They were skirting a ridge that had been formed by an old earthquake fault line, but it didn't really offer any hiding places. They had to face the fact that they were ducks on a platter out here in this desert.

"This trip was only supposed to cost me *one* diamond!" complained Deuce. "And now it's cost me *four!*"

As this was the two hundredth time he had complained about that particular injustice, Talia ignored him and pulled her wig and her hat down on her head. She guessed they were making good time for such a primitive craft, even if she was getting encrusted with sand; but it bothered her that she didn't know where they were going. Clement? It didn't ring a bell. They had to trust in Brother Sky's directions.

"You know, those kooks might not have seen anything!" snarled Deuce. "You didn't see a shuttlecraft, did you? Me neither!"

That thought hadn't occurred to her before, and Talia turned to look at the gangster. "Do you think they just wanted us out of there, so they made it up?"

"Sure, maybe they turn us in and say we stole their Hover-craft. I doubt if we're going to live to argue about it."

Talia banged on his shoulder and shouted, "Stop this thing! Park it somewhere!"

Deuce let up gradually on the accelerator, and the Hover-craft came to a stop and thudded into the sand. He wiped the sand off his face and demanded, "What's the matter with you?"

Talia jumped out of the craft and stretched her legs. "Stop and think about it," she said. "They got us out of the village because they know, one way or another, somebody is coming after us. Whether they sent for them, or they spotted us, or they intercepted a message, it doesn't matter. They know, and somebody's coming. There's no way to get across this desert by daylight without being spotted, so let's camouflage this thing and wait it out until nightfall."

Deuce stared at her for a moment, then stared into the unforgiving sun to the west of them. He grinned foolishly and scratched his stubbly chin. "Maybe we're doing this all wrong," he drawled. "Why should we run in a piddly Hover-craft, when they've got shuttles? Why should we run at all? Let's set a trap for *them*. How many of them can there be?"

"Well," said Talia, adjusting her wig, "assuming they're Psi Cops and they're after me, they won't alert any other authorities. They like to bring down a rogue themselves, without anybody interfering. They probably have several two-man shuttles spread out over this area."

Deuce grabbed the bumper of the Hovercraft and began to rock the vehicle. "Come on! Help me turn this thing over!"

"Why?" asked Talia, leaning down to grab the bumper.

"To make it looked like it wrecked."

CHAPTER 17

TALIA Winters watched a scorpion scuttle across the sand about a meter away from her face. The tan arachnid blended in perfectly with the sand, and she hadn't noticed it when she picked this place to lie down. Now its deadly tail was curving up and down, and its little pincers were looking for something to pinch. She was in horrendous fear that her nose would look delectable to the scorpion, but she couldn't possibly move or cry out. She would just have to let the scorpion sting her and take her chances with the venom.

Because a sleek, black shuttlecraft was about a kilometer away and swooping in for a landing.

Talia closed her eyes as the shuttlecraft landed and its thrusters blew sand all over her. After this sojourn in the desert, she wondered if she would ever feel clean again. She held her breath, waiting for the scorpion to get blown directly into the center of her face, stinger first. When that didn't happen, she held perfectly still, trying to look dead, or at least close to it.

She could imagine what the scene looked like from the air: an overturned Hovercraft which had skirted too close to the ridge, and the body of a woman lying a few meters away, broiling in what was left of the late-afternoon sun. It didn't look very threatening, she hoped.

Talia heard the door of the shuttlecraft open, and she heard their boots crunching across the sand. As she had guessed, there were only two of them, and she felt them probing her with their minds. Even though they were P12s and she was a mere P5, she had the advantage of all that contact with alien species; she was able to disrupt a casual mind-scan with bizarre images. Talia thought again about Ambassador Kosh and Invisible Isabel, knowing they wouldn't be able to make much sense out of that.

"She's alive," said one of them, "but she's delirious."

"Is that the rogue?" asked the other. "They said she had blond hair?"

"Hair color doesn't mean anything," said the first. "Besides, if we leave her here, she'll just die. Better take her in."

With her eyes closed, Talia wasn't able to see if they had returned their PPG weapons to their holsters. But they couldn't very well lift her, if they didn't. She heard their footsteps coming very close now, and it was time for her to give the prearranged signal.

She moaned loudly.

That drew their attention, and neither one of them heard Deuce as he rose up, covered with sand, and drilled the nearest Psi Cop in the arm with his PPG. The cop collapsed to his knees in shock, and the other one started to draw his weapon.

"Go ahead." Deuce grinned. "I promised the lady I wouldn't kill you, but I'm not great at keeping my promises."

Talia scrambled to her feet and grabbed the PPG out of the wounded Psi Cop's holster. Then she very carefully took the PPG from the other cop.

"You won't get away," said the black-suited telepath. "We'll bring you down."

Talia said nothing. She was busy gathering up the water bag and Deuce's briefcase and duffel bag from the fallen Hovercraft. As an afterthought, she left them the water bag.

"Oh, please let me kill them," begged Deuce. "Who would miss them? Even their mommas probably don't like them anymore."

Talia shot him a glare, and Deuce frowned disgruntledly and began to back toward the shuttlecraft. "Well," he said, "we are offering you gentlemen a great deal today—that perfectly good Hovercraft for this beat-up old shuttlecraft of yours. Now you just go northeast, and you'll get to civilization. I wouldn't go the other way, because we stole that Hovercraft from some folks, and they might shoot first and ask questions later."

Talia jumped into the shuttlecraft and kept her hand on the button to shut the hatch after Deuce.

"You got my briefcase?" asked the gangster.

"Yeah."

He nodded and jumped aboard. Talia quickly closed the hatch, and they scrambled into seats in the cockpit.

"Do you know how to fly one of these?" asked Talia.

Deuce laughed. "You think I never stole a shuttlecraft before? This is a hobby of mine."

Before she even had a chance to fasten her seat belt, he jammed the thrusters, and the little craft started to buck and shake. It wasn't a smooth takeoff, but they were soon in the air, with the dusty desert fading away beneath them.

Talia sighed and slumped back in her seat.

"Don't panic," said Deuce, "but you, uh, got a scorpion in your hair."

Talia panicked anyway—she screamed, yanked the wig off, and threw it on the floor. The startled scorpion tried to hide, but it was out of its element on the cold metal deck of the shuttlecraft. She took her shoe off to throw it at the arachnid.

"Don't kill him," said Deuce. "I'll take him with me to Guadalajara."

"Guadalajara," echoed Talia. "I need to go to Boston."

"Then I guess this is where you and I part company." To emphasize his determination, Deuce drew his PPG and aimed it at her.

"Can you let me off somewhere? A town, I mean."

"I'd have to let you off on the outskirts. You might have quite a walk."

Talia shrugged, too worn out to question whatever fate had in store for her next. "I haven't got any money," she added.

"Damnation," muttered Deuce, "what do I look like, a credit machine? This whole trip was only supposed to cost me *one* diamond, and now it's already cost me—"

"Four diamonds," she completed his sentence. "But you got a shuttlecraft out of it, and you wouldn't have gotten that without me."

"Yeah," Deuce conceded, putting his weapon away. "I guess you paid your debt. Hand me my case."

She handed him his briefcase, and he put the craft on autopilot as he rummaged through it.

"Here's a one-carat diamond," he said. "That should get you wherever you want to go. You know, you really should've let me kill those Psi Cops. As soon as they get to a link, everybody on Earth will know you're here."

"I know," said Talia somberly. She took the diamond from him and tried to smile. "Thank you."

"You're a tough one," said Deuce admiringly. "If we ever run into each other again—say, at my hanging—will you tell them I'm not totally bad? That I once did a favor for somebody, and let two Psi Cops live."

Talia gave him a real smile. "I will. I once heard somebody on B5 say that nobody is what they seem. I never knew what that meant before, but now I know—we have lots of people inside of us. Good, bad, right, wrong, it all gets blurred together. I'll never forget that you helped me, Deuce."

He smiled boyishly, and for a moment she could see the little kid who had put a firecracker in a teacher's wastebasket. Was that the moment he had gone bad? If it hadn't been for that incident, or if it hadn't been for the bombing, might they both be upstanding citizens now instead of fugitives on the run? She didn't know. She would never know.

"Phoenix coming up," said Deuce.

It was almost dark by the time Deuce landed the black shuttlecraft behind a grain elevator on the outskirts of the sprawling city.

"No time for long good-byes," he said, opening the hatch. "This is busy airspace around here."

Talia straightened her wig and her beret and made sure she had her only two possessions, the diamond and Emily Crane's address. She had thought about taking one of the extra PPGs, but shooting it out with the authorities was not really her style.

She paused in the doorway. "Bye."

"Good luck," drawled Deuce. "You'll need it."

Talia jumped out of the craft and ran for cover as he shot

the thrusters. A second later, the shuttlecraft and Deuce were gone, and she was alone again, surrounded by darkness and crickets. It felt soothing, like the darkness was a natural place for her these days. She saw the arcing lights of the city in the distance, and she found her way to an overgrown road and began walking.

Michael Garibaldi stood alone on the bridge, looking at the lights of Boston Harbor as they glinted off the black water. He had rushed back to Boston, for what? His efforts to find Emily Crane's home address had gone for naught, and he had no friends in the local police department to help him. The last thing he wanted to do was to try to explain all of this to a local cop—commercial telepaths pretending to be Martian terrorists in order to blow up Psi Cops on a space station several light-years away. You had to be there. Plus, they would keep him tied up in the squad room for days, making statements, checking statements.

With Malten having already skipped to Mars, Emily Crane was the only lead he had. Despite Gray's opinion that she wouldn't skip, he didn't trust her. As long as Talia was at large, they couldn't move against Crane, but she wasn't in the clear. If Talia showed up, protected and talking to the right people, Crane was in serious trouble. If only he could corner her at home, he reasoned, maybe he could throw enough fear into her to get *her* to confess to the police. But how could he get her unlisted address?

He snapped his fingers just as a barge announced its approach through the black waters with a woeful moan. Maybe he should go see the receptionist at the Mix office—what was his name? It had been right there on his nameplate: Ronald Trishman! A receptionist, even a sour one like him, was likely to have a listed address. Garibaldi dashed to the end of the bridge and into a bar along the waterfront.

The smell of booze was inviting—it always was—and the sight of all the lowlifes made him feel right at home, but Garibaldi had chosen another poison tonight. He went to the viewer and waited for a large guy with tattoos all over his arms to finish talking to his kids somewhere in Australia, then he grabbed the link before anybody else could. He punched up the information index and entered Ronald Trishman's name.

There were two Ronald Trishmans, but that wasn't bad for a city the size of Boston. The security officer jotted them both down in his electronic address book. It wasn't all that late, about 22:00, so he decided to pay these two Ronald Trishmans a call. One of them was bound to know where Emily Crane lived.

He knew the first one was wrong as soon as he got off the autotaxi. The place, called Flag Hill, was far too ritzy, a collection of townhouses built to look old but really quite elegant, with bay windows and a neo-colonial look. Well, he thought, maybe Ronald slummed by working as a receptionist.

He buzzed the outer door, and a sleepy woman's voice answered his call. "Yes?"

"Excuse me," said Garibaldi, "I need to speak to Ronald for a moment."

"He's taking a bath. What is it? Who are you?"

"I work with him at the Mix."

"Mix?" she asked. "He's a doctor." She rang off.

When Garibaldi got back to the street, he saw that his autotaxi had taken off. Well, he supposed, maybe he hadn't tipped it enough. He looked around the maze of dark streets and townhouses, all of it coated with a halo of city lights. After the sweltering closeness of Babylon 5, Boston seemed like an immense wilderness park, far too large to make sense out of and filled with exotic humans. He wondered what that said about his life—that Londo, G'Kar, and their alien brethren seemed normal compared to this mass of humanity.

The security chief had a pretty good sense of direction, and it was a pleasant night, so he decided to walk. He knew the second Ronald Trishman lived up some street named Beacon, and he wasn't far away from there. He would ask directions as he went. Within about three blocks, the oak trees thinned out to a standard urban sprawl of office buildings and shops, and he wasn't the only pedestrian anymore. The others looked better dressed, more affluent, and he felt like a soldier home from leave in his uniform. As he drew closer to a casino, his attention was snagged by a row of screens in the window.

Once again, there was Talia Winters's face. It was a good face for the screen—angular and confident, with lovely eyes —he could see why they liked to show it so much. This time they did a computer animation on Talia's face to turn her sleek blond hair into long, brown, curly locks. He couldn't hear the audio, so he ducked inside to see what the report was about.

"Based on the officers' description," said the newscaster, "Talia Winters was traveling with a man and wearing a dark hairstyle, probably a wig. She was last seen in Arizona, although she could be many kilometers from there by now. She and her companion are believed to have a shuttlecraft."

Traveling with a man, thought Garibaldi. She had found a protector. *That should be me,* he thought. Well, he was doing the best he could, building a case against the real bad guys. But he felt guilty about not doing more to find her. All he could think of doing was to stake out Emily Crane's office, believing she would find her way there, eventually. But what if she was just running and not trying to find Emily Crane?

At any rate, it was definite that she was on Earth, as he had figured. She would be lucky to escape from the planet before the Psi Cops got her. He wasn't going to count on her being able to testify on her own behalf, so the pressure was on him to find the real culprits. He wasn't telepathic, but he tried to send her a message:

Keep running, Talia.

"I have a diamond," said the tall woman with the curly brown hair.

She batted her eyelashes at the pawnbroker, hoping he didn't notice how filthy she was. Then she nearly swallowed her tongue as she caught sight of herself on the viewer behind him. It was her public relations photograph, taken last year for the brochures—only in this photo she was wearing the wig she was actually wearing! She gripped her beret tighter and looked down, waiting for the pawnbroker to yell for the cops.

"Yes?" he asked. "A diamond?"

He had been talking to another customer when she entered, Talia recalled, so he probably hadn't seen the newscast. She sighed and took the cut diamond out of her jacket pocket. With a hopeful smile, she handed it to him, and he placed it on the velvet pad.

"One carat," she said. "Gem quality."

"I'll be the judge of that," answered the pawnbroker, reaching for his scanner. He passed the diamond under the light beam for a few seconds, glanced at the readouts, and nodded. "Yes, it's top quality. Nothing like that left on Earth. Where did it come from?"

"Do you want it, or not?"

"Eight hundred credits."

She tried to stay calm. "I want to sell it, not a loan."

"Same price either way."

"I think it's worth more than that," Talia said slowly.

"Then go somewhere else."

She took the jewel off the velvet, but he called out to her before she could put it in her pocket. "Eight-fifty, no more."

She looked at him and thought how weary and dirty she was. At least with some money she could get a bath. This was robbery, anyway, but at least she would die or be captured with some money in her pocket.

"Yeah," she said, "eight-fifty."

"All right," said the man, "if you'll hand me your creditchit, I'll add it to your account."

She shook her head and looked down. "I don't have any credits. That's why I need to sell the diamond."

"All right," said the man, eager to conclude the deal any way he could, "give me your identicard, and I'll make you a creditchit. That's one of our services. It adds only one percent."

Another rip-off, she thought, but beggars can't be

choosers. At least she had an identicard. She handed it to the man, and he disappeared with both the card and the diamond.

She looked around the pawnshop, and she couldn't remember whether she had ever been inside a pawnshop before in her life. She imagined they hadn't changed in hundreds of years, with an odd assortment of jewelry, collectibles, small electronics, musical instruments, anything that was easy to carry and might be worth a few credits. There were also four teller windows for the various financial services that the shop offered.

"Here you go, Ms. Nelson," he said, returning her identicard and a new creditchit. "Thank you for coming in." She finally let out a breath and glanced at the two cards. It seemed for a moment almost that she was a real person again, even if she did have someone else's identity.

"Thank you," she said. "If I wanted a bullet train or shuttle to the east coast, where would I find it?"

"There's a U-rail at the corner that will take you to the bullet station. The trains leave frequently, so that would be the quickest way."

"Thank you," she said, feeling a bit woozy but straggling out the door. If it had been possible, she would've stretched out on the sidewalk and gone to sleep. *No,* she told herself, *you're a shark. Gotta keep moving. Keep moving.*

This was more like it, thought Garibaldi, surveying the nondescript skyscraper. It was the kind of silver monstrosity that housed a thousand families at once, and it already felt more comfortable to him than all that open space. The gate had a security lock, but so many people went in and out that anyone could time his approach to slip in with other tenants. Garibaldi did exactly that and slipped in with a family of Sikhs wearing turbans and white robes.

"Home on leave?" asked the patriarch of the group.

"Yes," said Garibaldi, "going to see my dad, Ronald Trishman. Do you know him?"

The family shook their heads in unison and headed for the escalator. Garibaldi checked his address keeper as if he were looking for the apartment number, but he hit the index screen as soon as they were out of sight. He found Ronald's apartment number on the forty-sixth floor, west wing, and he took a combination of escalators and high-speed elevators to get there.

It was getting late, he reminded himself. This was a planet, and they didn't live on a twenty-four-hour clock like he was used to, with no particular day or night. He had better not sound threatening when he asked for Ronald, or he might end up talking to regular cops after all.

He stopped in front of the correct door, found Trishman's name under the doorbell, and buzzed. A small viewer built into the door beeped on, and he could hear sounds of the apartment's built-in security coming alive. He buzzed again, figuring armed guards would be summoned if Ronald Trishman didn't answer the door soon.

Finally a puzzled face squinted at him from the view-screen. "Who the hell is it?"

He lowered his head apologetically. "I'm extremely sorry to bother you. I'm Michael Garibaldi, security chief of Babylon 5. We spoke today."

"Well, good God, what do you want at this hour?"

"We're extremely worried that Emily Crane may be in physical danger."

"What?" muttered the older man. "Why would you come here? Oh, what the hell, I'll let you in. I'll wake up all the neighbors if I don't."

He heard clicking sounds, and the door slid open. Garibaldi smiled to himself as he ducked inside. Trishman was wearing an expensive bathrobe and slippers; all he lacked was a pipe.

"Listen," said the receptionist, bustling around nervously, "if we're going to talk, I'm going to make some tea. Do you want some?"

"No, thanks," said Garibaldi, "you go ahead. I never liked tea much."

He heard Ronald knocking about in the kitchen, making a terrific amount of noise. The old man must've been nervous, thought Garibaldi, and he wondered if he knew something about the Mix's big ambitions. He took a seat on the sofa, marveling at the size of the living room, which was decorated tastefully all in white.

After living on Babylon 5 for a year, rooms in even the dinkiest apartments looked huge. This room even had a tinted picture window that gazed upon a small window of ocean between two similar apartment towers. It wasn't a thrilling view, thought Garibaldi, but it was better than a bulkhead.

After a few minutes, Ronald Trishman came back with a tray, a teapot, and two cups, as if he was still hopeful Garibaldi would try some tea.

"I made enough for four people," he said, "so you're welcome if you want some." Trishman leaned forward and asked in a gossipy way, "Now, what is this about Ms. Crane?"

"We just want to make sure she's safe, but we can't find her."

"Isn't she at home?" asked Trishman.

While Garibaldi was trying to decide how to finesse that question, Trishman clicked his fingers and added, "No, of course she wouldn't be at home. She's on her way to Mars, or maybe she's there by now."

"Mars," repeated Garibaldi without much surprise. That figured. "Are you sure?"

The older man shrugged and said, "That's my job. A receptionist knows who's in town and who isn't."

Okay, thought Garibaldi, he had gotten what he had come for. Now if he got anything else it would be gravy. "Do you know anything about a bill before the Senate that would place the Mix in charge of Psi Corps?"

The old man's eyes twinkled. "No. Do tell?"

Garibaldi started to say more, but then he realized that his job was to ask the questions, not answer them. Let this guy pontificate. "Is Mr. Malten around your office a lot?"

Trishman shook his head. "Not an exceptional amount.

Perhaps half a dozen times a year. Surely you can't suspect *him* of doing anything wrong.''

"Well," said Garibaldi, "putting a bill before the Senate isn't doing anything wrong. I suppose changing Psi Corps wouldn't be all that wrong either.''

"Then you're with us," said Trishman with satisfaction.

"Wait a minute," said the security chief. "We're not talking about a political debate—we're talking about two fatal bombings! If you know anything about this, I expect you to tell me.''

"I think you know about as much as I do," said the old man, rising and taking his cup to the kitchen. "Do you want to spend the night?''

"What?" asked Garibaldi.

"It's the middle of the night, Mr. Garibaldi. This is not the time to go running around knocking on doors. Don't they have night where you come from?''

"Is that a rhetorical question?" asked the security chief. He yawned and decided that he was getting tired. He had to meet Gray in the morning, in all likelihood to fly to Mars. No, he didn't have a hotel room; it just hadn't occurred to him to get one. On the other hand, could he trust this guy?

"I don't think so," he said, rising to his feet. "So are you in favor of the Mix taking over Psi Corps?''

"Instead of the other way around, like it is now?" asked Trishman. "Who wouldn't be? That doesn't mean I know anything about how this takeover is going to happen. I don't.''

"Well, that's a relief," said Garibaldi. "Do you know where Ms. Crane is staying on Mars?''

Trishman smiled. "I'm afraid not. You're welcome to that couch, or not. But I'm going back to bed.''

Garibaldi felt as if he had been dismissed, so he moved to the door and pressed the panel to open it. As he strode out, he was looking over his shoulder to say good night, when strong hands gripped his arms and shoulders. They dragged him back into the room.

He struggled, but there were three of them. They took him

by surprise and squirted some stuff in his face that made him
swoon. Garibaldi staggered backward, losing his senses, but
he managed a lucky swing that caught one of them in the
stomach and doubled him over. The other two were still in
his face, and one of them squirted him again with the seda-
tive. Garibaldi windmilled his fists in the air, but he wasn't
connecting.

He was slipping, falling, going where no one could reach
him.

CHAPTER 18

THE lure of the bullet station and immediate passage to Boston was strong, but the lure of a bed and a shower was stronger. When Talia passed a homey, old-fashioned hotel before she reached the station, she couldn't stop herself from going in and pressing the buzzer on the check-in counter. It was the middle of the night, but she hoped she would still be able to get a room.

A kindly older lady finally appeared. "What can we do for you, miss?"

"A single," she said. "Do you have one?"

"Yes, my dear, only sixty credits for a single. Interested?"

Talia found herself nodding before she even thought about it.

"Fine. I'll need your creditchit and your identicard."

Talia passed them over, thinking that was the second time she had used the fake identicard. She only had two more times. But she was so dirty and weary that she would risk facing a million Psi Cops to be clean and rested. Tomorrow would be time enough to get to Boston, she told herself, time enough to confront Emily Crane, clear her name, and get her life back.

She dragged herself to the room and ripped off the dirty clothes and the wig. Talia felt like throwing the entire outfit away, but she doubted if she would get very far naked. In the shower, she let the lukewarm water run over her hair and body, and she watched a river of sand snake from her feet to the drain. She was too weary to even adjust the water to make it warmer, although she had the strength to rub some shampoo in her hair.

When she staggered out of the shower, she collapsed into the droopy bed with beads of water still clinging to her back. She fell immediately into a sleep that was so deep it was beyond dreams.

* * *

Garibaldi, however, was having a dream. A nightmare, to be exact. In this dream, people were tying his hands behind his back, tying his feet together, and stuffing a gag in his mouth. He wanted to wake up, but he couldn't open his eyes. It wasn't until he began to squirm against his bindings that the dream turned really ugly. Someone slapped him across the mouth, knocking him to the floor, and his eyes bugged open. Unfortunately, the dream didn't end—he was still bound and gagged.

He was also still in Trishman's white living room, only the older man was not in sight. Instead, there were two brawny young men, well dressed in suits. One of them was standing over Garibaldi, glowering at him. Ah, yes, he thought, that was the guy he had punched in the stomach. Well, why was he upset? He wasn't the one bound and gagged, lying on the floor with a drugged-out hangover.

The man looked like he wanted to slap him again, when a woman's voice intruded. "Don't even think about it."

Garibaldi craned his neck as best he could to see who had entered from the bedroom. Lo and behold, it was Emily Crane! Only she wasn't dressed in her usual frumpy outfit but in a sleek gray jumpsuit, with her hair pulled back severely. He tried to ask her how her trip to Mars had been, but everything he said came out a mumble.

"Get him back on the couch," ordered the woman. The two goons complied and lifted him back into a semicomfortable position.

"Mr. Garibaldi," she said, "if you promise not to cry out, I will remove the gag."

He nodded. Crying out wasn't really his style, but he was looking forward to kicking the crap out of these guys at the first opportunity. She snapped her fingers, and the gag came off.

"That was a quick trip to Mars," he croaked.

"Don't blame Ronald for lying," she said, sitting beside him on the couch. "Or for calling us. We only have another twenty-four hours before we can put our plan into effect, and then we stage a bloodless coup of Psi Corps. Don't you want that—to get rid of Bester and his ilk?''

"Sister, right now, your ilk doesn't seem much better." One of the goons moved forward with his fists balled, and Garibaldi winced, awaiting the blow.

But Emily Crane waved the man off and looked back at Garibaldi. "Do you see why we have to keep you quiet for twenty-four hours, until the bill is passed and signed? Your detective work was quite good, but we can't let years of planning go down the drain to save one telepath."

She smiled pleasantly. "I'm hopeful you'll come around to our way of thinking. In twenty-four hours, after you see all that we've accomplished, you might want to forget about your investigation. The public is happy with Martian terrorists as the bombers—why can't you be?"

Garibaldi wasn't going to argue with the lady, because the alternative to agreeing with them was probably winding up as fish food in the harbor. "What are you going to do with me?" he asked.

Emily Crane got up, strode to the picture window, and looked out at the sleeping city. "Maybe we should move Mr. Garibaldi while it's still dark outside. If something happened to him here, it would reflect badly on Trishman. Gag him, untie his feet, and keep a PPG in his back."

The thugs untied the rope around Garibaldi's ankles and hauled him to his feet. They shoved the foul-tasting rag back into his mouth, but he was willing to give up his voice in exchange for having his legs free. His hands were still tied behind his back, but he could kick, he could run! He saw one of the goons pull a PPG out of his jacket pocket, and he felt the metal in his back. Maybe he wouldn't kick or run right now, thought Garibaldi.

Emily Crane opened the door and checked the corridor to make sure it was clear, then she motioned for them to follow her. Garibaldi stumbled out, sandwiched between the two thugs, one of whom had a PPG in his back. The only reason they were letting him walk, he decided, was to keep from having to carry his dead body. Nevertheless, he couldn't think of any way to get away from them, and he behaved himself all the way down the elevator and the escalator.

In the street, he told himself, maybe someone would see this obvious kidnapping and call the cops. But there was no one in the street in these dead hours just before dawn, nothing but a silent row of electric-powered vehicles. If he ran, thought Garibaldi, he was trying to decide how many meters he would get before the guy with the PPG drilled him. He figured three.

Suddenly, a strange voice seemed to speak in his head. It told him to duck! Garibaldi had nothing to lose, so he pretended to trip. He stumbled to the pavement a split second before a PPG blast ripped the head off the man behind him. The other goon was drawing his weapon when three blasts from entirely different directions turned his midsection a fiery orange. The two pieces of him fell to the ground.

Emily Crane ran for it, and her short height let her elude the first shots directed at her. Then two black-suited Psi Cops jumped out of the bushes directly in front of her. As she stumbled away from them, begging forgiveness, they executed her.

Strong arms picked Garibaldi off the pavement and guided him to a black shuttlecraft that awaited them in an adjacent parking lot. They tossed him in like a bag of potatoes, the hatch slammed shut, and the thrusters blasted the craft off the ground and into the black night.

"Hold still," said a familiar voice, and Garibaldi felt hands untying the ropes at his back. Once his hands were free, he ripped off the gag and rolled over to greet his saviors.

The first thing he saw was the relieved and smiling face of Harriman Gray. Behind him, swathed in bandages and holding a cane, sat Mr. Bester. The only other person in the shuttlecraft was the pilot, and she was concentrating on getting them through the skyscrapers of Boston.

"It would be polite to say 'thank you,' " suggested Bester.

"Yes, thank you," croaked Garibaldi. "You . . . you wasted them. Damn it, Emily Crane was the only one who could clear Talia Winters!"

"Rogue telepaths," said Bester. "All perfectly legal, although I doubt if we'll claim credit. Actually, you owe your life to Mr. Gray here. He got worried about you last night and contacted my office. When I spoke with him, he told me all about Emily Crane and the Mix. We just managed to get a tail on her before she came over here with her friends. We've been hoping you would come out soon."

Garibaldi touched his partner's arm. "Thanks, Gray."

The young telepath looked a bit sheepish. "I wasn't planning to tell Mr. Bester last night, but I got worried about you."

The security chief looked out the cockpit window at the vanishing lights of the city. "Did you warn me to duck?" he asked.

Gray nodded, and Garibaldi cleared his throat, thinking about what would have happened to him if he hadn't ducked. He lifted his hand, and it was still shaking.

"We'll leave the bodies there," said Bester contentedly. "I always say, if you can't talk to the person you want, leave a message."

Garibaldi rubbed his dry lips and looked back out the window. He shouldn't be an ingrate, because they had probably saved his life, but he felt rotten about the cold-blooded executions. That could be Talia lying down there in the street, he reminded himself.

"The person you want is Malten," he said hoarsely.

"It certainly is," agreed Bester. "I want to thank you two, you've done a wonderful job on this case. Beyond my expectations. You led us right to the rattlers' nest."

Garibaldi remained single-minded. "Then you'll let Talia Winters go now, right?"

Mr. Bester frowned. "That is a concern. To let her go would be to admit we made a mistake, and we don't like to air our dirty linen in public. Plus, we want to keep the Mix healthy and in place, with a few more controls and minus Malten. The Free Phobos group will never be heard from again, so what is the harm in letting them keep the blame?"

"Talia Winters!" barked Garibaldi. "Read my lips. She's not guilty, and you know it."

Bester swallowed and looked past him. "I've arranged for your passage back to Babylon 5, and Mr. Gray's passage to Berlin. There will be commendations for both of you in my report."

"Mr. Bester!" snapped Gray. "That is patently unfair! You know very well she is innocent."

The Psi Cop shook his head in amazement. "Don't you know how many agencies are after her now? I couldn't call them off even if I wanted to! If she turns herself in—to the right people—she might stand a chance."

"Then I'm going to keep after her," vowed Garibaldi.

"It is no longer your concern!" Bester seethed. He winced in pain as he shifted in his seat.

"Not true," said Garibaldi. "I'm bringing back a fugitive who escaped from Babylon 5. I can do that all day long. Put this shuttle down! I'm getting off."

"Me too," said Gray, jutting his chin.

"All right," snapped Bester. "Put them down."

"Is Miami okay?" asked the pilot. "That's the closest big city without backtracking."

"Fine," responded both Garibaldi and Gray. The security chief gave his partner a nod and glanced out the cockpit window. He saw that they were in space, in reentry, and half the globe was shimmering in the sunlight of a new day.

"One more thing," said Bester through clenched teeth.

"Yeah?"

"Stay away from Mars."

Garibaldi chuckled and looked at the Psi Cop. "You're talking about my old stomping grounds. Is that where Malten really is? On Mars. Why don't you get him?"

"We know he's on Mars, but we don't know where. If you find out where he is, call us. Let us handle him."

"Sure," said Garibaldi, "and if you find Talia, call me. Let me handle her."

They felt the thrusters of the shuttlecraft kick on, and the noise level increased. They strapped themselves into seats and braced for the descent into Miami.

Talia lay in the swaybacked bed, just watching the sun stream through the dirty lace curtains of the old hotel. It was not the kind of place she would have stayed a week earlier, but it felt so warm and friendly that she never wanted to leave. She knew she had to get up, keep moving, but her body told her to rest. It creaked with protest when she forced it out of the bed.

She strolled past the viewer and wondered if she should put the news on. She couldn't bear to see herself in that wig again, either in a computer mock-up or in real life, so she had decided to trim her regular hair a bit and stuff it all into the beret. Even though she dreaded seeing her face on the screen again, she couldn't resist the masochistic impulse to turn on the viewer. She dialed the news, hoping against hope that something good might have happened while she slept.

Thankfully, she caught the tail end of the report on her, which summed up that she was still at large. This came as some relief, she thought ruefully, just in case the hotel room was really an ingenious prison. At large, thought Talia. What a strange phrase—it sounded as if she were everywhere and nowhere at once, which was sort of true.

She was about to turn the viewer off when she heard the announcer mention a name, Emily Crane. Talia jumped back as if she had been shocked, and she stared at the image on the screen. It *was* Emily Crane, the one who had turned her into a hunted fugitive. Only she was dead, and her PR photo was replaced by a more grisly shot of a limp body on a sidewalk. Talia concentrated on the announcer's words:

"There are no suspects, and police are asking that anyone with information on the murder of Emily Crane, Michael Graham, and Barry Strump please come forward. Once again, three commercial telepaths from the Mix were brutally murdered about five o'clock this morning. There was no apparent robbery or motive. In sports, we have a new champion in field hockey . . ."

Talia punched it off and slumped back into the bed. Now, what the hell was she going to do? The one person who might be able to clear her was dead! She felt like curling up in the droopy bed and just staying there until her money ran out, or the Psi Cops found her, whichever came first.

After a moment, Talia sat up and wiped her eyes. She stared at the morning light as it streamed through the window, knowing what she had to do. She had to run for real. No more running *to* somewhere, just running away *from* everything. The one person who might have cleared her was dead, and she would never get a break.

Where could she go? In all the exotic places she thought about, such as Minbar, she would stick out and be easily recognizable. Earth was just too risky, and she couldn't get near where she really wanted to go—her childhood haunts. She needed someplace that was chaotic, with a thriving underground, because she was firmly a part of that social strata now. She could think of only one such place.

Mars.

Uncle Ted had been part of her undoing, so maybe he could help her now. Plus, Mars would be cheap to get to. She hurriedly put on her clothes and stuffed her hair under her beret. A glance in the mirror warned her that she looked too much like herself, and she resolved to do something about that later. First, she had to figure out a way to let Uncle Ted know she was coming.

She ran her chit through the viewer slot and punched in her mother's address. Then she entered her E-mail: "Hobo, Uhkhead."

It might be a message Ambassador Kosh would appreciate, she thought with a grim smile. Talia was sure her mother would get it, because "Hobo, Uhkhead" was her baby-talk way of saying "Hello, Uncle Ted." She had seen herself say it often enough in old home visuals. She wanted to say a lot more to her mother—like "Mom, I'm innocent!"—but that would have given away the sender. She hoped the cryptic message would look like garbled junk to whoever was reading her mom's mail.

Before she left the hotel, Talia took the card with Emily Crane's address on it and ripped it up.

"Now boarding shuttle 1312 for Clarke Spaceport," announced the computer. Gray and Garibaldi were already in line for the trip to the orbital spacedock, from where they would grab a flight to Mars.

Garibaldi glanced around the Miami Interstellar Port, marveling at the odd choice of colors. He had never seen a transportation center painted all in turquoise before. Ah, well, maybe they had gotten a deal on the paint. At any rate, the pastel color softened the hard look of many of the passengers in line with them.

He turned to Gray and said, "You know, you don't really have to come with me. You could just wipe your hands of this and go enjoy your place in Berlin for a few days."

"No," said the telepath, "we're a team. I was glad to have been of assistance this morning, when you needed it."

"There's something I didn't tell Bester," remarked Garibaldi, lowering his voice. "Emily Crane said that the plan would be put into effect within twenty-four hours. So if Bester doesn't find Malten by tonight, by tomorrow Malten may be his boss."

They shuffled ahead a few more steps in the line, and Gray replied, "That would be fittingly ironic, but I think Mr. Bester will be at the Senate today, twisting arms. His problem is how to bring down Malten without bringing down the entire Mix."

The two men strolled down the rampway and onto the shuttlecraft. It was a medium-sized craft and seated about forty people. Gray stopped midway down the aisle and pointed at two empty seats, then he remembered and shook his head.

"The rear, right?"

Garibaldi nodded, and they found seats once again in the next-to-last row. "You can see everybody from the back," he remarked.

"What makes you think that Ms. Winters will go to Mars?" asked Gray.

The chief shrugged and looked out the port window. "I don't know. It's close by, and that's where *I* would go if I were running. She needs to find an underground organization to hide her, and there are plenty of them on Mars. It's a good haystack, if you're a needle."

"She might be very useful to the Martian separatists," said Gray. "She's a telepath with a full knowledge of Psi Corps, plus she has her experience with aliens. I often wonder, what would we do if the Mars separatists allied themselves with an alien power?"

"Let's not think about it, okay?" asked Garibaldi. "Mars is a mess. We ignored it for too long, and now we don't know what to do with it. You wonder why the hell the alliance tries so hard to hang on to it."

"Yes, don't you," Gray remarked dryly.

In the gift store at Sky Harbor Travel Center, Talia bought an expensive print scarf, which she tied around her beret. Now it looked less as if she were tying to hide her hair color, she hoped. She bought some sunglasses, which were tinted lightly enough to wear indoors, and she glanced in the mirror at Frieda Nelson, the eccentric artist from Oregon. The real Frieda was probably a straight-laced professional, and she hoped that she wasn't destroying the woman's reputation.

"Announcing the departure of shuttle 512 to the Clarke Spaceport," droned the computer voice.

She glanced at her ticket—yes, that was her. She was booked all the way to Central Mars, and she wondered how often she would have to show her identicard. There would probably be a check-in when she reached the Clarke Spaceport, because space stations wanted to make sure that people were coming and going, not sticking around. Then she would have to show the card again when she disembarked at Mars. That would make four uses, right at the limit.

Talia tightened the scarf under her neck and headed for her gate. She walked briskly, to make it look as if she were a busy person, not a fugitive skulking about. She had become a bit more optimistic as she realized that there were other people who could clear her name. Deuce, for one; and surely Emily Crane had other accomplices. Some of them might be on Mars, and she would keep her eyes and ears open.

She darted importantly between two police officers, daring them to look at her. They did, but despite her thumping heart, they didn't rush after her. If she could make this last jump to Mars, and not get nabbed, maybe she could catch her breath. Unfortunately, she had begun to figure out who had killed Emily Crane. That was one way the Psi Cops handled rogues—to slaughter them in the street. Talia shuddered, but she shook off the panic attack and marched down the ramp to her shuttlecraft.

CHAPTER 19

"IDENTICARD, please?"

Talia took a breath and handed the card over to the security guard at the gate. If she got caught up here in the Clarke Spaceport, there wasn't anywhere for her to run. She adjusted her sunglasses as she waited for him to slide the card through his scanner.

"Thank you, Ms. Nelson," he replied, handing the card back to her. "Will you be staying long?"

"I'm catching a flight to Mars right away," she answered.

"Thank you," he repeated like a parrot. "Have a pleasant stay."

Talia moved past him, walking like a zombie with no particular sense of where she was going in the sprawling spaceport. She saw a bank of screens running news highlights, and she made a beeline in the opposite direction. She never wanted to see herself in the news again—from now on she would lead a life of quiet obscurity. She figured she had about fifty credits left on her creditchit, and food was the most logical thing to blow it on. If the Psi Cops brought her down, at least she would die with a full stomach.

She entered the restaurant as Gray and Garibaldi walked by. They didn't see each other.

"She may be traveling with a man," said Garibaldi. "At least, that's the report I saw."

"Then maybe she's run in a completely different direction," replied Gray. "After all, Mars is a stronghold for the Psi Cops. If I were running, I would certainly *not* go to Mars."

Garibaldi smiled. "I'll remember that if I'm ever chasing you." He looked back at the restaurant they had just passed. "You want something to eat?"

"No, thank you," answered Gray with a sour expression. "My stomach has been acting up. Too much excitement, too

many quick takeoffs and landings. You go ahead. I'd just like
to sit down until they announce our flight."

Garibaldi turned to go, and then something caught his eye.
He gripped Gray's arm and pointed. "What are they doing?"

About thirty meters away, a team of four black-uniformed
Psi Cops had stopped a young blond woman and were checking her identicard. She was protesting, but it didn't do her
much good.

"Spot-checking," said Gray. "They're still looking for
her."

Through clenched teeth, Garibaldi muttered, "Even
though they know she's innocent."

"Those four men don't know she's innocent. Only Bester
knows, and it's useful to him to blame Ms. Winters. If we
could find Malten, maybe we could get him to testify on her
behalf."

"If he's still alive," added Garibaldi.

The Psi Cops bowed and offered apologies to the woman,
who scurried to get away from them as quickly as possible.
They strode down the corridor, four abreast, scrutinizing every woman they passed.

"I just lost my appetite," growled Garibaldi. "Let's go
find the gate and be the first ones on for a change."

At the counter in the restaurant, Talia had just started to
eat her tuna fish sandwich when she saw the four black-
suited Psi Cops stop in the doorway. They entered and confronted a young woman seated close to the door. Talia
quickly lowered her head and wrapped the sandwich in her
napkin. When they headed her way, she bolted for the rest
room, hoping nobody would notice her quick departure. Fortunately, it was the kind of place where people often had to
run and eat at the same time. At least, that's what she told
herself as she burst through the swinging door into the
women's rest room.

Talia took refuge in one of the stalls and sat on the toilet
lid. Glumly, she unwrapped her squashed sandwich and tried
to eat it. But she only got through a few bites before she
dissolved into tears. Was this the life she had to face? Run-

ning from the sight of a uniform, eating in a bathroom stall?
She was so pathetic. Maybe she should just march up to the
Psi Cops and turn herself in. They could only kill her once,
but this way she was dying every minute.

The telepath hadn't realized how loudly she was sobbing
until she heard a knock on the door. "Are you all right?"
asked a kindly voice.

She grabbed some toilet paper and dabbed it at her eyes.
"Yes, yes," she lied. "I'm all right."

"Can I help you?"

This was ridiculous, talking through the door of a bathroom stall. "Just a second," she said. Talia stood up and
tossed the remains of her sandwich into the toilet, which she
loudly flushed.

When she emerged, she saw a kindly old lady, smiling
sweetly at her. "What's the problem, dearie?"

As Talia was trying to figure out what to say, she heard a
synthesized voice announce, "Transport *Bradley* to Mars is
now loading at docking bay three. Repeat, transport *Bradley*
to Mars is now loading at docking bay three."

"It's . . . it's my boyfriend!" Talia blurt out. "He beats
me, and I've been trying to run away from him. But everywhere I go, he follows me!"

The old lady frowned. "That sonofabitch. Let's sic the
police on him!"

"No," said Talia, "that will only bog me down in more
legal problems. I've got a ticket for the flight to Mars, and if
I can just get on it, I'll be rid of him for good. I've got family
who will protect me there."

"Is he out there now?" asked the lady, pointing to the
door leading to the restaurant.

"Yes," breathed Talia. "Perhaps if there was a diversion, I
could get past him."

The woman nodded thoughtfully. "You mean, like if a
little old lady ran out there, saying some guy was trying to
flash her?"

"Yes, that would do it," said Talia. "Direct everybody's

attention toward the back of the restaurant, if you can, and I'll run out the front. Thanks so much.''

''Fine,'' said the older lady, fluffing her hair in the mirror. ''I like to act.''

She walked calmly out of the rest room and went to the rear of the restaurant, where she commenced screaming. ''Help! Help! He flashed me! He's naked! He went that way!''

Talia edged out the door and skirted along the wall, as far as possible from the direction the lady was pointing. Even the four Psi Cops stopped their interrogations long enough to see what the fuss was about, and two of them moved to intercept the old lady.

''He doesn't have any pants on!'' she screamed.

No one noticed Talia as she slipped away from the restaurant.

At the gate, there was a long line waiting to board the transport to Mars, and at the end of the line were two different Psi Cops, questioning a young woman and her male companion. Talia nearly bolted in the opposite direction, but her reasoning faculties overruled her panic button. There had to be teams of Psi Cops all over the spacedock, the voice of self-preservation said. Hanging around here was suicide. She fished her ticket out of the pocket of her blue pantsuit and charged to the front of the line.

''Harold, Harold!'' she called, waving her ticket. ''Yoo-hoo! Wait for me!''

She stepped right in front of a middle-age couple waiting to board and stomped her foot. ''Oh, that man? Didn't he get my message?''

''Go ahead,'' said the man, motioning her to go first.

''Thank you,'' she said with a curtsey.

She stepped in front of the gate agent and offered him her ticket.

''I'll need to run your identicard, too,'' said the young man with a sigh.

''Oh,'' she answered, trying to sound nonplussed. ''I didn't think they carded you on this end.''

"Just for today. Extra security precautions. That's why the line's so backed up." He took her card and ran it through. When he handed the card back, he didn't bother to call her Ms. Nelson, but he did wave her through.

Twenty meters away, midway down the line, Harriman Gray clicked his tongue. "Did you see that woman cut in line? Some people have no class."

"Hmm," murmured Garibaldi. He had been watching the two Psi Cops roust all the young, attractive women. Some job they had. He wondered whether either of them had been part of the execution squad that had wasted Emily Crane in the wee hours.

Their patience was eventually rewarded, and Garibaldi and Gray boarded the *Bradley*. This was a big transport with a full complement, as the jump between Earth and Mars was a popular one, and Garibaldi panned the sea of faces as they made their way to the back of the craft. Gray didn't even question the seating rule anymore. For once, they settled in at the very last row, and Garibaldi stretched his long legs in the aisle.

Talia had been studying her identicard for several seconds, wondering if it was still a pass to freedom or a death certificate. She had used it four times, the last unexpectedly, and she would be asked for it again when she disembarked at Mars. She didn't have any other card she could use, and they wouldn't let her off without it—so she was going to use it a fifth time, like it or not. She hadn't planned to spend the entire flight in anguish over her identicard, but that's how it looked.

Then she saw two Psi Cops enter the transport and stop near the front of the cabin. Talia slouched in her seat, glad she had picked a row toward the rear of the craft, about two-thirds of the way back. She was in the last seat, against the bulkhead, and she leaned away from the aisle and put her chin in her hand to hide her face.

But the Psi Cops hadn't come on board searching for her; they were passengers traveling to Mars. They were among the last to find their seats. Great, thought Talia, two Psi Cops sitting a few rows away from her and a bum identicard that she couldn't use anymore. She gnawed on her thumbnail and wondered what else could go wrong.

"It's a full ship," observed Mr. Gray.

"There are still two Psi Cops," muttered Garibaldi. "Damn, they were beginning to get on my nerves back there. Who the hell do they think they are?"

"Psi Cops chasing a rogue telepath," said Gray. "You think we're only hard on you folks, the nontelepaths. We're much harder on ourselves. By running, Ms. Winters brought this on herself, remember that."

"We've got to find her first," vowed Garibaldi, although he realized that if hundreds of Psi Cops and a whole planetful of police couldn't find her, what chance did he have? Maybe her male companion was good; maybe he had gotten her out of it. After all, there was a lot of space out there, and maybe she could find a safe chunk of it. Garibaldi wished her well if she was running for daylight. But he would miss her.

"Please prepare for departure," said a computer voice. "Fasten seat restraints; stow all documents and carry-on items."

A few meters away, Talia relaxed in her chair. It was definite now—if she was going to be arrested, it would be on Mars. Of course, that would just feed the publicity mill that was grinding out stories about her connections to Mars. It couldn't be helped. This nightmare wanted to create its own internal logic, and she had to go with it.

Garibaldi settled back, crossed his arms, and closed his eyes. He told Gray, "Wake me up when we're there."

Halfway through the trip, Garibaldi got jostled awake by the man sitting across the aisle from him, who got up to stretch his legs. Gray was snoring softly to the right of him, and the lights in the cabin had been dimmed by half. Most people were asleep, but a handful were standing, milling about. He was just about to fall back to sleep when he saw the lithe figure of a woman moving about seven rows in front of him.

She was just the type he liked, classy and cultured, and she was wearing a pantsuit that hugged her slim torso. She was wearing a scarf and dark glasses, and he wondered if perhaps she wasn't older than he imagined. Ah, well, even if she was eighty, she still looked pretty good.

You pig, quit staring at her, he told himself. But the woman had almost struggled to the end of her row and was about to hit the aisle, so he thought he would hold on to catch her rear action. Garibaldi wasn't disappointed—it was the finest can he had seen in a long time. In fact, it was reminiscent. He sat up in his seat and stared at the woman's buttocks as she sauntered away from him. Then he gripped Gray's arm.

"Wake up!" he whispered. "Wake up!"

"What is it? What is it?" mumbled Gray.

He bent so close to Gray that it probably looked as if he was kissing him. "She's here on this transport with us," he whispered, "Talia."

"You saw her? You made positive identification?"

"Well," admitted Garibaldi, "all I saw was her rear end, but that's enough."

Gray wrinkled his nose. "Really, Garibaldi, that is disgusting! You see a woman's rear end, and you fantasize that you can identify Ms. Winters from *her* rear end? I hadn't realized you were such close associates."

"Trust me," claimed Garibaldi, "I have been watching that can very closely for the past year, and I know it by heart. But I want you to verify the ID—we'll be able to see her face when she comes back."

"I don't need to stare at her," said Gray with distaste. "All I have to do is scan her."

"No, don't do that. There are two Psi Cops on board, and I don't want to alert them. If she gets a mind-scan, she'll think it's them and she'll freak. The best we can do is let those two guys get off and try to approach her where we have some privacy."

Gray shook his head. "What am I doing? I'm talking as if you could identify a woman from her bottom!"

"Just look at her when she comes back, all right?"

Gray shook his head with disbelief and began to shut his eyes. That didn't last long, because Garibaldi elbowed him in the ribs.

"There she is!" he whispered.

With a look of contempt on his face, Mr. Gray peered around the seat in front of him. Garibaldi was holding the seat card with flight instructions in front of his face, in case she looked his way. The woman in the blue pantsuit stepped briskly back into her row, and she looked up only once. When she did, Garibaldi saw the chiseled features—a little more gaunt than before—and the determined eyes—darting and wary behind the sunglasses. She was a frightened woman, running on the edge, and he fought the temptation to leap out of his seat and wrap his arms around her. Hang in there, Talia, he told her with his thoughts.

She glanced up again, looking puzzled, as she made her way over people's knees to her seat. Finally she collapsed into the seat and molded herself into the shadows along the bulkhead.

"All right," admitted Gray, "that is either her or a very close proximity. And I'll pay more attention to women's rear ends in the future."

"You do that," whispered Garibaldi. "How should we handle this?"

"As you say, if we approach her in this crowded cabin, it might cause a scene. I suppose we have no choice but to wait until we get off the ship, then play it by ear. I suppose, if she's gotten this far, she has a fake identicard."

"Can you tell if there's someone with her?" asked Garibaldi.

"Somebody is sitting next to her. But all the seats are full, so that doesn't mean anything."

The man who was sitting across the aisle from Garibaldi chose that moment to return to his seat. The security chief smiled pleasantly at the passenger, knowing this was the end of his candid conversation with Gray. Besides, there was nothing left to say. They just had to sit tight until they could get Talia alone.

But at least they had found her! She was still in trouble, but she had friends around her.

Talia glanced behind her, thinking what a weird sensation that had been. She had been concentrating so hard on blocking her thoughts as she walked by the two Psi Cops that she had been stunned by a thought coming from the other direction. She hadn't been able to read it, because she had been blocking, but it troubled her to think that someone behind her was also watching her. Thinking about her.

She wanted to stare into the crowd of faces behind her, but she didn't dare. What if they were still watching? Really, was there anybody back there? It was probably just some guy giving her a leer, like Garibaldi always gave her on the lift. She even missed that part of Babylon 5. What was she doing to herself, wondered Talia, letting her paranoia get to her? Hadn't she come this far without a hitch? She would make it all the way. The worst part of running, she decided, was that the paranoia never let up. It only got worse.

Talia tried to sleep, knowing she wouldn't be able to.

Garibaldi sat nervously through the reentry into Mars' thin atmosphere. The transport was capable of docking on the Red Planet, with its fraction of Earth's gravity, so they didn't have to transfer from an orbital spacedock. As the long journey was about to come to an end, there was excited conversation in the cabin, and people moved about in their seats, anxious to be off the crowded vessel. But not him. The safe confines of the shuttle had been just fine; now they would have to chance the craziness of Mars. As far as he knew, Talia considered him the enemy, and she might freak when she saw him.

He could feel Gray tensing beside him, too. The timing of their actions would have to be perfect. There could be Psi Cops at the dock, eyeing everyone, rousting the attractive women. Maybe somebody would be meeting her—maybe the man she had traveled with. Or maybe that man was somewhere else on the craft, making it look as if they weren't traveling together.

No, he decided, it would be best to let Talia get through the security check-in alone, then they would make contact. But they had to be ready to move immediately if things went wrong. They might have to fight for jurisdiction over her. Despite being so close to her, he felt far away from Talia. What was her mental state like after the bombing, the accusations, and then running for her life? Not good, he imagined.

"This is where it all began for me," mused Mr. Gray. "About a week and a half ago, I got off this flight, and Mr. Bester was there waiting for me."

"Well, let's hope there's not a repeat of that," muttered Garibaldi.

They heard a heavy clanging and a thud as the air-lock mechanism latched on to the ship's hull. Everyone else heard it, too, and they rose from their seats in unison, ready to bolt from the transport as quickly as possible.

"Welcome to Mars," said a synthesized voice. "The time is 13:11, and the temperature is 379 degrees Celsius. It is hot and dry. Please watch your step as Mars has thirty-eight percent of the gravity of Earth."

The people in Talia's row began to file out, but she hung back, stricken with fear. She knew her identicard was going to get her arrested, and she couldn't go through that again! Not the lights, the accusations, the raised fists, and the angry shouts from people who wanted to punish her! Talia's heart was starting to do flip-flops in her rib cage, and she couldn't make her legs move. She felt ill, physically ill. *Come on,* she told herself, *you've felt ill for days now. If this is the end of the race, then so be it. Face it like a woman.*

For a moment, Garibaldi got excited, thinking that Talia would hang back in the cabin long enough for him and Gray to approach her there. But she suddenly got a determined look on her face and leaped from her seat, inserting herself forcefully into the herd of passengers moving toward the hatch. With maybe twenty people between them, he and Gray had to push and shove just to keep up. Even then, Talia's lithe body moved through the crowd faster than they could.

"She's getting away!" whispered Garibaldi.

"I can always send her a message," said Gray, "as long as she's in my line of sight."

"Hold off," ordered Garibaldi.

At least the two Psi Cops were already off the vessel, Talia noticed as she worked her way down the line. She hoped they got waved through the check-in and were long gone, but there was no such luck. When she reached the gate area, she could see the Psi Cops standing patiently to show their identicards to security. There were two more Psi Cops standing beyond the barriers, waiting for them.

Once again, Talia almost bolted, but there was no place to go. She held up her identicard and looked at it, hoping that Brother Lizard had outdone himself when he had chosen Frieda Nelson as her identity. Maybe Frieda was the stay-at-home type who never went anywhere, never had any call to use her real identicard. Maybe the system was not yet wise to there being two Frieda Nelsons. Right, she thought cynically, and maybe she would live to see her next birthday.

Behind her, two men inched forward, straining their necks to see what was happening. They were so close yet so far away, thought Garibaldi. With a few strides, he could touch her—and scare the daylights out of her. Her shoulders were hunched, and she moved as if she had aged ten years. More than anything, he just wanted to wrap his arms around Talia and tell her it was okay. There would be a happy ending.

He only hoped that was true.

The two Psi Cops met their friends, and there were hearty handshakes among gloved hands. To everyone's relief, they wandered off, apparently not on duty and not particularly interested in their fellow passengers.

Talia swallowed what was left of the saliva in her mouth. She would get through this—she would. The card would work one last time. Somehow, the people in the line in front of her melted away, and she found herself gliding forward in the light gravity, confidently presenting her card to the waiting security guard. The dock area was so much like B5's dock that it almost felt like home. Home, she thought wistfully. There's no place like home, except when they take it away from you.

"Thank you," said the security guard, taking the card from her trembling hand. "Are you all right, miss?"

She sniffled and gripped her hands to her chest. "Yes, just a bit air-sick."

"I get that way myself," remarked the guard pleasantly. He ran her card through the slot in his scanning device, and her heart and her breath held perfectly still.

"Hmm," he said puzzledly. "You are Ms. Frieda Nelson, aren't you?"

"Yes," she gasped.

"From Eugene, Oregon?"

"Last time I looked." She tried to sound disdainful, but she felt as if she was going to be stricken by a heart attack.

"Could you please step to the side for a moment while I finish with these other passengers." His tone wasn't so pleasant anymore, but it wasn't angry either. "There's an irregularity on your card. These glitches happen." To make sure she wasn't going anywhere, he put the card in his pocket.

Talia stood to the side, as ordered, and she wondered if she dared to send him a telepathic suggestion to the effect that her card was really okay. That was the sort of thing Mr. Bester could do with ease. Unfortunately, she felt so shaky and distressed that she didn't know if she could concentrate well enough to pull it off. Well, nothing ventured nothing gained.

Just as she had screwed up her courage to send the guard a message, an outside voice invaded her mind. Very clearly, it stated, "You are among friends. Do not panic."

Then, a monstrous explosion ripped the building!

CHAPTER 20

TALIA screamed, along with hundreds of others, as she staggered to the floor. She saw a flaming refreshment cart go rolling down the middle of the mall, spewing great clouds of choking, black smoke. The security guard was trying to hold back a panicked line of passengers while yelling into his link, and he wasn't paying any attention to her. She jumped to her feet and dashed through the smoke.

She bumped hard into a strange man, who wrapped his arms around her. Talia shrieked at his bizarre appearance, but then she realized he was a regular man wearing goggles and a breathing mask. She looked closer and saw his long white hair, like the mane of an old lion, and the devil-may-care smile under the mask.

"Hiya, Talia!" said his muffled voice.

"Uncle Ted," she gasped, and she dissolved into a coughing fit.

"This gas won't last forever," he warned, grabbing her arm and yanking her down the corridor. She staggered after him, her senses overcome by the smoke, shouts, and noise. Then a competing voice sounded in her head.

"Talia!" it called. It was a real voice, yelling above all the others. "Wait for me!"

She pulled away from Uncle Ted and whirled around. A telepathic voice popped into her head, saying, "Do not panic, Talia. It's Garibaldi and a friend."

Her uncle regained a grip on her arm and tried to pull her along. "What's the matter with you!" he growled.

"Stop!" she demanded. "I'm not alone!"

Two men came charging out of the smoke, hands over their mouths, coughing. A Psi Cop rushed by in the other direction, waving his PPG. Uncle Ted drew his own PPG and looked as if he was about to blast Garibaldi and Gray.

"No," she said, grabbing his arm. "Please wait."

"I don't want to shoot them!" He pulled on her arm, but Garibaldi reached her that same moment and started to pull on her free hand. The bare contact sent a shock of distracting intimacies through her mind.

There was no time for greetings or explanations, and Talia knew it. She pulled her hand away and saw the shock of the contact register in Garibaldi's eyes. "We've got to go with my uncle *now,*" she told Garibaldi. "Don't speak, just follow."

"But . . ."

She let her uncle drag her away, and she barely had time to glance over her shoulder to make sure Garibaldi and Gray were following. They were! As she and Uncle Ted approached a clearing in the smoke, he whipped his mask off and stuck it into the pockets of his greatcoat. As always, she marveled, he was quite a dashing figure. Even in his sixties, he had that handsome boyishness that had always gotten him into trouble. She hoped that she would age that well, although she felt as if she were aging fast at the moment.

Uncle Ted whipped out a cardkey and got them into a door marked EMPLOYEES ONLY. Talia stopped to hold the door open for Garibaldi and Gray. When the two men tried to talk, she put her fingers to her lips and glared at them. The telepathic message she sent them wasn't subtle either—it said they could follow or not, but they were not to stop her and Uncle Ted.

Garibaldi followed without question, and Gray looked around like he needed some encouragement. But with the others rushing away from him, he sprinted to catch up. The strange caravan of a dashing figure, a frightened woman, and two confused men swept through a sweltering kitchen where workers were baking doughnuts. The bakers glanced up from their work with minor interest, as if they were prepared for such intrusions.

After they rushed out another door, the group found themselves in a gray, unfinished corridor full of conduits and ducts for ventilation and life support. Uncle Ted suddenly pulled his PPG and pointed it squarely at Garibaldi.

"Honey, I wasn't expecting you to have friends from Earthforce."

Garibaldi just tried to ignore him. "Listen, Talia, we caught the real bombers—we all know you're innocent."

Talia scowled. "Oh, now you know! And I see what happens when you 'catch' someone—shot to pieces all over the sidewalk." Self-consciously, she pulled on her gloves. Garibaldi's eyes followed the action with fascination. She turned to Gray. "Are the Psi Cops still after me?"

"Yes," admitted the telepath.

"Then I'm still running."

"Please, we've got to talk," begged Garibaldi. "Let us come with you!"

"Out of the question," declared Uncle Ted.

"If you come with us," said Talia, "you've got to swear that you won't turn us in."

"I swear," he answered. "Besides, I know your Uncle Ted."

The flamboyant man squinted at him. "From where?"

"Here. It was almost two years ago, and I arrested you for creating a public nuisance, remember? You were railing against the new emigration rule—good speech. I was supposed to rough you up, if you'll remember, but I let you go with a warning."

"Yes, yes! Thank you!" beamed Uncle Ted. Then he frowned. "Those were the days when I could still speak in public. So, are you with the movement?"

"Not exactly," admitted Garibaldi. "But I'm not gonna let your niece out of my sight again. We have to talk somewhere about what to do next, and it might as well be at your place. Right, Gray?"

Mr. Gray looked stricken with fear at the thought of continuing with this dangerous group, but he didn't say no. Uncle Ted motioned for them to follow, and he took off at a jog down the dimly lit corridor. Talia could hear nothing but a rush of air coming from the ducts overhead, plus their pounding footsteps, echoing between the narrow walls.

Uncle Ted stopped at a large hatch in the center of the floor and motioned to Garibaldi. "Help me with this."

The security chief put his back into it, and the two men managed to twist the wheel enough to open the hatch. They threw back the cover, and Uncle Ted took a small flashlight out of his pocket. He turned it on and blinked the light three times into the hole. There was an answering beam of light that flashed three times across what looked like a river of coffee at the bottom of the conduit.

Talia leaned farther over the edge and peered down. She saw the flashlight beam sweeping eerily over the black water, and it was followed by the noses of three inflatable rafts gliding into view. The first raft had a young woman in it, and she was steering the other two rafts with her hands.

"With two people in each raft," grumbled Uncle Ted, "we'll probably all get wet. Don't worry, it's clean water. Or as clean as recycled water gets on Mars."

A metal ladder descended from one side of the cavity, and Uncle Ted started down. The woman floating below carefully positioned an empty raft underneath him, and he dropped into it with hardly a splash. He motioned for Talia to come down, and she did so without question. What was her fear of caves and tunnels anymore, when hundreds of Psi Cops were chasing after her?

She wasn't as adept at getting into the raft as Uncle Ted, and water came sloshing over the sides, coating the seat of her pants. Thankfully, it was warm water, almost the temperature of bathwater, although it did smell strongly of chemicals. Garibaldi came down next, and the young woman expertly guided the last empty raft underneath him. He alit in fine shape, only swamping it a bit. He grabbed a paddle and began to position the raft for Gray.

"You!" called Uncle Ted to Gray. "Shut the hatch before you come down. Don't worry about getting it tight."

Gray did as he was told, getting the hatch closed with no problem. He descended the ladder cautiously, doing everything right, but Garibaldi overshot him as he tried to position the raft. Gray landed half-on and half-off the inflated rubber, and he finally gave up and slid into the water when he realized how warm it was. He treaded water until Garibaldi extended the paddle to him and pulled him aboard, swamping the raft and getting both of them soaking wet.

"Earthlings," muttered Uncle Ted.

The young woman laughed heartily and said, "You're lucky. A lot of Martians don't know how to swim."

"Keep your voices down," ordered Uncle Ted as he put his paddle in the water and angled the raft into the current. With powerful strokes he took off, and the others followed, trembling flashlight beams leading the way. Soon the only noise in the darkness was the sound of paddles slipping through liquid and the steady drip of condensation over their heads.

After about an hour of steady paddling, it began to get extremely warm in the conduit, and the air was thin and dry. "Don't worry," Uncle Ted told the strangers. "We'll get out of the aqueduct before all the air is gone."

"That's good to know," said Garibaldi. "Does this aqueduct go outdoors?"

"Yes," answered Ted. "It's just a short stretch, and it's well insulated. Or we'd be cooked. We're getting out just before the turbines."

"Was that a real bomb you set off?" asked Gray with disapproval in his voice.

"Not really," answered Uncle Ted. "It was mainly sound and smoke, although I think we used one concussion cap. I'm not into violence anymore."

"Uncle Ted," said Talia, "I want you to know I'm innocent of that bombing on Babylon 5."

"Of course you are, honey," answered the charismatic figure with a toss of his leonine hair. "I'm innocent of sedition, or perdition, or whatever they've accused me of this week. But that doesn't matter—they have to have their villains."

He slapped his paddle on the water and said, "I plead guilty to wanting a Mars that is free from Earth's government and their greed. What are they to us? Do they know us? Do they care about us? Or do they want only what they can take out of our soil and our sweat?''

Uncle Ted chuckled. "Stop me before I start making a speech. I'm a Jainist now, a follower of Gandhi, and I truly have disavowed violence. Gandhi is sort of ancient history, and you young people probably don't know who he was.''

"I do," said Gray. "If you are really following the precepts of Mahatma Gandhi, I salute you. Many Martian revolutionaries do not.''

"Yes, I know," muttered Ted. "But we can't win by fighting Earthforce. We can only lose people and lose the moral high ground. What I do is organize nonviolent protests and tell my followers to resist passively. But it's hard being passive, when people are trying to kill you.''

He turned and smiled at his niece. "Sweetheart, I know what it's like to be in hiding, to run from every shadow. You and I can never be free, but then *none* of Mars is free. Maybe one day, you and I—and every Martian!—will be able to walk in the sun, free citizens.''

His lady friend lifted a fist and chanted, "Power to Mars!''

"This is Moira," said Uncle Ted. "She keeps me together.''

"What do you know about the Free Phobos movement?'' asked Garibaldi.

"Nothing!" said Ted with a scowl. "I never heard of them before now. But those two stupid bombings sure brought us a bad crackdown and a lot of biased media coverage. I'd like to have a word with this Free Phobos bunch, before they do a third bombing.''

"A third bombing?'' asked Garibaldi.

"Yes, Free Phobos released a statement this morning that they're planning a third bombing soon." He chuckled. "I have to admit, the threat of a real bombing made my little smoke bomb at the dock all the more effective.''

"We know who's behind Free Phobos," said Garibaldi. "If we put the right guy in jail, Talia can go free.''

"Right," muttered Ted sarcastically. He shined his flashlight on a grating that protected a line of pumping equipment recessed into the side of the aqueduct. They could hear a cascade of water somewhere in the darkness ahead of them, plus turbines churning. Uncle Ted steered his raft toward the pumps.

"Tie up on the grating," he ordered. "There's a narrow footpath—just try to follow me. Remember, we have to take out the rafts and deflate them, so don't let them get away. We can't leave anything that will give us away."

"Talia," said Garibaldi, "Arthur Malten is behind all of this. We've got to find him to clear you."

She looked back at him, stunned and hurt. Maybe she didn't want to hear that Arthur Malten had set her up to die, but he couldn't spare her the truth. Talia lowered her head and appeared to be thinking about it. After what she must have been through, thought Garibaldi, could anything surprise her?

"It's good to see you," she said finally.

"You, too," he admitted.

Uncle Ted grabbed the grating and hoisted himself onto a narrow ledge in front of it. He tied up his raft and helped Talia step out, then he caught the other two rafts and tied them at the grating. After everyone was safely on the ledge, hanging by their fingernails to the grating, Ted and Moira dragged the rafts out of the water and deflated them.

Very carefully, they skirted the narrow ledge. Through the soles of his shoes, Garibaldi could feel the heat rising up from the metal. They squeezed through a gap cut in the grating and walked carefully among the high-compression pumps, kerchunking away. Finally they reached a secured doorway, and Uncle Ted produced another keycard that opened the door.

They went through and found themselves in a storage room lined with shelves containing pipes, washers, fittings, and tools. There was a spiral stairway leading upward, and the air and temperature in the room were normal, or at least as normal as they got on Mars.

"I think this room is as far as I'm going to go with you boys," said Uncle Ted. "You can talk to Talia here."

For emphasis, he took his PPG out of his pocket. He studied the weapon for a moment before handing it to Moira. "I'm a pacifist, but I would fight to protect my Talia, after what they put her through."

"Believe me," said Garibaldi, "we came here to save her. In order to do that, we have to find Arthur Malten—he's the key to this Free Phobos group and everything else. Does anybody have any ideas?"

Gray stroked his chin thoughtfully. "Do your people have the ability to send out press releases to the media?"

"Of course," answered Ted, "that's about the only way I can make myself heard these days."

"Then let's expose him. Tell the press that Arthur Malten of the Mix is the man behind Free Phobos and the bombings. Coming from you, they're liable to believe it. Besides, it happens to be the truth."

A smile crept across Garibaldi's face. "That won't make Mr. Bester very happy. He wanted to keep that a secret."

"Well," answered Gray, "let's make them both unhappy, shall we? Once Malten is exposed, there's no reason for Bester to keep blaming Ms. Winters and the separatists. And Malten won't have to set off another bomb just to give his sham terrorist group some credence."

"What is this all about?" asked Talia wearily.

Briefly, Garibaldi told her, Ted, and Moira about Malten's attempt to privatize Psi Corps and have himself installed as head. They listened in rapt attention as he explained about the secret Senate bill, the fate of Emily Crane, and how closely the coup within Psi Corps had come to happening.

"In fact," said Garibaldi, "it might still happen if we don't move on it. I'd like to see Psi Corps disbanded, not fall under another tyrant."

"I'll be damned," muttered Uncle Ted. "Hey, I've got to tell this story right away, the whole bloody mess. And I think it's better Talia come with me, until she's officially absolved."

"Fine," agreed Garibaldi, turning to the blond woman in the dirty beret. "I just wanted to make sure you were safe, and that you knew we were trying to help you."

Talia stood up and gave him a grateful hug, allowing her head to rest on his shoulder for a moment. That made it all worthwhile for Garibaldi.

"Give us five minutes," said Uncle Ted, heading for the staircase. "Then come up after us. You'll find yourselves in a factory up there—just ignore everyone and keep climbing stairs until you find a monorail stop."

"Okay," said the security chief. "Give 'em hell."

Uncle Ted shepherded Moira and Talia up the stairs, and the weary telepath looked back one last time to give Garibaldi a smile. He waved until she was out of sight.

"What an experience she must've had," observed Gray with sympathy. "It's like she can barely talk."

"She doesn't need to talk," answered Garibaldi. "Just the way she is, I would walk across Mars for her."

"I know what you mean," Gray sighed. "Well, shall we go somewhere and wait for Mr. Bester to call us? He won't be very happy."

The two men grinned at one another.

With nowhere else to go to wait, Garibaldi and Gray took refuge in a nearby canteen devoted to military personnel from Earthforce. They arrived just in time to catch the news.

The newscaster raised an eyebrow as he reported the story, but he got it essentially correct when he said, "There has been a dramatic development in the Psi Corps bombing story. Noted Martian revolutionary Theodore Hamiliton is claiming that the Free Phobos terrorist group is actually one man—Arthur Malten, founder of the Mix!

"According to this report, Arthur Malten was poised to take over the leadership of Psi Corps with the passage of a privatization bill in the Senate. Details of this bill have now been verified by independent sources in the Senate. According to Hamilton, who is also Talia Winters's uncle, the bombing on Babylon 5 was really an attempt by Arthur

Malten to rid himself of political opponents within Psi Corps.''

In the canteen, there were gasps of surprise and an occasional ''I told you so!'' Everyone put down their Ping-Pong paddles and pool cues to listen to the gruesome details, which included two fatal bombings, dozens of deaths, and the murder of Emily Crane. Garibaldi frowned, because the report stuck it to the bad guys, but it didn't clear Talia. With Ted being her uncle, the news reports made it seem as if the information was coming from her. Public opinion would still figure her to be in the thick of it.

He looked at Gray and asked, ''Are you sure Bester knows where we are?''

''I was very clear about it,'' answered the telepath.

The commlink on the wall buzzed, and the closest officer answered it. After a moment, he called out, ''Is there somebody named Gray here?''

''That's me!'' called the telepath.

''There's a shuttlecraft on its way for you,'' reported the man, and he returned immediately to watching the news.

Gray and Garibaldi smiled at one another.

Because of Mars' thin atmosphere, every shuttlecraft had to dock with an air-lock, and most small shuttlecraft had a hatch at the bottom for that purpose. So Gray and Garibaldi had to climb up a ladder through the air-lock in order to board the black shuttlecraft through its underbelly. If Mr. Bester was surprised to see Garibaldi, he didn't say so, and Garibaldi certainly wasn't surprised to see him.

''I hope you two are proud of yourselves,'' he sneered. ''I ought to arrest you for collaborating with the enemy.''

''What are you talking about?'' asked Garibaldi. He and Gray looked innocently at one another.

''Thanks to you, there is no way we can handle this quietly now. The whole Alliance will know. . . .''

''That you made a mistake,'' offered Gray. ''That you're fallible.''

''No,'' muttered the Psi Cop, ''that Psi Corps is vulnerable to attacks from within. That's the one place we fear the most, attacks from within. And that's why we Psi Cops are so important to the Corps.''

"Aren't you forgetting one thing?" asked Garibaldi. "If it hadn't been for me and Gray, by this time tomorrow you would've been out of a job! I'll have second thoughts about that for a while, I can tell you."

Bester narrowed his eyes angrily. "I know what you want from me, and I'm not going to give it to you. Ms. Winters will remain a suspect *and* a rogue telepath. I imagine she will soon go on the list of known Martian terrorists."

Garibaldi nearly jumped out of his seat to strangle the pompous twit, but his inner voice warned him to keep calm. This was the only man who could remove the most damning of the charges against her—rogue telepath.

"I will testify in Ms. Winters's behalf," vowed Gray. "And when we capture Malten, he can testify."

Bester chuckled humorlessly. "Do you think I would let Arthur Malten go on the stand to testify? His trial would become a trial about Psi Corps itself, and the Mix would get destroyed in the process. To save us all a lot of embarrassment, we're negotiating with Arthur Malten."

Garibaldi sat up in his seat. "You know where he is? Why don't you bring him in?"

"Yes, bring him in!" echoed Gray.

"Well, we don't exactly know where he is. Mars is a big planet, and he's very clever. The Mix has a private underground transmitter, and we've been communicating over that. So we have a vague idea what area he's in."

Gray was sputtering with anger. "How . . . how can you negotiate with Malten? The man tried to kill you, remember, and he succeeded in killing two dozen innocent people!"

Bester scratched his nose. "There is that, of course. But we have some things we need from Mr. Malten. We need him to sign a confession, thanks to your loose lips. It'll have to be worded carefully to make it clear that he, Emily Crane, and those other two were the only telepaths involved from the Mix. His supporters in the Senate will have to officially condemn him. Then Malten will have to address the Mix employees—give them a pep talk and appoint a successor. We have several good candidates in mind.''

The Psi Cop paused in thought. "In exchange for saving the Mix, there will be a plea-bargained conviction, and he will be paroled to some distant planet."

"Then you'll kill him," said Gray.

Bester smiled but did not correct that assumption.

"What about Talia?" insisted Garibaldi.

Bester was distracted by his pilot, although she hadn't moved or said a word. "What did you just receive?"

"Finch is reporting that Malten broke off negotiations. He may be running. There was an echo on his last transmission, and we think we may have pinpointed his hideout. I have coordinates—we can be there in fifteen minutes."

"Go!"

CHAPTER 21

GARIBALDI stared out the starboard window of the shuttlecraft and watched the barren terrain of Mars streak by. Mars never looked real from the air, he thought to himself, with all those lifeless and craggy hills, broken up by the occasional dusty habitat, monorail tube, or factory dome. Mars was a place that couldn't possibly exist, yet here it was, a monument to humanity's determination to bring life to a dead planet. No matter how many buildings they put up, the edifices of man always looked tenuous on Mars, like vines trying to cling to a smooth metal door.

The terrain didn't look real from ground level either, he recalled. From that perspective, the mountains, chasms, and sheer cliffs looked too large and too vivid to be real. They rose at odd angles out of the pockmarked, reddish soil, like crystals growing in a culture. The mountains looked like sand castles, as if they would crumble in a strong wind.

"I hate this place," muttered Gray beside him.

"Yes, Mars is an acquired taste," agreed Garibaldi. He looked at Bester. "Psi Corps has certainly acquired it."

Bester was ignoring them as he leaned forward intently. "Status?"

"I'm running sonar," reported the pilot. "The readings indicate that there is a structure where we picked up the echo. It's the size and shape of a bunker."

"Underground?" asked Bester.

"Yes, but not too deep. I can hover over it and turn on the thrusters. That might blow away some of the camouflaged covering."

"Do it," ordered Bester.

Garibaldi braced himself as the pilot—who was damned good, he had to admit—positioned the craft directly over a small mound between two jagged mountains. The mound looked like a mogul on a ski slope, and he had seen hundreds of similar protrusions on Mars, formed by the pressures of lava flow. The pilot came so close to the mound that she nearly landed, then she popped the thrusters. The shuttlecraft rose like a shot between the two mountains, shuddering and rattling until she could regain control of it. Then she banked the craft away from the peaks and swerved around for another view.

True to her word, she had blasted a star-shaped hole in the artificial surface covering the mound. Under the singed material, sections of gray metal shone dully in the sun.

"Can you raise anybody in there?" asked Bester.

"I've been trying," she answered. "So has Mr. Finch. Malten has either left, or is keeping quiet."

"Damn," muttered Bester, "if we've lost him—if he ran for it—well, there will be no more negotiations!"

"I can land on the mound," the pilot offered. "We might be able to cut through, or find a hatch."

"If you've got a suit," said Garibaldi, "I'll go out and take a look."

"They're in the storage bin in the back," answered Bester. "Right beside the air-lock chamber. You can exit there."

Garibaldi started off, then stopped. "You won't leave me out here, will you?"

Bester scowled. "Leave you alone with Malten, or maybe a batch of his secret files? Not bloody likely."

Garibaldi found four environmental suits in the closet, and he was glad to see they were all roomy and optimized for use on Mars. With the low gravity, nobody had to worry about carrying around too much weight, so a Martian environmental suit could carry the maximum amount of high-grade insulation, plus cooling and air-processing equipment. He stripped off his uniform, figuring the pilot had seen it all before, and squeezed into the suit.

He lowered the helmet onto his head, locked it, and waved to the pilot. She set them down carefully on top of the camouflaged bunker, but they could still hear the grinding of metal against metal. There was a scary moment as something crunched and the ship shifted, but it settled down at an angle that wasn't too terribly dangerous. Garibaldi guessed that a few more pieces of the camouflage material had broken away under the weight of the shuttlecraft.

He pressed the button to open the air-lock chamber, then crammed himself into the tiny space. With a deep breath, he pressed the second air-lock and opened the hatch to the outside.

The brightness of the Martian landscape startled him at first, and he lifted his eyes to the dark sky until they could adjust. A few seconds later, he was scrambling like a mummified mountain goat over the top of the bunker, trying to find a way in. With his foot, he kicked off more chunks of the soil-colored camouflage material until he finally discovered a docking hatch.

He activated the radio inside his helmet and waved at the shuttle pilot in the cockpit. "I found a docking hatch. Do you want me to go in, or do you want to fly ten meters over here and try to dock?"

Garibaldi waited a few seconds, and the pilot replied, "Get clear. We're going to dock."

He bent his legs and jumped about twenty meters to the ground, landing so lightly that he had to run a few steps to slow himself down. That was when he saw the fresh rover tracks in the red soil. The sight of the tracks gave Garibaldi a very bad feeling in his stomach. He didn't know why, but he didn't think Malten would flee overland by rover. He just wasn't the survivalist type.

But it was too late to suggest caution, because the shuttlecraft lifted up again and came down expertly atop the hatch he had uncovered. Whatever Bester's bad qualities, thought Garibaldi, he had attracted a very good pilot for his shuttlecraft. When the thrusters went dead, Garibaldi jumped back on top of the bunker with one effortless leap. He peered under the shuttlecraft and saw the robotic mechanism of the air-lock twisting around by itself to find the hatch. They finally paired up and locked with a solid clunk.

He tapped his radio again. "Do you have atmosphere in the bunker?"

"Positive on that," answered the pilot. "Come back in. Mr. Bester is opening the hatch."

Garibaldi hurried as fast as the bulky suit would allow to the chamber at the rear of the craft. By the time he got through the air-lock and was stripping off his suit, Mr. Bester was halfway down the hatch. The Psi Cop groaned with pain at every rung of the ladder, and he pounded the head of his thick metal cane on the ladder.

Gray looked at Garibaldi and shrugged. "He insisted on going down."

The chief began putting on his uniform. "Be careful down there! I saw fresh rover tracks outside."

Bester's head disappeared into the hatch, and he was gone. Gray scrambled down after him, and Garibaldi tried to be patient as he waited his turn. He glanced at the young pilot.

"Keep the motor running," he advised her.

Then he heard a shout. "Oh, my God—stay back!"

Garibaldi was so anxious to see what was happening that he dropped the last few meters of the ladder onto very plush blue carpeting. He was amazed when he saw the vast layout of viewers, computers, and editing equipment—it was truly a decked-out communications bunker. There were hardly any other furnishings in the room, except for a workbench and a few chairs. It was one of the chairs that Bester and Gray were staring at.

Arthur Malten, wide awake but looking haggard, was tied to one of the chairs, with a bomb strapped to his head. He was trying to hold perfectly still, but the sweat was running a marathon race down his face. Pinned to his chest was a note that read: "Compliments of the real revolutionaries."

"They came in," he gasped. "Martians! I didn't see them!"

Garibaldi edged forward. "Can we disable it."

"No, no!" screamed Arthur Malten. "It's got a motion detector on it. You get too close—*kaboom!* If I move too much—*kaboom!* They explained it to me in loving detail. They also have a remote!"

That last admission made Bester start hobbling toward the

ladder with his cane. "Listen, Malten, we're not the bomb squad. I'll send for some specialists."

"Bester!" called the desperate telepath. "I didn't mean it personally! You understand, it was politics."

"Of course," said the Psi Cop. "It was a damn good try, too. You took me by surprise and nearly succeeded. I'll remember that."

"The Mix," croaked Arthur Malten. "Try to save it."

"We will. Come on, gentlemen."

"But we just can't leave him here," Gray protested. "Garibaldi, do something!"

The security chief rubbed his hands together and tried to think. "We need some small clippers, but if we can't get close to him . . ."

"Mr. Bester!" called the pilot from above. "An unidentified man is telling us we have thirty seconds to get off . . . or else!"

"I am sorry about Talia Winters, too!" wailed Malten from the chair. "And *Emily!*" He began to sob, and his head bounced around, which made Bester squirt up the ladder.

"That's a deathbed confession," said Garibaldi, pushing Gray toward the ladder. "Let's move it!"

"There's no hope for him?" asked the telepath.

"Not unless we get help. Move it!"

The light gravity allowed them to bound hand-over-hand up the ladder, as Malten's sobs grew louder and more pitiful. When they reached the shuttlecraft cabin, Bester was already strapped in, and the pilot was going through her preignition checklist. Bester stumbled to his seat, and Garibaldi struggled to get the hatch shut. He fell backward as the robotic link broke and the mechanism retracted into the shuttlecraft.

"Five seconds!" called the pilot.

They heard a low rumble beneath them, and Garibaldi shouted, "Now!"

She jammed on the thrusters as a fireball and concussion rocked the little craft, sending it spinning around. Garibaldi was tossed into Bester's legs, and the Psi Cop screamed in anguish. The pilot bore down and never gave up on the bucking craft, yet Garibaldi could see one of the jagged peaks looming ever closer in the window. He braced himself for impact, but the pilot hit the thrusters again and spun them away from the mountain.

She picked up altitude as quickly as she could, and everyone craned their necks toward the ports to see what had happened. All that was left of Arthur Malten's secret bunker was a huge, black crater with a few smoldering sparks at its edges. Debris and twisted bits of metal were scattered for half a kilometer around the site.

"Oh, my," murmured Gray, slumping back in his seat.

Bester looked reflective. "Maybe it had to end this way. Well, I suppose we can tell the press that he died constructing a bomb."

Garibaldi scowled and shook his head. "You never want to give the right people credit for anything, do you? The revolutionaries found him before you did, and they weren't in a negotiating mood. Face it, Bester, you have been one step behind everybody this whole chain of events."

The Psi Cop bristled. "I'm still going to take down Talia Winters and her uncle."

"No, you're not," said Garibaldi confidently. "I didn't want to use this, because I'm ashamed of it, but you force my hand. Do you remember the reception on Babylon 5 the first night of the conference? It was our only successful event."

"Yes, what of it?" asked Bester, sounding wary.

"That night I made a visual of several of your Psi Cops *gambling* in the private quarters of Ambassador Londo Mollari. I believe he was teaching them three-card monte."

Mr. Bester looked pale, but he still managed a smile. "That can't be true. You're bluffing."

"Am I?" Garibaldi countered. "You can ask Ambassador Mollari for confirmation. He was, shall we say, my accomplice."

Bester's lips thinned, and he stared hard at Garibaldi. But Harriman Gray inserted himself between the men and warned, "Don't scan him, Mr. Bester. I will help him block it. Suffice to say, Garibaldi told me about this incriminating visual, but I begged him not to use it.''

Gray looked with disgust at Garibaldi. "He must feel you gave him no choice.''

The security chief picked some Martian dirt out of his fingernails. "You will drop all charges against Talia Winters, especially the rogue telepath. And you'll do it right this minute, or the next thing you'll see on the news will be Psi Cops gambling. Won't the press enjoy that right after this juicy scandal with the Mix? Maybe the Senate will have enough courage to throw you out on their own.''

"I don't believe you did it," muttered Bester, "but it's the kind of thing Ambassador Mollari *would* do." He called out to the pilot, "Get me a channel to headquarters.''

"Yes, sir. You're on-line.''

"This is Mr. Bester with a final report on the Babylon 5 bombing. This information is cleared for immediate release to the media. Arthur Malten confessed to forming a terrorist organization called Free Phobos, and his only accomplices were three other telepaths from the Mix—Emily Crane, Michael Graham, and Barry Strump. Unbeknownst to anyone, they were Martian sympathizers. Mr. Malten died this afternoon, the victim of an accidental bomb explosion.

"In light of this new information, all charges against Talia Winters have been dropped. She is to be taken off the list of rogue telepaths, with all her duties and rights as a member of Psi Corps restored to her, effective immediately. Bester out.''

Garibaldi nodded, leaned back in his seat, and closed his eyes.

At the Clarke Spaceport orbiting Earth, two men stood among the crowds, shaking hands. One man wore gloves, and the other didn't. One was catching a quick shuttle to Berlin, and the other was headed in the opposite direction to catch a two-day transport to Babylon 5.

"Are you sure you don't want to come back with me?" asked Garibaldi. "If you've blown your expense account, I'll put you up on my couch.''

Gray chuckled. "I *have* blown my expense account, thanks to you. But that's not the reason. I don't want to go back to B5 just to see Susan—that would be making a nuisance of myself. I'll have business on B5 again someday, and I'll be looking forward to seeing all of you."

"Just don't bring Bester with you."

The two men laughed, and Gray lowered his head. "I have one request. Will you tell Susan that I did something worthwhile. Something that would win her over."

"You bet I'll tell her," said Garibaldi. "I plan to get a lot of free meals out of this—by recounting our adventures over and over again. I'll leave out the part where you fell in the water."

"That was *your* fault," Gray reminded him.

"That's why I'll leave it out."

"And how is Ms. Winters?"

"Still a little shaken," answered Garibaldi. "I understand she's staying with her parents for a few days before she goes back. I bet she'll have some pretty good stories to tell, too." He sighed. "These are classy women we're talking about, and we're a couple of lugs. We may never stand a chance with them."

"I know," said Gray.

A synthesized voice announced, "Transport *Starfish* is now boarding for Babylon 5."

"That's me," said Garibaldi. He started off but stopped to wave back. "You're okay, Gray."

"You too."

Two hundred kilometers below them, a young woman with sleek blond hair stood watching the stars from her parents' porch. The nightmare was finally over, but she still didn't feel like talking much, about her escape or anything else. So much of what had happened to her in the last few days Talia didn't understand. She had to parse it slowly in the light of time, and pick out those pieces that were worth saving, and worth puzzling over.

As she watched the stars glimmer, she marveled at the fact

that she lived among them. She called them home. Talia had
seen enough of both Earth and Mars to last her for a while,
and she looked forward to going back to the cold blackness
of space. She longed to see the aliens, who were less judg-
mental and prejudiced than her own species. Among aliens,
you could be whoever you were, she realized, but among
humans you had to be whoever they wanted you to be.

And nobody was what they seemed.

Out of all the weirdness, the duplicity, the good masquerading as bad, and the bad masquerading as good, there was
one piece of her journey she wanted badly to understand. It
was Invisible Isabel. She wanted to talk to Ambassador Kosh
as soon as possible, but she knew the Vorlon would speak in
riddles and tell her nothing outright. Kosh would want her to
figure it out for herself.

The part of Invisible Isabel she recognized was her nascent
telekinetic abilities, a gift from an old friend; but it was
Isabel's voice that was new to her. That voice was confident
and independent, and it could get her out of tough scrapes.
She couldn't hear it all the time, but she would like to hear it
more often.

"Talia, honey, we're going to have some ice cream!"
called her mom, sounding a lot like her Uncle Ted. His nightmare was still going on, but at least he had chosen it.

And what about the dogged persistence of Garibaldi? That
was something. She had to think about all of it, but not
tonight. Tonight she would eat ice cream and listen to stories
about her extended family and parents' friends. Then she
would return to her home, Babylon 5.

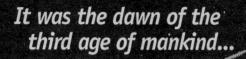

It was the dawn of the third age of mankind...

...and the last best hope for peace is the last of the Babylon stations.

BABYLON 5